"BOSH! I CANNOT THINK BUT THAT ANY YOUNG LADY WOULD FEEL PRIVILEGED TO DANCE WITH YOU, MY LORD."

"Yes, well, that is because you see me through entirely different eyes than Miss Beatrice. Toby accompanies me tonight."

"Oh! Ought he to be out and about so very soon?" Melody asked.

"Yes, I think so. It is his shoulder merely. It is not as though his leg is broken. The fever has left him and the shoulder will heal if he is in bed or out of it. But he may not dance. He will likely sit in your pocket the entire evening, Miss Harriman. But I daresay you will not particularly mind that."

"No, of course I will not. I shall be pleased to have his company and I shall do my best to entertain him."

"Yes, well, we shall see you this evening then," Stoneforth replied with the oddest look upon his face. Then he leaned down from his horse and held out his hand and Melody put her own hand into it. He raised the hand to his lips and pressed a kiss upon the back of it. "Farewell, Miss Harriman."

He was off with a nudge of his spurs against the black's sides, and he did not once look back. And it was a very good thing that he did not, because he would have seen Melody staring at the back of her gloved hand in wonder as her cheeks colored up to a bright pink, and he would have hated himself for being unable to resist kissing her—merely her hand—just this one time—and bringing that most bewildered expression to her face.

MUTINY AT ALMACK'S

Judith A. Lansdowne

Zebra Books
Kensington Publishing Corp.
http://www.zebrabooks.com

ZEBRA BOOKS are published by

Kensington Publishing Corp.
850 Third Avenue
New York, NY 10022

First Printing: October, 1999
10 9 8 7 6 5 4 3 2 1

Printed in the United States of America

One

Adam Gregory Attenbury, Viscount Stoneforth, stood at the back of the chapel in St. Agnes Lane amongst the empty pews, the lazy dust motes and the filtered sunlight and attempted to pray. His shoulders square, his back straight, he allowed only his head to bow the slightest bit as he whispered into the silence. "God, please do not let Toby die. I will do anything You wish if only You will spare his life."

Stoneforth's face was pale beneath a weathered tan but there were no tears. He was not the sort of gentleman who did cry. He had grown into manhood solid and impenetrable, and what pierced him to the heart he was accustomed to endure dry-eyed and in silence.

"He ought not have done it. He was a fool," Stoneforth muttered awkwardly. "But young men are foolish." And then he began to pace up and down the aisle, boot heels cracking like pistol shots against the stones.

Before he was thirteen Stoneforth had attended three younger sisters, two infant brothers, his mother and his father to their graves. Each of those journeys had served to stiffen his spine the more. Each had taught him more forcefully to bury his feelings deep in his heart just as he had buried his loved ones deep in the earth. "But I will not bury Toby!" he shouted abruptly, glaring at the altar that stood abandoned before him. "I vow I will not!"

At the age of seventeen, secure in the fact that young Toby would be well cared for by his uncle and that the title of Stoneforth would pass without contention into Toby's hands should he himself die, a stoic Stoneforth had joined the dragoons and had soldiered his way through Egypt, across a major portion of Europe and into Spain. Blown from his horse by a mortar shell in the Battle of the Pyramids, downed by a long gun at the Battle of Alexandria, pierced through by a French sword at Talavera, always he had continued the fight—his back straight, his countenance composed and his voice urging his men to carry on as his blood and theirs mixed with that of their foes. Grief for his fallen compatriots burrowed deep down inside of him battle after battle to mingle with the pain that already dwelt there, but he did never acknowledge it. The soldiering had tempered his spine to steel and had sent his already suppressed emotions plummeting into the farthestmost reaches of his heart where they had huddled—unexpressed and undiscovered by anyone—until Nora.

Stoneforth ceased pacing and stared at the glorious rainbow filtering into the chapel through one of the stained-glass windows. "Nora," he whispered, and he remembered her gazing up at him and the warmth of her body against his own as she rested for one last time in his arms. "Nora, I am making a muck of things already. I cannot even pray properly!" He slipped into one of the benches, sat down, glowered at the chancel laid out before him and sighed.

On February the tenth, the Year of Our Lord 1810, the only person who had dared to explore the tangled path that led to the hidden depths of Stoneforth's heart, Mrs. Nora Huston, had succumbed to influenza. Stoneforth, on the march, had been obliged to bury her without ceremony beside a muddy track in Portugal. That ought to have been his final lesson. Nora's illness and death had wrenched, twisted and battered his heart until he thought it should be forged into steel like his spine. But Nora had begun to teach him the value of being other than steel. She had wrung from him his word to try to open his heart, to attempt to share his feelings with those who craved to know them, to loose the bittersweet font of love and sorrow that was dammed up inside of him and send it pouring out into the world. And so, when nearly a year later at Albuera, Stoneforth had lost the sight in his right eye, he had taken stock of what there remained in him to offer to England and what he had promised Nora. He had taken stock and then he had sold out and gone home to try his luck at opening his heart and sharing his love and sorrow, his grief and joy with his remaining family, only to discover that his uncle had gone from town and his brother lay abed with a raging fever contracted from an infection inflicted by a pistol ball.

"Help me, Nora," Stoneforth whispered into the dank, silent chancel. "Can you not tell God that I have just now got home? How can I learn to open my heart when first thing back I discover that my brother lies dying so that all I wish to do is to steel myself against the possibility of his death?"

Stoneforth shivered in the dampness. "I expect Toby thought it the honorable thing," he muttered, running his fingers through his hair. "I expect he thought not to call the man out would be cowardly. And to appear a coward when you are twenty-two—it is not to be borne. But You cannot take Toby from me because of such a stupid thing, God! Not now. Not when I have finally got the courage to make a new attempt at life."

* * *

The Right Honorable Melody Harriman swiped angrily at the tears that persisted in wetting her cheeks. "I will not go back to London," she managed in a wavering voice. "I will not."

"Bosh," responded her cousin Kate. "You most certainly will. I cannot think what has gotten into you, Mel. You are not generally so fainthearted."

"No, but she has never before been forced to face such rudeness," offered a second young lady from behind the sopha. "Rudeness takes great fortitude to overlook, and to effectively combat it, one must be outrageously rude oneself." Melody's cousin Allisandra, who had the same hair—the color of autumn leaves—and the same sparkling gray eyes as her sister Katherine, placed her hands upon Melody's shoulders and gave them a reassuring squeeze before she came around to the front of the sopha and settled down beside her. "Mel has not got the least notion how to go about being rude. That is exactly the problem. But the answer is obvious, Kate."

"It is?" asked Melody with a sniff.

"Certainly," grinned Ally. "We shall send Bea to London with you. I will wager there is no one in London who can out-rude Bea once she sets her mind to it. I know that there is no one in Wicken who can do so."

Melody sniffed and giggled at one and the same time. "Th-that is a terrible thing to say," she managed as the giggle won out over the sniff. "It is a very good thing that Beatrice is not present to hear you speak so of her."

"No, but it is true!" exclaimed Kate. "Ally, you have hit upon the very thing. We shall pack up Bea and send her off to London directly she sets foot in the door."

"And we will go with her," Ally replied happily. "Well, we must go with her, Kate. We cannot possibly turn Bea loose upon Society—not even upon such rudesbys as

Melody describes—without the two of us to rein her in when she goes too far."

"Do you think your mama would have us, Mel?" asked Kate, her eyes alight with laughter. "What a lark it would be for the four of us to descend upon London Society together! Ally and Beatrice and I are seventeen now, you know—we are quite out of the schoolroom and longing for excitement."

Melody's smile widened at the thought, and the tears that had come and gone for most of a week ceased to flow on the spot. "Oh, would you? Would you come? But what would your papa say?"

"I expect that Papa would give thanks to the Lord to be without us for a time. Especially if Aunt Lydia is to be looking after us," Kate declared. "Papa is writing a new operetta, you know, and he is in great need of some peace in which to do it."

"Another? Truly?"

"Yes," nodded Allisandra, "and this one is the very best of the lot, I think."

"How do you know?" asked Kate.

"I peeked at it two weeks ago. The very day that you and Bea took Papa off to Wicken to buy him a new hat. You are the heroine, Kate. I know it is you, for Papa describes her as a beauty with flashing eyes and a heart of gold and a brain stuffed with dreams and melodies."

"Yes, that is Kate all right," nodded Melody. "A heart of gold and a brain stuffed with dreams and melodies. Is it a comic opera like the others?"

"Indeed. Mr. Kemble at Covent Garden is begging for another comic opera from the pen of Herbert Van Cleef. Do you know that the theatre has been sold out for every performance of *The Innocent Isolda* since it first began? And Miss Gorsky is so very fond of it that she has requested permission to perform it in St. Petersburg."

"Thank goodness no one knows that Herbert Van Cleef is Papa," giggled Kate. "He would be so very embarrassed."

"No, would he? But his operettas are so wonderful!" Melody exclaimed.

"When Papa first showed *The Innocent Isolda* to Miss Gorsky, she immediately determined to come to London and perform in it," Ally replied with a nod. "Her enthusiasm was one of the main reasons, Papa said, that things began to go well for England with the Tsar."

"One day I am going to perform in one of Papa's operettas," stated Kate with enormous determination. "But Papa does not think they are at all the thing. He thinks he ought to be writing treatises upon the folly of mankind."

"Which is where he is very much mistaken," said Ally, "for Papa's operettas *are* treatises upon the folly of mankind. That is why so many people take such pleasure in them. Everyone recognizes someone of their acquaintance in the cast of characters."

"I am always the villain," announced an energetic voice from the doorway. "It never fails that there is something in the villain that cries out: 'Here is Bea; look, everyone; here is Bea; just see what she has become by not listening to her papa!' " The young lady who entered the morning room was dressed outrageously in pantaloons and shirt, waistcoat and jacket. Her feet were encased in Hussar's boots and her short, crisp curls, windblown and wild, captured beneath a forager's cap. "What's afoot?" asked the youngest of the Lange triplets with a wide, sparkling smile. "Some mischief, I think. Will I like it?"

Stoneforth entered the town house, tossed his hat and gloves on to the table in the vestibule and climbed the staircase, proceeding directly to his brother's chambers. From the depths of the bedclothes two bleary blue eyes blinked up at him.

"I expect you thought that I would never return, eh, Toby? Well, but you know how it is. Always something to be done when one has been gone from London for so long a time as I have been." He laid one cool hand upon his brother's brow. The fever still raged. The eyes blinking up at him were likely not seeing him at all. "Toby? Do you know who I am?"

"You are Papa," replied his brother. "And I will not never climb that tree again."

"No, I am certain that you will not," responded Stoneforth, the memory of Toby's childhood encounter with the old oak outside the nursery window in Doncaster tugging vaguely at his heart. "Look, here is Watlow with your medicine. You will take it, will you not, if I help you to sit up properly?" Without waiting for an answer, Stoneforth lifted his brother into a sitting position and held him steady until Watlow had got the dose effectively down the lad. Then Stoneforth straightened the pillows with one hand and laid Toby gently back down upon them. He began to bathe his brother's face with lavender water and watched as the blue eyes flickered closed. "He is no better," Stoneforth murmured.

"He be a demmed sight better, Colonel," replied Stoneforth's batman. "When we first come home, I reckon as I thought he'd not make it through the night. An' here it be a full week later and him a-breathin' yet."

"Yes, but he will not be shed of the fever, Watlow."

"Well, an' that's goin' ta take a bit longer, now, Colonel. You may not be rememberin' how long it took fer you ta shed yer ravin's an' rise up inta the present them times when you was wounded, but I remember well enough. I was sure-certain each time how ye was never goin' ta reckernize me agin."

"Yes," sighed Stoneforth, refreshing the bit of muslin. "I expect it took me forever, did it not?"

"Ferever," nodded Watlow, straightening the sheets and blankets around the lad. "An' I were as near certain that you were goin' ta die as you are that Mr. Toby will. But he willn't."

"No?"

"No, sir, Colonel. This 'ere lad would not dare ta die when you be opposed to it."

That brought a slow smile to Stoneforth's rugged face. "I am not as frightening as all that, Watlow. I cannot frighten a gentleman into living."

"I reckon ye can," responded Watlow quietly. "An' I reckon ye ought ta be glad of bein' fearsome, Colonel."

"I ought?"

"Aye, 'cause once this boy does be wakin' up, I reckon as how he'll be frettin' an' fussin' an' as hard ta handle as you always was after you was wounded. Ye'll be thankful then that you got the power ta frighten the lad inta doin' as ye bid."

Stoneforth hoped with all his heart that Watlow was correct, that if he could not pray Toby into living he could somehow frighten him into it. Because if he could not, he knew for a certainty that the heart he had promised Nora to open and share with those he loved would explode like a mortar shell and he would be as good as dead himself.

Waving Watlow away, Stoneforth set the lavender water aside and moved from the edge of the bed to the wing chair he had set beside it. He picked up a volume of poems by William Blake, the Engraver, from the cricket table, found his place and continued painstakingly on. It was not a great bother to be blind in one eye. There was no difference in the appearance of the orb, nor did it jump about or do anything else unusual except twitch from time to time when he was very angry. But letters appeared to move of their own accord upon a page when he sat down to read. They began to undulate and blur, and he could make little sense of print or hand-writing without tremendous effort. Stoneforth thought that he could prevent the letters from acting so oddly if only he persisted in reading for an hour or so each day. And so he persisted, struggling through volume after volume until the letters should settle into words and the words behave properly. So far, they had not.

"I doubt I ever will read comfortably again," he sighed aloud, marking his place with a red riband from which a tarnished silver medal dangled. His gaze drifted to Toby but what he actually saw, for the briefest moment, was a boy of five standing beside a coffin, a veritable cherub of a boy, with hair as brown and thick as a beaver's pelt and eyes as blue as sunlit summer skies, eyes that stared with such innocent horror at that coffin, that Stoneforth had never seen the like, even among the first-timers upon the battlefield. "I love you, Tobias Attenbury," he whispered hoarsely. "I have never told you so but it is true. I love you and I will do anything to keep you safe and happy."

"Melody," whispered his brother in return. "I love you."

"Yes. You love Melody. I know that, Scamp. And let us hope that she knows it as well, eh?"

It had preyed upon Stoneforth's mind for several days that Toby's Melody had not once sent anyone around to ask after his brother. But then Ridgeworth, Toby's valet, had informed him that Miss Harriman had not known the first thing about the duel and had, in fact, departed for the country on the very morning that Toby had met his man upon the dueling ground. And Toby's second in the duel, Mr. Frederick Haversham, had informed him, much to his surprise, that Miss Harriman quite possibly knew nothing of Toby's infatuation with her.

"I will wager she did not think him at all serious," Haversham had muttered. "We none of us did. Not even Wentworth. Which is why Wentworth made the remarks he did in Toby's presence, you know. Because he thought Toby would laugh like everyone else."

"Except you did not laugh, did you, Scamp?" sighed Stoneforth, reaching over to lay a cool hand upon his brother's burning brow. "I cannot think, if you loved the girl, why you did not tell her so straight out, especially when you intended to place yourself in the gravest danger—and all for her honor. I should think that would be the best way to do it. But what do I know?" A haunted smile twisted at Stoneforth's lips. "My only experience with love occurred across a panoptic collage of battlefields and ended in disaster. I have never attempted to romance a young lady in a drawing room. No, nor at such a place as Ridgeworth and Haversham say that this Almack's is."

Lady Harriman was both amused and relieved by the missive that arrived upon her butler's silver salver late that afternoon. "Does Frederick's groom await an answer, Higgens?"

"Indeed, my lady."

"Go to him then and say that he shall have a reply shortly and then send Mrs. Claymore to me in the library if you please."

"Yes, my lady," replied Higgens, exiting the chamber.

"What a lark!" exclaimed Lady Harriman, rising. "The Lange triplets in London! I am amazed that Frederick should acquiesce to the idea. Why, he has not let those girls out of his sight from the day they were born."

Her cotton twill skirt swishing about her ankles, Lady Harriman strolled down the corridor to the library, and taking a seat behind the oak table, she gathered pen and paper about her. *By all means bring the cousins with you!* she wrote, the smile never leaving her face. *I look forward to it eagerly. What a gay time we shall have! Give my love to their papa and say that he must not worry a bit about them.* She signed it with a flourish, folded the paper and sealed it with a wafer.

"My lady?" asked a voice from the threshold.

"Yes, Mrs. Claymore. My daughter returns on Tuesday and her cousins accompany her. We shall need to prepare chambers for them. I expect it must be the striped chamber. That is quite the largest. You will need Robert's help to bring two of the old feather beds down from the attic."

"Yes, my lady."

"Good. And the girls will doubtless bring Annie. Have you room in the servants' quarters for an abigail? She is a tiny thing as I recall and will not require a great deal of space."

"She may share with Dorabelle," replied the housekeeper.

"Yes, good. Take this missive to the groom in the kitchen before you begin, if you will." With a wave of her hand, Lady Harriman dismissed the woman and, rising from behind the table, began to pace the library excitedly.

This is just the thing, she thought, clasping her hands behind her back. I cannot think why it did not occur to me. Well, it did not because I did never think that Frederick would allow them to come. But they are quite old enough to be gaining some town bronze. They are seventeen now and will enjoy a taste of the Season. And with the triplets beside her, Melody will not take the rudeness of strangers so much to heart. A frown puckered Lady Harriman's brow as she remembered the particularly rude reception her daughter had met with at the hands of Lord Wentworth and his devoted entourage.

"And it is all my fault," she murmured to herself. "I took such great pleasure in accompanying Arthur on one mission after another that I did not once think to return to London in time for Melody's presentation. I have been most selfish and most remiss."

What Lady Harriman had been remiss about had been time. The years of her marriage had veritably flown by. Before she had so much as blinked her eyes, Melody had turned twenty-four. That realization had startled her ladyship into action.

"Twenty-four," she whispered now. "How could I have allowed her to reach twenty-four without ever bringing her to London and presenting her properly? Arthur and I were married three years and I expecting Melody when I was twenty-four. What sort of mother am I? It is my fault that these young ladies and gentlemen call her a spinster and ignore her and say that she is upon the shelf. But things will be better now. The cousins will shine a new light upon everything. Melody will smile again and that smile will win her the attention and the friendships she deserves and perhaps a young gentleman's devotion as well."

Stoneforth was not smiling as he stood in morning dress, ramrod straight before Lord Castlereagh of the Foreign Office.

"I wondered if I was ever to have the honor of making your acquaintance, Colonel," stated the newly appointed Secretary of Foreign Affairs. "It is a pleasure, believe me. Although I think you have got the wrong person. Liverpool is in charge at the War Office now. Doubtless it is he whom you wish to see."

"No," replied Stoneforth. "You are the one I need. Nothing to do with the war. A—personal matter."

"Take a seat then," Castlereagh offered, slipping back down into the chair behind his desk.

Stoneforth sat and crossed one knee over the other. He rested his elbows upon the chair arms and made a steeple of his hands. "It is, ah, something considerably stupid actually," he said gruffly.

"Is it? Do continue," urged Castlereagh, curious.

"I ought to know how to go about it myself," Stoneforth sighed, "but I have been a soldier too long. I am not accustomed to London Society. I have not been here in some fifteen years. Soldiering, you know."

"Just so," nodded Castlereagh, "and we do all of us wish you were soldiering still. Wellesley and I especially. Attenbury was born to fight, Wellesley always says."

Stoneforth's deep blue eyes flickered with humor. "Just so," he nodded. "Born to fight. Not born to dance."

"Not born to dance?" Generally a solemn, formal man, Castlereagh grinned. His sense of humor—which his subordinates took leave to doubt he had—began to tickle like a long-lost feather at his insides. "You have come to me on a matter involved with dancing?"

"Somewhat, yes, though I do not expect that they can actually require me to dance. I expect a gentleman may simply go and stand about."

Castlereagh leaned forward, spreading his arms across his desk. The name of Colonel Attenbury had figured in innumerable conversations, discussions and field despatches while Castlereagh had been in charge at the War Office. A list of battle decorations the length of a man's arm had been bestowed upon the gentleman before him. Yet Castlereagh had never before had so much as a glimpse of the man. Now he was getting that glimpse and finding the colonel oddly beguiling. "Join me in a glass of port?" Castlereagh asked, pushing himself back from the desk and rising to fill two glasses from the decanter upon the credenza behind him. He carried one to Stoneforth, took the other for himself and, leaning one hip against the desk top, he toasted, "To His Majesty."

"To His Majesty," responded Stoneforth.

"Now, you need not be circumspect with me, Colonel. Just spit it out. I would consider it a privilege to be of assistance."

Stoneforth downed the wine in one quick gulp, leaned forward and set the empty glass upon Castlereagh's desk. Then he sat back, folded his arms across his chest and looked straight up into the foreign secretary's puzzled eyes. "I hesitate to speak of it, but my Uncle North—Sanshire, you know—wrote to me a few years back that things between yourself and Mr. Canning had come to a head and that the two of you had dueled. No, do not glare, Castlereagh. I know it is not a matter you care to discuss. I would not refer to it at all, except that because of it, I think you will understand me better. My younger brother has been involved in a duel. He took a ball in the shoulder and is lying abed this moment raving like a lunatic from the subsequent infection."

"My God," murmured Castlereagh, his glare diminishing. "He is not like to die?"

"The surgeon who removed the ball says he hopes not. My batman says he thinks not. But neither one of them is certain and Toby continues to rave. It has been over a week and he grows no better, Castlereagh."

"What is it I can do?" asked Castlereagh grimly.

"The entire thing, I am told, was over some young lady with whom Toby has fallen in love. I cannot think what she must be like to provoke Tobias into challenging this Wentworth person to a duel, but I think that I must bring her to Toby whether or not I am like to approve of her, and to bring her as soon as I possibly can. If she speaks to him, if once he hears her voice, perhaps. . . . Well, I was very close to death once and Nora—she is dead now, Nora Huston—but hers was the only voice that could reach me in the midst of my delusions."

"Wentworth? Your brother dueled with the Earl of Wentworth? Over a woman?"

"Indeed."

"Damnation, Colonel. Wentworth is notorious. They say he has downed more men than anyone cares to count. Your brother had no business to—"

"My brother had not the least business to point a pistol at anyone regardless of whether he stood to win or lose," growled Stoneforth. "I am the Attenbury who kills people. Tobias is the Attenbury who was raised to be a respectable young gentleman."

"What is it that you need?" asked Castlereagh. "Name it, Colonel, and it is yours."

"I wish to meet this young woman, this Miss Harriman, in a most unexceptionable way and convince her to come to Toby. Word of the duel cannot get about, Castlereagh. I have thought over all that Ridgeworth— he is my brother's valet, Ridgeworth—I have thought over all that he has told me about Society's rules these days and I have concluded that the best way to go about meeting Miss Harriman is to gain entrance to a particular establishment where she and I may be introduced without arousing the least curiosity. Ridgeworth tells me, however, that the place requires a ticket, which cannot be purchased without a voucher, which cannot be got without the approval of certain ladies."

"Almack's," hissed Castlereagh.

"Yes, that would be the name Ridgeworth gave me. He appeared to think that Lady Castlereagh might be one of the ladies who—"

"Gawd, I should say Emily Anne is 'one of the ladies

who,' " interrupted Castlereagh as he set his empty glass aside and sat upon his desktop, his legs dangling. "But Emily Anne and the other patronesses will make you jump through hoops and still not give you a voucher for weeks. They love it—wielding power. No, forget vouchers and tickets, Colonel. I shall get you in myself. You will meet me in King Street this Wednesday evening shortly before eleven. We will not give Mr. Willis so much as time to breathe before he closes the doors. You will make Miss Harriman's acquaintance, I promise you."

Two

On the very Wednesday evening to which Castlereagh had referred, Miss Melody Harriman, in a most delightful gown of white muslin with an empire waist accentuated by a forest green riband, stepped lightly down from her mama's coach. Similar ribands accented the sleeves and the square neckline and the hem of the deceptively simple fashion that floated enticingly about her slim figure. Equally as deceptive as the simplicity of her gown was the smile that touched Miss Harriman's lips. At first glance anyone would have deduced that she, like all of the other young ladies converging upon the boring brick building in King Street, St. James's, was both pleased and becomingly grateful to have been acknowledged as a member of London's elite and thus invited within Almack's Ionic doorcase. Not the merest flicker of a frown betrayed the anger written large in Melody's heart. Not one of the remembered insults that buzzed about her brain made the slightest appearance in the mysterious sea green depths of her eyes.

"I say, Melody, it is distressingly ordinary," murmured Bea as she descended onto the flagway directly behind her cousin. "Are you certain this is the correct place?"

"Well, of course it is, Bea," declared Ally as she joined them. "Uncle Arthur's coachman is not such a ninny as to mistake the building. But it is not at all as I imagined it to be."

"No, I realize," responded Melody. "It is not what I imagined it to be either. And the inside is much worse. There is nothing the least bit enticing about it. The dance floor is warped and the food and drink are terrible and the people are haughty and pretentious. Mr. Gow's musicians play with some talent, but otherwise Almack's is a positively dreadful place. It depends upon the prestige of its patrons to give it allure. That is what Mama says. One must be considered to be the *crème de la crème* of Society to enter here, though why the *crème de la crème* wish to have anything to do with such a place I cannot say."

"Humph!" said Kate, who had just gained the flagway and turned to assist Lady Harriman from the enormous coach.

"Humph, indeed," giggled Bea. "If one must be the cream of Society to enter, how do Ally and Kate and I come to be here?"

"You come to be here because your lineage, my dears, is impeccable. And because I have procured vouchers for you from Lady Sefton," smiled Lady Harriman. "Maria remembers your papa fondly. It was your papa who introduced her to Lord Sefton."

"It was?" asked Ally. "Papa? A matchmaker?"

"Only through the greatest necessity," laughed Lady Harriman. "Your papa was forced to introduce them or have Lord Sefton punch him in the nose."

The small party strolled under the bright canopy and Lady Harriman handed in their tickets to a smiling, bowing Mr. Willis at the door. Then she herded her charges up the staircase and into the ballroom on the second floor, where she paused to introduce each of her nieces to the patronesses present that evening. Lady Jersey's eyes came near to starting from her head at the sight of the lovely Lange triplets bedecked in matching muslin gowns, their fine gray eyes aglow with excitement and their autumn-colored curls becomingly dressed—except for the one—the one Lady Harriman had called Beatrice. Her curls were really quite short and refused to be dressed in any manner that resembled her sisters' hair at all.

Well, at the least I will not be confused as to which one is Beatrice, Lady Jersey thought. But how any of us shall tell the other two apart, I cannot think.

Lady Sefton cooed and kissed each of the triplets upon the cheek and called them Frederick's angels and declared that the gentlemen were certainly in for a treat this evening.

Mrs. Drummond-Burrell lifted an eyebrow and nodded.

"Which is the very best anyone can expect from Mrs. Drummond-Burrell," whispered Melody into Bea's ear. "She is the most arrogant of the lot, I think. She frowns down upon everyone. Oh, I am so grateful that you came. I should be shaking in my slippers else, to be forced to face another evening in this wretched place. Look, there in the far corner, just near the potted plant. That is the Earl of Wentworth. He is such a—a—"

"A what?" asked Beatrice, studying the gentleman in a most forthright manner.

"A beast," sputtered Melody.

"That splendid gentleman?"

"Is merely splendid on the outside," Melody declared. "Beneath all his fine feathers he is a savage beast."

Bea's eyes lighted with interest. "Did you hear that, Kate?" she asked, tugging at the skirt of her sister's gown.

"Yes," grinned Kate, "and I gather that you intend to debeast that particular fellow yourself."

"Indeed I do," nodded Bea. "You may be certain of it."

The Earl of Wentworth glanced about him at the bevy of beauties who filled the ballroom and sighed a well-practiced, world-weary sigh and then choked right in the middle of it. Who the devil was that? And what did she think she was doing looking him up and down in such a forthright manner as though he were some stud on the block at Tattersall's? The devil!

Thinking to set the staring maiden to the blush for such impertinence, Wentworth raised his quizzing glass, took one step in the girl's direction, then studied her outrageously. And then he gulped, lowered his glass and turned away himself, because rather than blushing, the young woman had continued to stare at him, her smile had widened and she had winked.

"That will give him pause," declared Bea triumphantly.

"Indeed," agreed Ally. "Now instead of some cheeky little chit, he probably considers you a veritable strumpet."

"Pooh! As if I care. I know I am not a strumpet, and what he thinks can make no difference to me. I am cheeky, though," Bea added with a giggle. "Even Papa says that I am cheeky."

Melody felt like laughing aloud. Never had she seen Lord Wentworth's cool, bored composure shaken. She had assumed it was beyond anyone's ability to strike beneath his lordship's ennui to the very heart of the fiend. And now Bea had noticeably done so with one short, swift thrust. "You are the most remarkable girl, Beatrice," she said, as they followed Lady Harriman to the side of the chamber and sat down in little gilded chairs all in a row, Lady Harriman first and then Bea and Melody, Kate and Ally.

"What exactly did that gentleman do to make you

think him such a great beast?" asked Ally, leaning across Kate to get Melody's attention.

"He danced one dance with me and then wandered around town for an entire week proclaiming to everyone who would listen that I was quite as boring as he had expected me to be. He said that I was dull, lacked conversation and that it was the first time he had ever discovered himself dozing off in the midst of a reel."

"Oh!" exclaimed Ally, Kate and Bea.

"And then he named me The Harriman Lullaby because I put him to sleep, and all the gentlemen snickered behind my back for a fortnight and the young ladies laughed and laughed about it. I thought I should die of embarrassment. I do not understand why he takes me in dislike. I was most polite to him."

"Well, you ought never be polite to him again," declared Bea. "And you ought to have done something exceptionally *dire* to him the very moment you heard what he had said."

"Do not waste time in regret over missing that opportunity, however," offered Kate. "Bea will certainly do something exceptionally *dire* to him on your behalf, will you not, dearest?"

"Indeed. I must only discover more about him so that when I lunge and thrust home I prick him to the very core."

"And you must not feel sad or waste your anger upon any of the other ladies and gentlemen who laughed with him, Mel," Ally added, giving her cousin's hand a pat. "Anyone can see that they are not worth it. How such a flock of nobodies could send you crying into our arms I cannot think. Honestly, to name you elderly and a spinster and boring as well, and then to flounce and prance about with such pomposity themselves as though they had not one ugly feather among them! Well, we

will put an end to that. But we must make their acquaintances first before we can devise a workable plan."

And then all private conversation among the four
young ladies ceased as, singly and in groups, gentlemen
came to be introduced properly to the Lange triplets
and to request dances of them. Young ladies approached as well, some with their mamas in tow, others
upon the arms of chaperones, to be made known to
the three young ladies whose exquisite youth and
beauty, so amazingly replicated, marked them as quite
likely to become all the rage. Though jealousy murmured in a number of feminine hearts at the mere sight
of the triplets and envy arose in many others, all realized
the virtue of being able to claim close acquaintanceship
with any one of the sought-after debutantes of the Season, and without doubt the Lange triplets were going
to be sought after. Anyone with a mind had known *that*
the very instant they had entered the ballroom.

Stoneforth stared at himself in the looking glass and
thought seriously about digging his sword out from his
trunk, unsheathing the thing and falling down upon it.

"Ye look splendid!" declared Watlow encouragingly.
"A reg'lar dandy, Colonel. Why, that little Ridgeworth
has done you up right han'somelike!" Stoneforth's batman moved in a slow circle around him, studying him
every inch of the way. "I shouldn't a-given ye a penny
fer sich a twit as Ridgeworth a week ago yeste'day, but
jist see what he has wrought. Aye, jist look at what he has
gone an' wrought."

"What exactly is it that you think he has wrought,
Watlow?"

"Why, he has maked you inta a reg'lar gen'leman, he
has."

"I was born a gentleman."

"Aye, but I ain't never afore seen ye look like one."

Stoneforth's grim countenance brightened. "You do not think I looked like a gentleman in my uniform, Watlow?"

"No, sir. That is, I reckon as how you might have once. The time it were cleanlike. I did not know ye then."

A smile flickered in Stoneforth's eyes. "It was clean more than once, Watlow, my uniform."

"It were? Well, I'll be demmed. I never seen it without it were covered in dust, er mud, er blood."

"No, I expect not. But when first I purchased my commission, I was a dazzling sight, let me tell you."

"And now you be dazzlin' once again."

Stoneforth's attention returned to his reflection in the looking glass. Perhaps he did not look as dreadful as he thought. Watlow did not seem to think so. Perhaps it was simply the fact that he was unaccustomed to such things as knee breeches and silk hose and dancing slippers. Perhaps every gentleman he met would *not* double over in laughter at the very sight of him. "But every young lady will run screaming for her mother," he mumbled.

"Balderdash," replied Watlow.

"What?"

"Balderdash, Colonel. Ever' young lady willn't run screamin' fer their mamas."

"Oh, I said that aloud, did I?"

"Aye."

That is something that I am going to need to watch, Stoneforth thought as he accepted the gloves Ridgeworth brought him and tugged them on. I cannot go about speaking aloud to myself or everyone will think me mad. Although, I must be mad to have gone to Castlereagh and actually asked him to get me into this place. I cannot think why I did it. "Yes, I can," he muttered. "Yes, I can."

"Pardon, my lord?" asked Ridgeworth.

"Not speakin' at you," snickered Watlow. "Speakin' ta hisself, the colonel were."

"I see." Ridgeworth did not truly see, but he thought it best to say that he did, just as he thought it best not to take a swat at the annoying, plebeian Watlow. Ridgeworth did not, after all, have endless opportunities for employment and he was quite certain that his position with Mr. Attenbury could come to an abrupt end if he should somehow displease Mr. Attenbury's elder brother. Doubtless, taking a swat at Watlow would displease him.

"Well, you have done your best, Ridgeworth," sighed Stoneforth, placing the *chapeau bras* upon his carefully arranged curls. "I only hope that I do not prove a disappointment to you."

"Never, my lord," breathed Ridgeworth. How Lord Stoneforth could speak so of himself, he could not imagine. Lord Stoneforth was the very sort of gentleman upon whom a valet might build his reputation. His broad shoulders and narrow waist, his well-formed limbs and marvelous posture—all combined to display clothing to perfection. Every bit of taste and advice that Ridgeworth had invested in the gentleman was now repaid a hundredfold.

"Has John brought the carriage around, Watlow?"

"Awaitin' ye at the front door, Colonel—I mean Lor'ship."

"Colonel will do, Watlow. It has been Colonel between us for five years now. I do not expect that you will remember the lordship part for another five. You will both of you keep a close watch over Toby, eh? And you know where I am to be reached if I am required. Do not hesitate to send for me."

"Ye willn't be required, Colonel," grinned Watlow. "That boy be strong as a ox. An' once you 'ave fetched this Miss Harriman o' his, why he'll be a-poppin' out o' that fever within a day er two."

"Just so, my lord," Ridgeworth nodded. "Mr. Attenbury will be well tended in your absence, I assure you."

And then Stoneforth was exiting the chamber and off down the corridor to the main staircase.

Robert Stewart, Lord Castlereagh, stood waiting for Stoneforth beneath Almack's canopy and welcomed him with an unaccustomed smile and a warm handshake. "So, are you quite prepared?" he asked.

"Prepared?"

"For the stir you are about to cause, Attenbury. No, I ought not be calling you that. You have sold out and I ought to be calling you Stoneforth now. I will not forget again."

"It makes no matter."

"Yes, it does. The King Street Cabal will be a deal more impressed by a viscount than by a lieutenant colonel. Believe me, I know. And you will be forced to meet at least three of them tonight. Thank God, my Emily is not here nor Princess Esterhazy. They have gone off to Bath together to pay a call upon Emily's aunt. That, at least, is in our favor."

"In our favor?"

"Yes. We need a number of things to be in our favor if we are to get you into these hallowed halls tonight," explained Castlereagh. "Do you know the time?"

"Near eleven, I expect." Stoneforth tugged his watch from his pocket and squinted intently down at it. "Very near five minutes of eleven."

"Good. Perfect," murmured Castlereagh, taking Stoneforth's arm and leading him toward Mr. Willis, who stood smiling and nodding at the entrance.

"Good evening, Willis."

"Good evening, my lord."

"Fine night, is it not? Seems likely that everyone who is coming has come, eh?"

"Quite, Lord Castlereagh."

"Just so. We are the last then," he added most unnecessarily. "Stoneforth, may I present to you Mr. Willis, the guardian of the doors. Willis, Lord Stoneforth."

Mr. Willis, his eyes smiling, bowed respectfully and looked from one to the other of the gentlemen. "Your tickets?" he asked.

"Yes, well, that is just the thing, Willis. We have not got our tickets," announced Castlereagh.

"You have not? But, my lord, you know I cannot—"

"I am aware of the rules, Willis." Castlereagh took Mr. Willis by the arm and led him the merest bit away from Stoneforth, ostensibly so as not to be overheard. "The truth of the matter is, Willis, that Lady Castlereagh and I had a row last week and I tore up my tickets. Stupid of me, I know."

"Yes, my lord. I mean—"

"No, never mind, Willis. It *was* stupid of me. I thought never to wish to enter Almack's again, but I have changed my mind since. I wonder if you might, just this once—Well, you do know me, Willis, and you are quite aware that my Emily is one of the patronesses, and you do know that my presence here is most acceptable to the others."

"Indeed, my lord. I should not think to forbid you entrance."

"No. Good. Then Lord Stoneforth and I will simply—"

"I do not know Lord Stoneforth," murmured Mr. Willis.

"He is my guest, Willis."

"Yes, but even one's guests must receive the nod from

one of the patronesses and—I shall simply step upstairs and request a word from one of her ladyships."

"It is two minutes until eleven, Willis," Castlereagh declared, tugging his watch from his pocket and offering it with a flourish to the man's view. "It will be time to close the doors by the time you gain the ballroom."

"Yes, but, I cannot merely—Perhaps you might bring Lord Stoneforth back next Wednesday," suggested Willis hopefully.

"No, I have brought him this Wednesday. Listen to me very carefully, Mr. Willis." Castlereagh once again took Willis' arm and tugged him even farther away from Stoneforth. "Until recently, Lord Stoneforth was better known as Colonel Attenbury of His Majesty's Dragoons, and he has what he considers a monumental reason to require entrance here tonight. It is not a social matter."

"Yes, my lord, but—"

"I have not finished, Mr. Willis. Lord Stoneforth has been upon battlefield after battlefield since 1796. He has lived in the midst of war longer than he has lived in the midst of Society. Because of it, he has grown most accustomed to killing, Mr. Willis, as well he might. Why, the gentleman kills as naturally as he walks, without thought or hesitation or guilt whenever he deems it necessary to do so."

Mr. Willis' eyes widened considerably. "Are you suggesting, my lord, that—"

"I suggest nothing, Willis. I merely point out that Lord Stoneforth sees his entrance into Almack's tonight as a grim necessity, and I cannot help but worry that he might—"

"In," declared Mr. Willis on a great gulp. "Take him in at once, my lord. The bells chime eleven. I must lock the doors."

"Thank you, Willis," replied Castlereagh soberly, turning about on his heel, stepping up to Stoneforth, taking his arm and leading him inside the building and up the staircase.

"What the devil was all that about?" asked Stoneforth.

"Never mind, Colonel. Never mind," chuckled Castlereagh. "My gawd, I have not enjoyed myself in so long a time that I have forgotten how it feels to actually laugh. The ballroom is just above us on the second floor. I shall introduce you to whichever of the patronesses is standing guard, eh? Your brother has been here before?"

Stoneforth nodded.

"Good. I shall point that out at once and the ladies will be certain that Emily Anne has bestowed vouchers upon you."

Lady Jersey's jaw, which had not ceased to move since the Lange triplets had first appeared at the top of the staircase, froze instantly open as Lord Castlereagh crossed the threshold to the ballroom accompanied by the most ruggedly handsome gentleman she had ever seen. Her heart gave a large thump. Her mind screamed, *Who is he? Who is he?* And then her jaw snapped closed and she veritably flew to welcome Lady Castlereagh's dour husband and his perfectly awe-inspiring companion.

Castlereagh made the introductions quite soberly and then drew Sally Jersey a few steps aside and began to whisper seriously in her ear. Her eyes grew large and she glanced at Lord Stoneforth and then back at Castlereagh, who nodded and then began to whisper in her ear again.

"You cannot be serious, Robert."

"Oh yes, my dear. Deadly serious. He is Sanshire's nephew, you know. And you know very well how dangerous Sanshire was in his youth. You have heard the stories as well as I."

Lady Jersey gulped. Her heart gave a great lurch and in a moment she was smiling widely and offering to escort Lord Stoneforth from group to group to introduce him around.

"No need, Sally," interrupted Lord Castlereagh. "I have brought him; I will introduce him about. Just go on with your visiting, my dear. You did not want her to introduce you about, did you?" asked Castlereagh as Lady Jersey curtsied most seductively to Stoneforth and departed.

"Not if you can do it instead," Stoneforth replied. "Do you truly know all of these people?"

"No. Barely a one of them."

"Well, do you know Toby's Miss Harriman?"

"No. But I do know Lady Harriman. Lord Harriman is presently in the service of the Foreign Office and a member of our envoy to Russia. We met once, she and I, at a dinner. That will be her seated across the room. The blond lady in the green silk. I expect that will be Miss Harriman in white seated beside her. Come, Stoneforth. No better time than the present."

"But it will look to everyone as though I came especially to seek the girl out and that is precisely what I wish to avoid."

"Not to worry, Stoneforth, I shall go on to introduce you to several other people afterward and then we will go off to the card room and you may return and approach Miss Harriman whenever and however you think best, eh?"

Lady Harriman smiled benignly upon Lord Castlereagh and expressed a deal of pleasure at making the acquaintance of his guest for the evening. She then made both of the gentlemen known to her daughter and, as a country dance was just then ending, urged them to remain and make the acquaintance of her nieces.

Melody watched as Lord Castlereagh and Lord Stoneforth bowed over the triplets' hands and murmured pleasantries much the same as they had murmured to her. She was quite astonished at them. All evening long gentlemen had been falling over each other to make the triplets' acquaintances and to gain a dance with one or the other of them. Yes, and they had all been making perfect cakes of themselves about gaining a dance, too. But apparently the love-inspiring vision of Ally, Beatrice and Kate, all similarly attired and all delightfully flushed from the exercise of dancing, had no such effect upon these two gentlemen.

Melody's bemused gaze followed Lord Castlereagh and Lord Stoneforth as they wandered off through the side door into the card room. "Mama," she asked quietly, "if he is Lord Stoneforth, does that not mean that he is Mr. Attenbury's elder brother?"

"Indeed," nodded her mama.

"He is Colonel Attenbury?" exclaimed Bea excitedly. *"The* Colonel Attenbury?"

"Oh no," sighed Ally. "I do hope he is not *the* Colonel Attenbury or the poor man will not have a moment's peace while we are in London."

"Stoneforth," murmured Beatrice, signaling for the gentleman who had come to lead her into the next dance to wait a moment. "Stoneforth. Of course he is one and the same. He must be. Oh, it is so confusing when gentlemen join in the fighting, because they will abandon their titles and be known by their ranks. But I am almost certain that Papa said Colonel Attenbury was Stoneforth."

"Yes, he did," groaned Kate, "but we have not come to London to traipse about on that particular gentleman's heels, Bea. We have come to—" The gentleman who had scrawled his name across Kate's dance card for this particular dance came forward to take her hand, and Kate thought better of announcing why she and her sisters had come to London. Instead, she curtsied and took Lord Emerson's arm and allowed him to escort her to the floor.

Ally took Lord Danforth's arm and physically placed Bea's hand upon Mr. Bridges' arm, and in a moment the breathless rush that seemed always to be the Lange triplets vanished.

"Well, I cannot think what that was all about," offered Lady Harriman, noting with some despair that once again her daughter did not dance. "Would you care for something to drink, Mel? I shall fetch us something, shall I?"

Melody nodded and watched as her mama rose and departed the ballroom. Mr. Attenbury's elder brother? For the very first time she noted that Mr. Attenbury was absent this evening. Why he was always at Almack's. And most generally he took pity upon her at some time during the evening and requested her to dance with him, too. Melody smiled. She liked Mr. Attenbury. He had never treated her poorly. He had never been condescending to her. He had never once laughed at Lord Wentworth's devastating observations upon herself and her age—at least, she did not think that he ever had. Mr. Attenbury had always seemed simply to accept her and he required only that she smile at him from time to time when they were dancing. Yes, one evening, she remembered, he had said as sweetly as could be, *"Do smile upon me, princess, or I shall think myself doomed in your eyes before I have even begun to hope."*

"I wonder if his brother is at all like him?" Melody whispered to herself, gazing about to see if perhaps Lord Stoneforth had reentered the ballroom. "I wonder if he is?"

Three

It took Stoneforth almost a quarter hour to gather his considerable courage about him and depart the card room.

"Are you thinking to ask Miss Harriman to dance?" Castlereagh inquired, following behind, sipping at a glass of orgeat. "I should think that a waltz would be best. You might speak to her quite privately while you are waltzing. Do you know how to waltz?"

"In theory," muttered Stoneforth. "I have never actually done the thing. But it cannot be any more complicated than the sword exercise, do you think?"

"It is quite uncomplicated, actually." Castlereagh could not quite deduce what it was about Stoneforth that urged him to it, but nevertheless, he gave the gentleman a pat upon the back and smiled encouragingly into the colonel's worried eyes. "You shall need to ask one of the patronesses to give Miss Harriman permission to waltz. She may already have permission, but it will be better to request it regardless, because she cannot waltz with you, Stoneforth, if one of them has not given her the nod. Besides, the carnivores will like you all the better for it."

Stoneforth paused in his wandering about the edges of the floor and turned to cock an eyebrow at Castlereagh. "Why do you call them that?" he asked. "Carnivores?"

"Because they tear people up into little shreds and eat them," replied Castlereagh blandly. "Even Emily Anne does it."

"Not literally."

"No, but figuratively—and figuratively is messy enough, believe me. There is Sally. Walk up to her and ask if Miss Harriman may waltz with you."

Stoneforth followed Castlereagh's gaze, discovered Lady Jersey among a group of chattering ladies and gentlemen and wandered in that direction. The moment he approached, Lady Jersey's eyes took on a most interested gleam. "Lord Stoneforth, may I present Lady Sefton and Mrs. Drummond-Burrell and Lord Wentworth and Miss Pascale and Mr. Davies."

Wentworth? Stoneforth's eyes fairly glittered as he bowed to the group and his gaze focused upon the splendidly dressed earl.

"Lord Stoneforth has but recently returned from Portugal," continued Lady Jersey, quite brazenly taking Stoneforth's arm. "We must all be most hospitable to him, my dears. Not only is he a hero, but he is quite likely the most dangerous gentleman in all of England. I have that from Robert's own lips."

Stoneforth heard not a word she said. His deep blue eyes iced with suppressed fury as he glared at Wentworth. "You are an acquaintance of my brother, I think," he growled deep in his throat, the muscles about his blind eye twitching the merest bit.

"And your brother would be—?" drawled Wentworth with obvious disinterest.

"Attenbury. Mr. Tobias Attenbury."

"And I am amazed not to see Mr. Attenbury here," interrupted Lady Jersey, feeling the instant tension between the two gentlemen but not in the least understanding it. She gave Stoneforth's strong forearm a squeeze and laughed the oddest laugh. "Mr. Attenbury is one of our favorite young gentlemen and we miss him."

"Toby is occupied elsewhere this evening," Stoneforth responded, without removing his frigid gaze from Wentworth. "You are acquainted with my brother, are you not, Wentworth?"

The Earl of Wentworth's dark eyes flickered. He raised one hand to his mouth to cover an artificial yawn. Then he lifted his chin and stared at Stoneforth with an annoying insouciance. "Yes. We are known to each other, Mr. Attenbury and I."

"So I thought. You and I, Wentworth, shall come to know each other equally as well. I assure you of it." And then Stoneforth's gaze turned to the lady beside him and one gloved hand moved to cover her hand, which clung to his sleeve. "My lady," he said with the most serious of expressions, "I have come to request that you give Miss Harriman permission to dance the waltz if you have not already done so. Lord Castlereagh claims that all the young ladies must have your approval before they attempt that particular dance."

"Miss Harriman?" asked Lady Jersey, a slender eyebrow rising in surprise. "Not one of the Lange triplets, my lord? I have had every gentleman in the room approach me with requests to allow those three young ladies to waltz, which they cannot, of course. Not so very soon."

"The Lange triplets? Who the deuce are the Lange triplets?"

Lady Jersey's lips parted in surprise. "Who are they? Why, they are Miss Harriman's cousins, my lord, and have been collecting gentlemen's hearts since first they entered the chamber. They are quite the most bewitching trio of young ladies to enter our establishment this Season and will quite likely become all the rage even before the night is out. You met them shortly after you entered. Lady Harriman presented them to you."

"I fear I did not take much note of them," sighed Stoneforth. "I am not much for remembering people when I am forced to meet so many at one time. But I am quite certain that it is Miss Harriman with whom I wish to waltz." Stoneforth's attention turned from Lady Jersey in response to a mumbled word from Wentworth. "What was it you said, my lord?" he asked quietly. "I did not quite hear."

Wentworth shifted his weight from one leg to the other. His fingers fumbled with his quizzing glass, but he did not raise it to his eye. "I said, merely, that apparently all the Attenburys prefer ladies who are well out of the schoolroom."

Miss Pascale tittered. Mr. Davies hushed her with a glance.

"You take a peculiar interest in the sort of ladies we Attenburys prefer, Wentworth, do you not? I cannot think why you should. However, we shall meet in the near future, you and I, and address your concerns properly. You may depend upon it."

"I do believe that Miss Harriman has waited quite long enough to waltz," interrupted Lady Jersey, confused by the conversation between the gentlemen and wondering why Lord Stoneforth's words should make Lord Wentworth blanch. "Most certainly you have my permission, Lord Stoneforth, to lead Miss Harriman out. But I do believe it is my responsibility to protect the dear girl."

"Protect her?" Stoneforth's devilishly blue eyes glanced down at Lady Jersey with a hint of a smile in them. "How so, protect her? From me do you mean?"

"Exactly so. I do believe you must waltz with me before you waltz with Miss Harriman," declared Lady Jersey boldly. "In fact, I am quite certain it is my duty to insist that you do so. How else will I know that you *can* waltz and without stepping upon the girl's toes and putting her to the blush?"

Mrs. Drummond-Burrell made the oddest gasping sound in her throat. Lady Sefton stared wide-eyed at Lady Jersey. Miss Pascale and Mr. Davies stared in equal astonishment at each other, and Lord Wentworth's jaw dropped open.

"Neil is striking up for a waltz even as we speak!" exclaimed Lady Jersey, her grip upon Stoneforth's arm tightening. "How fortuitous for us!" And without another word, she veritably dragged Stoneforth out onto the floor.

"Of all things!" declared Mrs. Drummond-Burrell. "What in heaven's name has got into Sally?"

Lady Jersey wondered that very same thing herself. But then Lord Stoneforth's hand caressed the small of her back and the muscles in his arm rippled beneath her fingertips and they whirled together into the dance, and she knew without one single doubt exactly what it was that had got into her. Lord Stoneforth's back was ramrod straight and his shoulders were broad and strong and his face was a most delectable confusion of shadows and light and every movement of his enticing, well-muscled body so close to her own tempted her mercilessly toward downright lust.

"You have not been back in England long?" she managed, finding her breath coming in rather short gasps.

"Not yet a fortnight," responded Stoneforth. "Much has altered over the years. Or perhaps I have forgotten a good deal. England seems foreign to me. Am I doing this correctly?"

"Indeed. You have practiced your waltzing upon the Continent, I think. You do it quite wonderfully."

Stoneforth's first notion was to disregard the compliment and speak of the weather, but something in Lady

Jersey did much to remind him of Nora and his promise. His face abandoned its austere facade and crinkled into a most endearing grin. "No. I have not practiced upon the Continent. I have never waltzed before in all my life. You are taking a great gamble, dear lady, to be my very first dancing partner."

"I should never have guessed, my lord. Why, you waltz as though you were born to it."

Stoneforth's eyes narrowed and glittered, which made Lady Jersey gulp a most magnificent gulp, because those eyes quite abruptly suggested to her that this powerful and dangerous gentleman likely did other—more intimate—things as though he were born to them as well. For the first time in years, Lady Jersey's face grew warm and her cheeks developed a pinkish tinge. "You are a most extraordinary gentleman," she whispered, narrowing the gap between them considerably.

"An old soldier, merely," murmured Stoneforth, stepping back and widening the gap.

"Never old, my lord," Lady Jersey whispered, stepping in.

"Ancient, I assure you," Stoneforth replied, stepping back. And when he saw that she intended to close the space between them once again, he allowed himself to chuckle and add, "No, no, do not step in again, my lady, I beg of you."

Lady Jersey's eyes simmered with a mixture of pique and passion and she deliberately stepped in, leaving but a whisker of space between them.

"I have never held so—delectable—a lady in my arms," Stoneforth managed in an amused growl, amazed at the imp within him that prompted this response. "You must understand, Lady Jersey, that I have—"

"Sally," whispered Lady Jersey.

"Sally. I have long been deprived, Sally, of any—that is to say—well—if you do not step away just a bit, my dear, I cannot promise that I will not embarrass us both right here in the middle of this dance floor. And then, though I should like to meet Lord Jersey sometime, it is beyond a doubt that I shall be forced to make his acquaintance much too soon and under the most trying of circumstances." Stoneforth then whirled her into a turn, taking her breath away and giving her actual palpitations of the heart. Lady Jersey grew quite positive that if the dance lasted much longer, she would not give a fig about any embarrassment or Jersey and would quite likely melt into a puddle at Stoneforth's feet.

"What the devil were you doing?" asked Castlereagh as Stoneforth delivered Lady Jersey back to her companions at the close of the dance and then arrived at Castlereagh's side.

"Waltzing."

"Oh no. That, my bucko, was not waltzing. That was something else entirely. I have never seen Silence become so silent before."

"Silence?"

"Yes. Silence. Because she never ceases to chatter, you know. At least, she never did until now. By Jove, Stoneforth, she is not speaking yet, just staring after you while Smiley and Cuddles argue behind her. I cannot believe it."

"I am not going to inquire," drawled Stoneforth, "which of the patronesses is Smiley and which is Cuddles. I assure you, I am not. I do hope they do not intend to play the next waltz for a while. I do not think I could manage another just at the moment."

"You do look a bit dazed, Stoneforth. Are you not feeling quite the thing? Did dancing with Silence make you ill?"

"Dizzy. It is not so simple to be turning in circles when

you cannot see out of one eye. It did not bother me until the fifth turn, but by then, it was much too late to stop. There is Miss Harriman, just across the way. I shall go and request the next waltz, eh? Then we can go and sit down in the card room until it is played. Once I have danced with Miss Harriman, we can both be quit of this place."

The dancers were just taking their positions for a Scottish reel as Stoneforth stepped out onto the ballroom floor intending to cross it before the music began and to arrive in a most inconspicuous manner before Miss Harriman. But Stoneforth was dizzy and warm. Very warm. And he had been wearing boots for so many years that the dancing shoes upon his feet felt terribly foreign when it came to walking. They made his normally commanding, determined stride seem most awkward and incredibly wrong to him.

And Almack's dance floor was warped in some places.

Castlereagh gasped as Stoneforth struck the toe of one shoe against a slightly raised board, lost his balance and hit the planking with a thud. Then he gasped again as Stoneforth slid across the highly polished floor all the way to the line of chairs where Miss Harriman and her mama sat, arriving facedown at Miss Harriman's feet.

Miss Harriman's dancing slippers, Stoneforth took immediate and unavoidable note, were a forest green satin that matched the ribands which decorated her gown. Cursing under his breath, he hurriedly gained his knees and then his feet. "I—I—" he stuttered, his ears growing bright red.

"Are you all right, my lord?" asked Miss Harriman, wide-eyed.

"Come, there is a chair right here," offered Lady Harriman, taking the gentleman's arm. "Sit for a moment."

"No, thank you. I am fine. Thoroughly abashed is all."

"And bloody," observed Melody.

"Bloody? Am I?"

"Your chin is bleeding," Melody informed him, searching hurriedly through an enormous reticule for a handkerchief. "Please do sit, Lord Stoneforth. You cannot convince me that you feel at all the thing after such a wretched experience."

Stoneforth accepted the bit of lace that passed for a handkerchief from Melody's hand and dabbed blindly at his chin with it. For the longest moment he said nothing at all, simply staring down at her. "I do not think a chair is the answer," he muttered at last. "A hole would be much better. A very deep, dark hole into which I may crawl. Preferably one with a cover that I can pull tightly closed over the top of me."

Melody laughed.

"Well," sighed Stoneforth, "at least something good has come of my *faux pas.*"

"And what is that?" asked Melody.

"I have made you laugh and now you are smiling a smile that glows in your eyes instead of one which just sits arbitrarily upon your lips. You have not truly smiled the entire evening, I think. At least not at any time that I have peeked out of the card room to have a look at you. No, nor you have not danced either, have you? I dread to tell you this, now that I have managed to make a perfect spectacle of myself, but I have got permission from Lady Jersey for you to waltz."

"Is that what you were doing with Lady Jersey?" interrupted Melody's mama.

"Yes," nodded Stoneforth curtly. "Waltzing."

"Oh." Lady Harriman's eyebrows rose into a perfectly doubtful vee.

"At any rate," Stoneforth continued, "I have come to ask you to waltz with me, Miss Harriman, at the next opportunity. I will not fall again," he added. "I give you my word upon it."

* * *

Beatrice would have rushed directly to him if he had not fallen at Melody's feet. As it was, her eyes lingered upon Stoneforth as the music began and she missed three full measures before she remembered she was supposed to be dancing a reel.

"It is nothing," murmured her partner of the moment, the most curious and condescending Lord Wentworth, who had finally decided to meet the audacious girl face-to-face and foot-to-foot, so to speak. "You were distracted, my dear, as anyone might be by Miss Harriman's newly acquired admirer. He will be all the talk tomorrow, let me tell you."

"He will?" asked Bea, glancing up at the earl.

"Indeed. To dance so licentiously with Sally and then to fall on the dance floor and slide to a stop at Miss Harriman's feet? Well, I should think his name will be on everyone's lips."

"His name is Lord Stoneforth and before that Colonel Attenbury. Do not mistake it," declared Beatrice with a toss of her glossy curls and a steely flash of her speaking gray eyes. "Take pause before you think to make jest of him, my lord. He is one hundred times the man of any fellow in this chamber up to and including yourself." And lifting her nose as high into the air as it could go without abandoning her face, Bea twirled away from Wentworth into the next figure of the dance.

"Wentworth has said something dreadfully wrong," laughed Mr. Lionel Trent as he advanced to touch Kate's fingertips with his own. "Your sister has danced away from him and left him with the most amusing look of utter confusion upon his face."

"No, truly, Mr. Trent? How very odd. May I ask why you are watching Beatrice so closely when you are dancing with me?"

Mr. Trent stared at the girl, blinked, and stared again as the figure of the dance parted them.

"Do let me see if I have got it aright," pronounced Ally with a most elegant tilt of her head as the dance brought her back to Lord Henley's side. "Lady Jersey may dance with whomever and however she pleases. I may dance quite properly with any gentleman who asks me, but not the waltz, because I have not the patronesses' permission to waltz. And my cousin, Melody, does not dance at all because you and the other gentlemen do not care to disagree with Lord Wentworth's declaration that Melody is boring, practically a spinster and upon the shelf?"

"Yes, just so," nodded Lord Henley, registering most of her words but not a bit of her tone as his green-eyed gaze fastened admiringly just above the low-cut bodice of her gown. "And a gentleman may dance whenever and with whomever he chooses, providing the chit has the dance open and does not decline him. If she declines him, then she can dance with no one else for the remainder of the evening. Those are the rules."

"How aggravating," pouted Ally, a frown puckering her brow. "I shall not be able to dance one more dance for the rest of the evening once the cotillion begins. I shall be dreadfully bored, I expect, but if those are indeed the rules—"

"What?" asked Henley, his eyes rising to meet hers in surprise.

"Well, you have signed your name a second time to my card for the cotillion, have you not, Lord Henley?"

"Yes."

"Just so. And since you admit that you do not dare to disagree with Lord Wentworth upon his opinion of my cousin, well, I shall tell you that in my eyes that makes you simply one sheep of many amongst Lord Wentworth's flock. And I do not dance with sheep, my lord. So I must, of course, decline to dance the cotillion with you. It is a pity, but then, I much prefer to spend the remainder of the evening upon the shelf with my poor, boring spinster cousin than to dance with a sheep. How very sad for you," she added, as she floated away from him. "People will notice that I dance no more, will they not? And then they will conclude that I have turned you down. They will wonder why I have done so, but I expect that the rules here must be obeyed, must they not?"

Melody felt uncommonly nervous as Lord Stoneforth escorted her to the dance floor and placed his hand in the small of her back. She looked up hesitantly at his most austere and sober countenance and took a sharp little breath. Really, she did not wish to do this thing. To waltz. With him. At Almack's. He was so very tall and straight and intimidating. And absolutely everyone would be watching, especially Lord Wentworth, waiting for her to make a mistake or for Lord Stoneforth to doze off in the midst of a turn. But she had felt so very sorry for him after his fall. And he had been kind enough to seek Lady Jersey's permission for her to waltz. And he wished to dance with her even though he knew that not one gentleman had asked her to dance the entire evening.

"Do not fret, little one, I am not about to chew you up and spit you out," rumbled Stoneforth.

"Pardon me, my lord?"

"Why? What did you do?"

"I—I—you said something and I—"

"Oh," mumbled Stoneforth as the music began and he twirled her into the dance. "I must beg your pardon then. It was nothing. Sometimes I say things aloud that are not actually meant for anyone else's ears."

"Truly?"

"Yes. A habit come by long ago. Not only am I old and a soldier and clumsy, but I speak thoughts aloud that are not meant for human ears. You are kind to put up with me for even the length of one dance."

His eyes, so deeply blue that stars might shine in them at midnight, studied her with a seriousness that Melody could not understand. She had never met the gentleman before this evening. Why should he look at her so? He ought to be smiling and speaking to her of the weather or some such—or he ought to be gazing about him, bored to death, she thought with a tiny frown.

"Do you not wonder how I came by the temerity to ask you to waltz with me?" he asked quietly.

"Yes. That is, no. I do not think it audacious of you to dance with me. I think it compassionate."

"I am not known as a compassionate man."

"You are not?"

"No, not generally. No one I know would use such a word to describe me. But I wished to speak with you privately, Miss Harriman, about my brother and this seemed like the most expedient way. I could not wait much longer than tonight to gain your ear and meeting you in the midst of a crowd seemed the most inconspicuous means of doing so."

"About your brother?" Melody could not think why this overwhelming gentleman should have the least cause to speak with her about Mr. Tobias Attenbury.

"Ridgeworth and Haversham were correct. You know nothing at all about it."

"Pardon, my lord?"

"It is evident in your expression, Miss Harriman, that you cannot guess why I should wish a private word with you. I cannot think where Toby's mind was not to declare himself and tell you that he loves you before he— well, I might not have done so, because I have never been able to—to—say things—you know. But Toby cannot possibly have grown to be as silent as I."

"Lord Stoneforth," Melody managed, her mind in a whirl. "What is it that you are attempting to say?"

"That Toby has fought a duel, Miss Harriman. He took a pistol ball in the shoulder and is even now lying in his bed in Leicester Square about to succumb to a raging fever, but declaring that he loves you with every tortured breath."

"Oh!" cried Melody, stumbling against him in her astonishment. "Oh! I cannot—this cannot be true!"

"It is," Stoneforth assured her as he tightened his hold upon her and directed her back into the dance. "And what I thought was—well—there was a time that I was very near death, Miss Harriman. I raved just as feverishly as Toby, they tell me, though I do not remember that. I remember only bits of a nightmare world from which I could not escape. Still, when Nora—when the woman I loved—was fetched and came and spoke to me, the sound of her voice led me up through the frightening land into which I had fallen and back into the real world again. And I thought—I hoped—that you might come to Sanshire House and attempt to do likewise for Toby. My brother requires your help, Miss Harriman. Desperately."

"Mr. Attenbury f-fought a duel? Mr. Attenbury loves—me?" Melody was so utterly overwhelmed by Stoneforth's words that she did not notice in the least how much closer he danced to her than he had at first, nor how the strength of his hands was all that kept her upright and moving. Had he loosed his grip, she would have sat down flat upon the floor.

"Will you come, Miss Harriman? Tomorrow? You may come alone or with your maid or bring your mama and all your cousins if you wish. I will send a carriage for you if you require one or I will give you fare for a hackney cab or I will come and fetch you myself in Toby's curricle. However such things are done—you must only say and I will comply. Only please, will you come?"

There were unshed tears in Stoneforth's voice, though they were quite well hidden and no one of his old acquaintance other than Nora Huston would have taken note of them. But suppressed and unacknowledged as they were, the sound of them did not escape Melody's ears. They tugged at her heart and she knew she would do anything at all that he asked of her because of them. But she could not bring herself to believe that Mr. Attenbury loved her. Surely there was some mistake. She could not be the woman for whom Mr. Attenbury called. How could she be? And therefore she would likely be of no help to the gentleman at all.

Melody straightened and stiffened in Stoneforth's arms and lifted her chin. She studied those bluest of eyes. There were no tears in them. Not a single one.

But he cries nonetheless, she thought. He cries somewhere deep in his soul and the grief trembles upon his lips even though he refuses to acknowledge it. And even if he is mistaken—and he must be mistaken—about Mr. Attenbury being in love with me, I will not, cannot deny him my assistance.

"I will come," she said steadily. "I am not quite certain how or with whom, but I shall be at Sanshire House tomorrow by one. I promise you. Only are you quite certain that it is me for whom Mr. Attenbury calls? Perhaps you have mistaken the name."

"No, Toby's friend Haversham assures me that the Melody he calls for is Miss Melody Harriman, Viscount Harriman's daughter."

Melody nodded, puzzled. "Yes, well, that is certainly me."

Four

Lady Harriman gave her daughter's hand a squeeze as they stood upon the threshold to the chamber where Mr. Attenbury tossed restlessly in his bed. "Do not be afraid, Melody," she whispered. "Go to the young man."

"I am not afraid. But what must I say to him?"

"It makes no difference, dearest. He will not understand you. Say that you are come to visit and that you are very sorry to find him not feeling just the thing. Say that you have missed him at Almack's. Say anything. It is your voice that will reach out to him, not your words."

Melody crossed the chamber and took the chair that Stoneforth offered her near the head of the bed. She reached out and captured one of Mr. Attenbury's flailing hands in her own. "Mr. Attenbury," she murmured, "can you hear me? It is Miss Harriman. I am come to visit you for a time. I am most sorry to find you so very ill."

The hand she held, so warm that she could feel the heat of it through her gloves, immediately ceased to flail about uselessly and clasped her own, but weakly. "M-Melody?" The dry lips barely managed to pronounce the word. "M-Melody?"

"Yes, it is Melody. And I have come to tell you that

you must do all that you are told so that you will be well again, Mr. Attenbury, for I cannot bear to see you in such a state as this."

"I l-love you," trembled the soft, boyish voice. Mr. Attenbury's head turned toward her upon the pillow and his bleary blue eyes peeked open the merest bit. "Melody," he gasped. "You are truly here!"

"Indeed she is, Scamp," declared Stoneforth from the opposite side of the bedstead. "She has come especially to see you, my lad."

"Yes," agreed Melody. "Your brother told me that you were not feeling just the thing, you see. I knew I must come the moment I heard how ill you were."

"S-stay," mumbled Attenbury.

"For a while. I will stay for a while—"

"Toby," whispered Stoneforth.

"Toby," repeated Miss Harriman with a thankful glance. His name is Tobias, she thought. I must remember that. Toby.

Mr. Attenbury's eyes fluttered closed. He smiled a wobbly smile and the hand that clasped Melody's fell limp.

"He has fallen asleep—truly asleep," observed Stoneforth, the relief in his voice obvious. "I do thank you with all my heart for coming, Miss Harriman. And thank you, Lady Harriman, for allowing her to do so. The scamp has not truly slept for days."

"Ought I to let go of his hand, do you think?"

"No," answered Stoneforth at once. "It is because you have come that he has ceased to fight the medicine. If you keep his hand in yours he will know that you are near even in his sleep and he will be at peace." Stoneforth's eyes caught at Melody's, his gratitude evident in them. "Until this very moment, Toby has not had a moment's peace."

"I daresay that you, Lord Stoneforth, have not had

a moment's peace either," Lady Harriman observed, sitting upon a settee before the bedchamber windows.

"No, m'lady," replied a gruff voice from the adjoining dressing room, " 'e ain't had him a unruffled minit since we comed ta Lunnon."

"Ladies, my batman, Watlow," Stoneforth sighed, as Watlow wandered into the bedchamber, a stack of linen in his hands. "And a more interfering companion no gentleman has ever suffered."

"Ha!" exclaimed Watlow as he bowed over his bundle to the ladies. " 'Tis a privilege, I am sure, ladies. An' if the colonel din't have me ta pester at him from mornin' till night, he would not so much as slept one time since he comed 'ome ta find Mr. Attenbury ill. Not that he has slept much atall."

"Then you must escort his lordship to his own chambers so that he may get some sleep at last," Melody urged. "Yes, you will go," she added with a glance at Stoneforth. "I am here now. I will not let Mr. Attenbury die, I promise you."

At the Harriman town house the vestibule was rapidly filling with flowers and calling cards. But everyone who sought entrance was determinedly turned away. "Her ladyship is not at home," declared Higgens over and over again, appearing as calm and unruffled as the perfect butler ought.

"Well, I think Higgens ought to let some of them come in regardless," declared Bea. She watched from the top of the stairs as another gentleman bowed and turned about on his heel. "We might convince Mrs. Claymore to chaperon, you know."

"Never!" giggled Kate. "Aunt Lydia's housekeeper? Why, she would faint dead away to be in the same room with a gentleman."

"Do come back into the parlor and let us discuss what we are to do next," urged Ally, tugging at Bea's arm. "It is a perfect time to lay our plans with Aunt Lydia gone. Then when Mel returns we will have something to set before her."

"Certainly," nodded Bea. "But I will tell you straight out, Ally, that my plans include bringing this Lord Wentworth fellow to his knees. And I will, too. What a coxcomb the man is. And to think that he should not only criticize Melody but Lord Stoneforth as well. Oh, I could just—"

"I do most heartily wish that he had kept his mouth closed concerning Lord Stoneforth," sighed Ally, urging her sisters toward the comfortable little parlor. "Now we will never hear the end of Lord Wentworth."

"Well, but you cannot blame Bea for detesting the beast," Kate declared. "Not only did he insult Melody and intimidate the other gentlemen into treating her quite heartlessly—and some of the young ladies, too— but he had the sheer audacity to remark negatively upon Bea's colonel."

"Yes, Bea's colonel," nodded Ally. "I am well aware. The great Colonel Attenbury has owned Bea's heart since she was old enough to understand what Papa said of him."

"He does not own my heart," protested Bea, flopping nonchalantly upon an enormous wing chair.

"He does not?" asked Ally, her eyebrows rising in disbelief.

"No. He merely seethes and simmers in my imagination and has cordonned off my soul."

"Now you sound like Kate."

"Yes, I know. I was attempting to achieve a most dramatic flair. And I did like the sound of it, too. Now, what sort of plan have you in mind, Ally? We are still to put a tarnish upon some of the bronze we met last evening, are we not?"

"Indeed," Ally assured as she settled upon the chaise longue, "or perhaps, in a few cases, turn a few faces green with envy or purple with rage. I observed last evening that Lord Wentworth ruffled up like a fighting cock when you had the audacity to look him up and down, Bea. And whatever you said during your dance with him, turned him a vibrant violet. I do think, with a bit more prodding upon your part, he will definitely achieve a fine shade of purple. You ought to concentrate particularly upon him, I think, since you wish to anyway, and Kate and I will take it upon ourselves to deal with all the other guilty gentlemen."

"But how shall we deal with the other gentlemen?" asked Kate, resting her elbows upon the back of Bea's chair and her chin upon her fists.

"First we must all think quite seriously about the matter and put forth suggestions. And then we shall discuss the suggestions quite rationally and choose whichever appears to be the most workable. That is how Papa and the squire would do it. And we must include in our discussion a method of instructing a considerable number of the young ladies in plain, honest humility and civility as well, do not you think? I thought some of them quite as rude as the gentlemen," declared Ally with a frown. "Did you not see, Kate, how arrogantly some of them acted, especially toward the others like Mel who were not often asked to dance? I vow, I should have liked to step upon any number of toes last evening—gentlemen's toes and ladies' toes as well."

Lady Jersey whistled. It was one o'clock in the afternoon and she had just strolled into Gunter's in the company of Lady Castlereagh. Amazed to hear herself whistling, she quickly unpuckered her lips and seated herself upon the little gilded chair that the waiter held out for her.

"Whatever has gotten into you, Sally?" asked Lady Castlereagh, once the waiter had taken their orders and disappeared. "Good heavens, has Jersey died and made you an even greater heiress?"

"Not at all, Emily. It would not make me whistle to have my husband die. I am fond of George."

"What then?"

"I was merely thinking of last evening and what a splendid time I had and a whistle slipped out. I shall not let it happen again, I promise you."

"Well, I should hope not," replied Lady Castlereagh. "It is not at all the thing."

"I know it is not. You need not persist in instructing me in the rules of polite society, Emily. I am not some simpleminded schoolgirl. You will be sorry that you did not attend at Almack's last evening, dearest. Mr. Frederick Lange's daughters appeared. You do remember Mr. Frederick Lange? He is Lady Harriman's youngest brother. Well, his daughters caused quite a stir, let me tell you. Maria presented them with vouchers of course. What else could she do? Frederick Lange introduced Maria to Lord Sefton."

"I know," sighed Lady Castlereagh. "And even if he had not, Maria would have given them the vouchers. I vow, Maria Sefton is impossible. She scatters vouchers about as though they are rose petals."

"Indeed. But we shall never cure her of that, you know. It is merely because she is so kindhearted. The Lange girls are triplets, Emily. I did never realize that Ellena Lange gave birth to triplets. Of course, I did never know Ellena well. She was a good deal older than myself. Oh, you ought to have seen the stir those girls caused among the gentlemen."

"Do they remain for the entire Season?"

"I have no idea. They are visiting with Lady and Miss Harriman. I was amazed to see Robert last evening as well, my dear. We did not expect him, you know. He comes so seldom."

"My Robert?"

"Indeed."

"At Almack's?"

"Yes, Emily. And he brought Lord Stoneforth with him. You were devilishly deceitful not to tell us about Lord Stoneforth, my girl. You might at the very least have warned us that you had presented vouchers to such an incredibly alluring gentleman."

Lady Castlereagh blinked and then stared from beneath the brim of her bleached straw bonnet as though Lady Jersey were speaking in tongues.

"I mean to say, Emily Anne," Lady Jersey continued, her neck feeling for some reason inordinately warm and a red blush creeping up into her cheeks, causing her to make use of a brightly painted fan that dangled from one wrist. "I mean to say, dearest, the very thought of a gentleman the size and style of Lord Stoneforth— well—it would set the most innocent girl to whistling. I have never been so very peeved and so very pleased with you all at one and the same time. But such a secret to take to Bath with you, never once hinting at his arrival to the rest of us! Did you think that Robert would not bring him to Almack's until you returned?"

Lady Castlereagh continued to stare, her lovely lips parted the merest bit so as to allow air to pass between them.

"I confess, I have not felt so utterly shameless since I ran off to Gretna Green with Jersey," declared Lady Jersey on a tiny gurgle. "Oh, how everyone must have wondered last evening what had come over me. I am certain I acted the perfect hoyden, but of course, I could not help myself. He is so very overwhelming, Emily. Such an intensely interesting face and such broad shoulders, and his hair—Well, I had the most difficult time to keep from twisting my fingers into those taunting curls of his. And I did waltz much too ardently with the poor man. I admit it. I was a wretched example to all of the young ladies present. I vow, I must watch myself most carefully the next time we meet or guiltless of all intent though Lord Stoneforth may be, I shall do something most unacceptable and George will feel obliged to call the fellow out."

Lady Castlereagh made the tiniest noise in her throat as the waiter reappeared and set their ices before them. She took not the least note of the man, nor did she pick up her spoon when he departed. The strawberry ice sat before her for a full sixty seconds before she even thought to blink down at it. "Robert attended Almack's last evening? My Robert?"

"Yes, Emily, I said he did, though why you are so amazed—"

"He tore up his tickets in a rage the day before I went to Bath," Lady Castlereagh interrupted hoarsely. "We had the most terrible row and—well, you know how he can be, Sally. He is such a—a—dour individual. He tore them up right before my eyes and declared that he never wished to hear the name of Almack's upon my lips again, for if he did, he would move to his club on the instant and never return home."

"Yes, but no one ever takes Robert seriously, Emily. Not even you. He has always been—overly dramatic. And I have never seen him when he did not have one thing or another to fly up into the boughs about. Obviously he has gotten over it, whatever it was upon which you disagreed, because he was amazingly pleasant last evening to everyone."

"No, he has not got over it. This is some plot, rather,

to make me go completely out of my mind. I have never met a Lord Stoneforth," Lady Castlereagh murmured into her ice, "and I did never present a gentleman by that name with vouchers."

"You did not? That is odd indeed," mused Lady Jersey. "Robert, we must assume, presented Mr. Willis with a ticket in pieces, but if you did not present Lord Stoneforth with vouchers, then what did he present to Mr. Willis? Are you quite certain that you did not present him with a voucher, Emily? I merely assumed that you— come to think of it, Mr. Attenbury did not attend last evening, and Lord Stoneforth is Mr. Attenbury's brother. Perhaps it is as simple as Mr. Attenbury bestowing his own ticket upon his brother."

"It is against all of the rules for Mr. Attenbury to have given his ticket to anyone," Lady Castlereagh glowered. "We had best speak to him about it at once."

"Yes," nodded Lady Jersey thoughtfully. "Someone had best discover if the rules were broken. But it had best be me, I think, Emily. Lord Stoneforth is a friend of Robert's after all. They arrived quite arm in arm, so to speak. You would not like to get into another row with Robert, especially not over anything to do with Almack's, would you? Not on the very day of your return? I shall look into it myself. Eat your ice, dearest. It is melting at an abominable rate."

Giles Mackenzie Harding, Earl of Wentworth, dismounted, handed his horse's reins over to a most untrustworthy-looking urchin and strolled through the rear door into the Redding Warehouse in Newgate Street. He passed unchallenged a goodly number of laborers, all intent upon the building of carriages, and made his way with long strides but a lazy gait to a small office that sat upon a raised platform in the center of all the activity. Once there, he pulled a ladder-back chair up before a much abused desk, sat down and leaned back in it and clunked his boot heels upon the desktop, his spurs scratching what remained of the finish even more.

"So, Peter, is it near completion?"

The man behind the desk, who had not so much as thought to stand at the earl's entrance, nodded. "But what you intend to use such a coach for, I cannot think."

"My business, dear boy. Only say that I shall have the thing by Friday next."

"Without a doubt. Friday next."

"May I take a look at it?"

"If you like. It is over there beside the second column. Harris is in charge. Thinks anyone is balmy to want it. He has asked me a number of times if the design is correct."

"And you told him that it was."

"Yes, but I think you are balmy as well, Giles. It will be the ugliest coach in London. I shall be much obliged if you will not mention that I had a thing to do with the building of it."

"No, no, I will not so much as whisper your name, dear brother," Wentworth assured the man with a smile. "And the use I have for it is a secret, so you will kindly remember not to mention my name either, eh, if anyone should ask? How are you fixed these days, Peter, for money?"

"I make a decent living," replied Peter Redding, arching an eyebrow. "I have no complaints."

"Indeed. I am pleased to hear it. Not forced to dun my friends to death in order to get your bills paid, eh?"

"Not a carriage leaves this place without it is paid for in full, Giles. I am not such a simpleton as to place more stock in a man's title than in his banknotes. Father taught me that."

"Yes. Taught you any number of things, I'll wager, when he found the time. I often wonder when he found the time. But then he was a most resourceful gentleman, Papa."

"Yes. And you owe one hundred and fifty pounds before that vehicle of yours exits this place, Giles. Please prove yourself equally as resourceful as Papa by appearing on Friday next with that amount in hand. And not a bank draft either."

"You do not trust me?" exclaimed Wentworth in the most amazed tone. "Peter, how can you not trust me? I am your very own kith and kin."

"Not by any choice of mine," responded the man behind the desk. "I am nothing but a mistake Papa made in his early years. You are an earl. We have nothing in common, Giles, but the length of our noses and the color of our eyes and hair."

"Not even so much," grinned Wentworth maliciously. "Your hair is turning quite gray, brother."

"As will yours someday, if you live long enough."

"What does that mean?"

"You know very well what it means. I heard that you met a Mr. Attenbury in a duel last week. I hear things, you know, Giles. Gentlemen speak amongst themselves in here and never notice me and my men. That makes six duels that have come to my ears in the past two years. If you are not more cautious and less predatory, Giles, my lad, it will be you who they carry from the field someday, bleeding your guts out onto the ground."

If anyone had asked him, Peter Redding could not have said exactly what he had expected to see upon Wentworth's face at those words, but a quickly hooded tinge of fear in the eyes and a slight paling and a hurried licking of suddenly dry lips was not it. The sight of his young half-brother's audacity so briefly yet so obviously overturned amazed the man.

My gawd, there is someone he actually fears, Redding thought, setting aside a stack of papers and planting his elbows upon the desk and his chin upon his hands. "Who is it?" he asked.

"Who is who? I cannot think of what you speak."

"The gentleman you fear will lay you open upon the field."

"You mistake, brother. There is none I fear on that score."

"No? I thought I saw—never mind. It makes no matter to me. One dead earl more or less will not keep me from going about my business, I think. It is not at all difficult, Giles," he added in a low rumble, "to avoid a fight. You simply refuse to be stirred into a meeting on the grounds that it is quite illegal. No one will think the less of you for it, lad."

"Ho, no!" sneered Wentworth. "I will only become the finest jest in all London. 'What happened, Wentworth?' the jesters will inquire once they hear of it. 'Grown tail feathers, have you?' That they will say and any number of other equally witty things."

"Bah! What do you care? Lift your chin and tell them that you are the Earl of Wentworth and that the Earl of Wentworth is all you need to be. And add that it is a good deal better to be the Earl of Wentworth than the late, lamented Earl of Wentworth. Then they will laugh with you, Giles, and not at you. Courage is a fine thing, but only when it is accompanied by the presence of a working brain."

"Who did this thing?" asked Lady Harriman without the least roundaboutation as she turned a most astonished Ridgeworth about in his tracks and dragged him out into the corridor by his elbow, leaving Melody behind to look after Attenbury. "Mr. Attenbury is not merely ill as I supposed. He has been shot. I wish to know who is responsible for it."

"I cannot say, my lady," managed Ridgeworth, amazed.

"You are Mr. Attenbury's valet, are you not?"

"Yes, my lady. And Mr. Attenbury must have a dose of this tonic now if he is to get well again. Please let me enter."

"The tonic can wait for a moment, Mr. Ridgeworth. You will inform me this minute how Mr. Attenbury came to be shot and who it was did the shooting. You are his valet and valets know everything about their gentlemen. I know that to be true. Was the young man set upon by thieves?"

"No, my lady."

"No. It was a freakish accident then at one of his clubs?"

"I hardly know, my lady."

"You do know and you will tell me, Mr. Ridgeworth."

Ridgeworth could not think what to do. The gray eyes glowering at him looked amazingly like storm clouds and he felt lightning in the air, ready to strike if he did not reply satisfactorily. But it was not his place to speak. If the lady had been meant to know, Lord Stoneforth would have provided her with the information.

"I do not care for that thoughtful look upon your countenance, Mr. Ridgeworth," proclaimed Lady Harriman at her most regal. "You are contemplating a lie, sir, and I will not tolerate a lie, I promise you."

"And I will put you out into the street if you tell her the truth," growled a deep voice from just down the corridor. "What will you do, Ridgeworth?"

"I shall take Mr. Attenbury his tonic," the valet replied hastily and dodged around Lady Harriman into the bedchamber.

"That was most unkind of us," murmured Stoneforth, advancing upon Lady Harriman. "I shall be forced to apologize to him before the day is out. If you will step in here, my lady," he added, opening the door directly across from his brother's chambers, "I will tell you what you wish to know myself. I thought Miss Harriman would have explained all, but I see she has not."

"She told me that Mr. Attenbury was gravely ill and calling for her," declared Lady Harriman, entering the chamber, which turned out to be the nicest little sunroom with chairs and tables strewn negligently about. "Though why he should be calling for her, I could not guess. Still, when someone is ill, that is not the time to question, but to act. He has been shot, my lord!"

"Yes. In a duel. I did warn Miss Harriman that it was not something to be bantered about because it is quite illegal to duel, you know, but I did never think she would not so much as tell her own mother. She is very much to be depended upon, is she not, when one says something must be kept secret?"

"Indeed. Melody never reveals secrets. Her father is a diplomat and in a diplomat's family secrets must be kept. That poor boy fought a duel? And it is Melody for whom he calls? Good gracious! Must I assume that Melody was the reason for the duel?"

"No, certainly not. One thing might well have nothing to do with the other," Stoneforth replied as he closed the door behind them. "A man may call for the woman he loves when he believes himself to be dying, whether or not she is the cause of his predicament. I called for Nora over and over, they said, when I was near death, and she was certainly not the cause of my being felled upon the battlefield."

"Your brother, sir," Lady Harriman declared, sitting

down upon the very edge of a white wicker chair, "has never to my knowledge been upon a battlefield."

"Well, no, he has not but the analogy still stands."

"Perhaps it does. But I am not a slowtop, my lord, nor am I unaware of why London gentlemen fight duels, and unless your brother or his opponent was cheating at cards, I highly suspect that my daughter's name came somehow into the conversation."

Stoneforth lowered himself into a chair opposite hers and leaned forward, his arms resting upon his knees, his hands clasped together and dangling between them. "You will not tell Miss Harriman, will you? If I say what I know of the truth?"

"Not a word."

"I have not told her that it was Lord Wentworth with whom Toby fought or that the duel was on her behalf. I did not wish to upset her because—because she seems a remarkably nice young woman, your daughter."

"She *is* a remarkably nice young woman, my daughter. Now tell me what was said of her. I shall have no peace until I know. Lord Wentworth has never been one of my favorite young gentlemen."

Stoneforth studied his hands. "This Wentworth fellow meant it as a jest, Haversham said, though Toby, apparently, did not find anything the least bit humorous in it."

"Lord Stoneforth, do just come out with it!"

"Yes, well, apparently this Wentworth fellow remarked that Miss Harriman got about quite nicely for a lady of her advanced years. This was not the first time that he had remarked adversely upon Miss Harriman's age, I understand, and Toby had just got his fill of it, I assume, because he whacked the man across the cheek with his glove and it came to pistols at dawn."

Stoneforth expected to hear a most indignant word or two from the lady at the very least, but not a sound escaped her lips. He eyed her expectantly. And at last, she inhaled deeply and her eyes sought his. "It is all my fault. Every bit of it," she stated quietly. "I was so enjoying myself with Arthur, flitting here and there about the Continent on one mission after another, that I forgot. I forgot to bring Melody out properly until now—when she is already twenty-four."

"And that is the only reason that this Wentworth sharpens his wit upon her? By Jove, now, most certainly, I shall have that gentleman's guts for garters. Why should it make the least difference," Stoneforth muttered with a shake of his head. "Twenty-four is not old at all."

"Oh, yes, it is," sighed Lady Harriman. "Twenty-four for a young lady, my lord, is a mere whisper away from spinsterhood."

Stoneforth straightened, his deep blue eyes widening, his eyebrows jumping about in the oddest manner. "Spinsterhood? A young lady as fine as your daughter considered a spinster at twenty-four? By Jove, ma'am, has all England gone mad?"

Five

Lord Castlereagh frowned down at the missive upon his desk. He sat back in his chair and ran his fingers through his hair. Then he sat forward again and glared down at the communication once more. "Devil it," he mumbled. "Why must it happen now, when we are so very close to reaching an agreement? If it is true, if it should happen, we will lose every inch we have gained. Tsar Alexander will continue to honor his treaty with Napoleon. He will send our envoy packing and keep the blockade alive. Most certainly he will. Liverpool is correct on that point. If the lady is attacked here in London, it will set us back years with the Russians. But what the devil Liverpool expects me to do about it, I cannot guess. He is in charge at the War Office now. He has all the resources. All I have are blasted diplomats!"

The message that had come to Castlereagh by way of the Earl of Liverpool warned that Miss Tallia Gorsky, a Russian diva who had come to London through the auspices of her grand patron, Tsar Alexander I, to appear in Mr. Herbert Van Cleef's comic opera, *The Innocent Isolda*, at the Covent Garden Theatre, was in grave danger. Word had come from a number of his sources, Liverpool wrote, that a request for Miss Gorsky's demise while in London was being secretly passed throughout the very real network of French spies and French sympathizers in and around the metropolis and the request had come from Napoleon himself. It was, of course, an effort to quash the alliance that the Little Corporal already suspected was imminent between Russia and Great Britain.

"But what the devil Liverpool expects me to do about it, I cannot think," grumbled Castlereagh, standing and beginning to pace. He had never liked Liverpool. He did not like him to this day. And he could not understand why Liverpool had risen to be Secretary of War. "I ought not to have abandoned that particular office," Castlereagh growled to himself. "I ought to have kept it, duel with Canning or not. Instead, here I am without the least resources and forced to do Liverpool's job for him. And what the devil can I do with nothing but a troop of diplomats?"

It was a task that required the subtleties and nuances of split-second military maneuvering upon the battlefield. Miss Gorsky must be got safely from London back to St. Petersburg. She must be got there as soon as possible and without anyone suspecting that she would depart before the announced date of her final performance. And all must be accomplished with a minimal number of people involved in it, because Liverpool's men had not been able to provide so much as one name in reference to the likely assassination attempt. They had not the least idea who, if anyone, would accept or had accepted the generous payment Napoleon offered. Barely anyone near the girl, including the other members of the theatre company, could be trusted in the matter either. Word of any plan to remove Miss Gorsky to the safety of her homeland might travel from that theatre as far and as freely as had the request for her demise. That could prove fatal, not only for Miss Gorsky but for whomever proposed to rescue her. One never did know whose ears were listening, whose lips might whisper into them or whose finger might be poised upon the trigger of a pistol.

The names of spies, double agents and ruffians for hire whirled with tornadic violence through Castlereagh's brain. He had been gone from the War Office for over three years and was no longer certain who was to be relied upon and who not. Barely anyone could be trusted with this and worse yet, Liverpool's spies had not got the least idea when the attempt on her life might be made or if it was to be made at all. It could be tonight or tomorrow or not until June sixth, the night of her farewell performance—or perhaps never.

"Bloody hell!" grumbled Castlereagh. "I need The Rogue, or Wellesley! I need a man who can put together all the fine points and gather men and means about him to do the thing with the least possible fuss in the shortest possible time. I need a master spy or a battlefield commander or—" Castlereagh ceased to mumble. His hand went to rub at his chin; his eyelids lowered slightly in concentration and then he nodded slowly, surely. "And I know just the man," he whispered. "By gawd, I know just the man! He has proved his acumen, his courage and his loyalty time and time again. Stoneforth could do this thing. He *could* do this thing!"

Stoneforth stared down at his brother with a most beguiled grin. "You do not think that I am Papa anymore, eh, Scamp?"

"Papa? Why would I imagine you to be Papa?"

"I have not the least idea, Toby, but you have been thinking that for over a week. Are you hungry?"

"Ravenous."

"Better and better. Of course, you will get nothing but the most fortifying of meals for a while, you know. Uncle

North's Mrs. Peel in the kitchen has been cooking up the most awful stuff in anticipation of your recovery."

Mr. Attenbury gazed up at his elder brother and managed a boyish grin. "When did you come home, Adam? You did not send word to Uncle North or he would never have gone off to Witherbe Hall. I know you did not send word to me."

"I was so excited to be coming home at last, Scamp, that I actually beat my own message to London," Stoneforth replied, settling into the chair beside the bed. "And a good thing I did, too. To challenge some rapscallion to a duel—really, Toby. I did think you had grown up with more sense than that."

"I grew up exactly as you and Papa and Uncle North wished me to do," protested Mr. Attenbury. "I *had* to challenge Wentworth. He made himself inordinately free with Miss Harriman's name and he said—he insulted her, Adam. Most grievously. Time and time again. I could not stand by and ignore him another moment. You would not have wished me to do so. *You* would have challenged him. Yes, and Papa or Uncle North would have done so as well. I know that to be the case."

Stoneforth doubted heartily that he would have challenged the gentleman to a duel over a jest, though he certainly would have taken his fists to the insufferable fribble and beaten a pound or two of humility and good manners into him.

I would have thrashed him to within an inch of his life, he thought with a silent sigh, but I would not have gone so far as to challenge the brat to a duel. Still, I was thinking to do just that when I met him at Almack's. Had Toby not thrown off that blasted fever—had Toby died—I would have met the man and, no matter his choice of weapon, he would not have left the dueling ground alive.

"Never mind, Scamp," he said. "I did not mean to

criticize you. It is merely that I thought for days and
days on end that I would lose you before I had even
come to know you again and you cannot imagine how
devastated I was at that prospect. To lose my only
brother—I would much rather die myself than to watch
you totter upon the bank of the river Styx. Thank goodness that Miss Harriman seized you before you fell into
that dread bit of water. It was she managed to drag you
back to us, you know."

"M-Miss Harriman?"

"Indeed. You do not remember her speaking to you
and holding your hand? She has come the past five afternoons in a row, Toby, to sit beside you and hold your
hand and encourage you to take your medicine. It is
because of Miss Harriman that you have lived through
that horrendous fever and are awake and making sense
this morning. She will be overjoyed to see that you are
practically your old self again."

"Miss Harriman came here?"

"Yes, indeed."

"She knows?"

"That you dueled, yes. I had to tell her, Toby, to convince her to come. Just as I was forced to tell her that
you loved her and were calling out for her. But I did
not explain what Wentworth said, or even that it was
Wentworth with whom you dueled. She did not need
to hear that, I thought. It would make her feel frightful
to know what it was all about and how you challenged
him because he spoke of her in jest. But I told Lady
Harriman everything. She demanded it of me and I
could not think but that she deserved to know. Now
why are you frowning? Lady Harriman will not tell her
daughter, I assure you. She gave me her word upon it."

"You ought not to have told Miss Harriman about
the duel at all," murmured Mr. Attenbury, his brow re-

maining puckered. "I did not wish her to know anything at all about it."

"Bosh, Toby. You love the young lady and you fought for her honor. What is there to fear in her knowing that? Surely she will love you all the more for it."

"Y-yes," murmured Mr. Attenbury, his blue eyes flickering closed. "I expect so. Only I—" And then he was asleep.

Stoneforth leaned back in the chair and stared at the morning shadows upon the wall across the room. One of them appeared determined to form itself into a gray image of Miss Harriman. He smiled to himself as he watched it. Miss Melody Harriman of the ash blond curls and the emerald eyes and the lips that seemed to smile so seldom. Well, but Toby would bring a smile to those lips. Perhaps a permanent smile once he had recovered completely.

How odd it will be, Stoneforth thought, to see Tobias married and dandling kiddies upon his knee. I wonder if he and his Melody will allow me to dandle one or two of the rascals from time to time? I wonder if I could? Would I know how? Would the children allow me to do so? Or will they come to think of me as crotchety old Uncle Adam, the ugly old gentleman from whom they must run and hide whenever he appears?

"That is more likely to be the case," he mumbled. "Run from me as though I were a hobgoblin, I expect."

Melody bid her mama and her cousins farewell and watched as the Harriman coach trundled off in the direction of Bond Street. Uncle Frederick, dear gentleman that he was, had provided each of his daughters with a little pocketbook filled with banknotes and instructed them each to procure whatever frocks and folderols young ladies found attractive these days, and the girls were determined to do just that as soon as possible.

Uncle Frederick is a dear, thought Melody as she wandered back up the stairs to the first floor and stepped into the morning room. A cup of hot chocolate awaited her there beside the overstuffed chair next to the window. She settled herself comfortably and, taking up the chocolate, gazed at the portrait that hung above the fireplace across the room. A young woman with powdered curls and large green eyes gazed back at her. Dressed in shimmering gold and white satin and wearing the panniers of a time before Melody's birth, the lady in this particular portrait had always fascinated her. And here, her grandmother wore the most intriguing smile.

Were you thinking of Grandfather? Melody wondered now, sipping at her chocolate. Had you met him for the very first time or had he just requested your papa's permission to court you? I know you were not married as yet.

The thought of marriage produced a crease above the bridge of Melody's nose. She had come to London to discover a gentleman whom she might wish to marry and who might wish to marry her. She had discovered instead a bevy of self-centered dandies more concerned with the cut of their coats and the tying of their neckcloths than they were with forming lasting alliances. And they were more concerned as well with the impressions they made upon each other than with the impressions they made upon the opposite sex.

Except for Mr. Attenbury. Since the very beginning of the Season, Mr. Attenbury had been kind to her. He had spoken to her at the open houses and the dinners and the routs. He had even gone so far as to sit beside her at Lady Ashbury's musical evening and to escort her to the supper room. And he had danced with her at Almack's. He had determinedly led her out on the very

Wednesday following the one on which Lord Wentworth had danced with her and proclaimed her a perfect bore. No other gentleman had had the courage to escort her out onto the floor that evening, but Mr. Attenbury had walked straight up to her and bowed over her hand and begged the privilege of leading her out. She had thought him merely being kind. Never once had it entered her head that he was in love with her. Oh, he had spoken phrases designed to be flirtatious and vaguely naughty, but in love with her? How could it be?

"He is most handsome," Melody whispered, pausing to take another sip of her chocolate. "With his light blue eyes and dark locks and cherub's face, he is quite boyishly handsome. But whoever would have thought him in love with me? He sent me posies twice after we danced but he did never so much as come once to pay a morning call. No, and he did never take me driving either. I cannot believe that he loves me. But he must. He must, or he would not have been lying abed in a wretched fever moaning my name. But he is better now. The worst of the fever is over, I think. I do hope so, for I cannot bear to see that terrible anxiety for him flickering in Lord Stoneforth's eyes."

Lord Stoneforth's eyes.

Melody continued to stare up at her grandmother's portrait but now she noticed nothing about it, not even the color of her grandmother's gown. A vision of Lord Stoneforth's eyes arose before her instead. How strange they were and how overwhelming. It seemed as though the very essence of all that it was to be human—the joys, the sorrows, the passions, the fears—all—smoldered and sparked and blazed in the midnight blue brilliance of Lord Stoneforth's incredible and most speaking eyes.

* * *

The sight of the Lange triplets shopping in Bond Street was enough to make any gentleman stop in his tracks with a bemused and thoroughly delighted smile. And one particular gentleman out and about at the most unreasonable hour of eleven discovered that the sight of the triplets being ushered along the flagway by Lady Harriman with a footman traipsing along behind fostered a thoroughly bemused and delighted smile not only upon his face but within his heart as well.

"I'll be deviled," declared Mr. Davies roundly, "if that is not the prettiest picture to be had in all of London. Do come to a halt, Wentworth, and allow me to enjoy more than a fleeting glimpse of it, eh?"

"What?" Wentworth, discovering himself to be suddenly strolling alone, paused in his tracks and glanced over his shoulder to see what could have happened to Davies. What he saw was that gentleman gazing, enthralled, at the little convoy of ladies just turning into Madame Gallier's. With a mumbled epithet, Wentworth walked back and drew up at Davies' side.

"Do not look quite so sour, Wentworth. What have you against those chicks? I have never seen such a fine covey of quail in all my life. I shall join in the hunt for them, I think."

"They are children," scoffed Wentworth.

"Ha! You are off there, my lad. They are seventeen and out of the schoolroom. I cannot think what has come over you of late. Miss Harriman is too old to be considered acceptable; her cousins are too young to be of notice. What have you against the family, Giles? Did Harriman step upon your toes at one time or another?"

"Of course not. I do not even know the man."

"No, I should not think so. He has been a member of one diplomatic mission after another for years now. Perhaps it is his brother-in-law has offended you?

Though I do not recall Mr. Lange having come to London in years."

"It is nothing of the kind. Miss Harriman is long in the tooth and deadly dull as well. I merely stated what I observed to be the truth and have been plagued about it ever since."

"Yes, after one dance with the girl. And you have stated those observations over and over again with great cleverness, Wentworth, until every gentleman at Almack's fears to approach Miss Harriman lest he become an object of your wit as well. The only one who took it into his head to contradict you upon Miss Harriman's desirability was Attenbury. I say, Wentworth! Look! What the deuce has happened? Come along, do. Apparently one of the Misses Lange requires our assistance." And without pausing once to discover if Wentworth would actually deign to accompany him, Mr. Davies made his way across the street to the opposite flagway.

"Good morning. It is Miss Beatrice, is it not?" Davies said as he came up beside her. "Have you lost something?"

"Oh, Mr. Davies, what a welcome surprise," grinned Beatrice impishly, glancing only for a moment beyond that gentleman to assure herself that Lord Wentworth was also approaching. "I am such a stupid! I have dropped my reticule and my things have gone bouncing out all over the flagway."

"Never fear, dear lady, I shall be most happy to help you retrieve them," smiled Davies, looking about him and then bending from the waist to pick up a lace handkerchief, a scent bottle encased and protected by a stiff silver filigree and a leather case that apparently had kept the bottle of salts inside of it from breaking. These he placed into the reticule that Bea held expectantly open.

"Beatrice, what on earth!" exclaimed Lady Harriman, popping back out of the shop. "I thought you were right behind me."

"No, Aunt Lydia. That is, I was, but then I turned to look at that delicious bonnet in the window and I dropped my reticule and it came open and—"

"Yes, so I see," sighed Lady Harriman. "Thank you, Mr. Davies, for coming to Bea's aid. Good morning, Lord Wentworth," she added as the earl managed to make his way at last around a farm wagon and up onto the flagstones.

"Oh, there is my fan!" exclaimed Beatrice stepping aside just as Wentworth began his bow, ignoring him completely.

"Where?" asked Mr. Davies, peering about.

"Just there, beside the wheel of that curricle. And my coin purse lies right next to it. Thank goodness! I should be most unhappy to lose my coin purse now, when it is full. I shall not mind nearly so much once we depart Bond Street, I think."

"You plan to empty it completely this morning, do you?" Mr. Davies laughed as he stooped to fetch the fan and the purse and place them back into Beatrice's reticule. "Is there anything else gone missing, Miss Beatrice?"

"No, no, I cannot think there was anything else. Oh, dear," she added, one silk-gloved hand going to her prettily pink cheek. "I completely forgot. My silver snuffbox. Oh, please, it cannot be lost. It is the verimost beautiful thing."

"Might that be it glittering amongst all that muck between the horses at the hitching rail?" asked Wentworth with barely restrained anger. By Jove, the child had given him the cut direct. He ought to take her over his knee and beat the chit, not point out the whereabouts of her snuffbox. And what was she doing with a snuffbox? Of all things for a young lady to be carrying about.

"Oh, Beatrice! No!" exclaimed Lady Harriman as Bea stepped toward the pair of horses and peered beneath them. "You will soil your new half-boots and the stain will never come off from your hem. Get back up here on the flagway at once."

"Well, but I cannot ask Mr. Davies to ruin his clothes, Aunt Lydia, by crawling about in the muck of the gutter under a pair of horses," Bea replied. "And I must have it. Papa gave it to me on Christmas to carry my little sweets about in and I cannot abandon it. I do not expect," she added, turning her wide gray eyes upon Lord Wentworth with what he considered the most disdainful look, and then flicking on past him to Lady Harriman. "I do not expect that anyone else here would be willing to fetch it for me. No, you must not, Mr. Davies," she added as he came to stand beside her and bent to peer under the horses himself. "It was I who dropped it and I shall fetch it. I would never forgive myself if you were to get anything at all as ugly as that"—she pointed daintily at the filth—"upon those lovely primrose pantaloons. No, I shall fetch it myself, if only you will hold my hand while I do so."

"Of all the—" began Wentworth, his collar seeming of a sudden to become uncommonly tight and causing him to tug at it with one finger. "Stand away, Miss Beatrice, and you, too, Davies. I shall simply get the handle of my cane behind it and tug it out into the open." And with a glower and a glare at Beatrice, Wentworth stepped down into the gutter and up beside Mr. Davies and did as he proposed, tugging the tiny silver box out from beneath the horses and then bending to pick it up in his fashionably York tan-gloved hand. A great glob of sludge came off from it upon his glove and he held it away from him between thumb and index finger and shook it, sending droplets of filth and slime spraying about.

Mr. Davies dug hurriedly into his coat pocket, produced his handkerchief, and taking the snuffbox from Wentworth, wiped it as clean as he possibly could, then presented it with a smile and a flourish to Bea. "But you must be certain to wash it thoroughly when you get home," he told her. "Inside and out."

"Yes, I will. Thank you so very much, Mr. Davies," Beatrice replied, taking the box from his hand, her own hand lingering just long enough to send Mr. Davies' heart to racing. "I am so very, very grateful to you. Oh, yes, and to you as well, my lord," she added, throwing Wentworth a negligent curtsy and then hurrying back to Lady Harriman's side.

"My thanks as well, gentlemen," smiled Lady Harriman, once more opening the shop door and this time ushering Beatrice in ahead of her.

Both Davies and Wentworth remained motionless in the gutter staring as the shop door slowly closed.

"What an absolute angel," murmured Davies, staring down raptly at the hand Beatrice had held.

"What a devil, you mean," growled Wentworth. "By Jove, to give me the cut direct. Me! And then, when I have deigned to overlook such impertinence and help the chit out, to thank you so exceedingly and add me as an afterthought!"

"She never did," grinned Davies, making his way back across to the other side of the street, dodging between a peddler's cart and a milk wagon with Wentworth directly upon his heels.

"Never did what?" muttered Wentworth, glaring down in disgust at the muck that stained his glove, as he stepped up onto the flagway.

"Never gave you the cut direct."

"She most certainly did."

"Wentworth, she is a child. You said so yourself. I will wager Miss Beatrice Lange does not even know what the cut direct is. She was excited and upset is all."

"Ha!"

"Her dearest treasures were strewn all over the street. She was simply not thinking."

"Ha!"

"You shall not hold it against her, Wentworth, regardless of whether she meant to cut you or not. You cannot afford to hold it against her. You sank Miss Harriman easily enough with your wit and your jesting, but you will only make yourself look foolish to attempt the same with Miss Beatrice and her sisters. They are about to become all the rage. Take my word for it. And you will look the perfect fool to be opposing them. By Jupiter but I should like to take Miss Beatrice into my arms and place a kiss upon those most devastating lips this very moment."

"Really, Charles? I should like to take her lovely neck into my hands and squeeze until those oh too innocent eyes of hers pop right out of her head."

Six

Mr. Attenbury, snuggled in a red wool banyan and supported by an inordinate number of pillows that his brother thought necessary to his comfort, sat up in his bed and played nervously with his fingers, glancing sideways from time to time at Melody in the shyest fashion. His cheeks were shaved and his hair was combed and his bedclothes were smoothly perfect around him. Someone had carefully tied a red cravat around his neck and he looked most respectable.

And very, very young, thought Lady Harriman with a smile as she looked up once again from her embroidery just in time to see Melody's eyes crinkle in laughter.

"I am so pleased that you are feeling more the thing, Mr. Attenbury," Melody laughed. "I have missed your sense of humor."

"You have?" asked Mr. Attenbury, for the first time that afternoon meeting her lovely green eyes.

"Indeed. You are so very droll. And I do so enjoy your observations."

"Well. Well. I am—pleased to make them then," managed Mr. Attenbury, plucking nervously at the counterpane. "And may I observe that you are looking quite—quite—lovely today. I am—I was—I would—what I mean to say," produced Mr. Attenbury at last with a frustrated sigh, "what I mean to say is that I am most grateful that you have come to sit with me this afternoon. And—and all the other afternoons as well. Adam told me how often you came to sit beside me while I was feverish. I did never—never expect—Well, I am most grateful and that's a fact. I heard you speaking to me, you know. I thought that I was dreaming, but I was not."

"No, you were not."

"No. And you held my hand, too, did you not?"

Melody nodded.

"I knew you had. I mean, I thought that you had. This hand," he murmured, shyly raising his right hand into the air and then concealing it beneath the counterpane and lowering his gaze to rest upon the flowered coverlet. "Doubtless you have met my brother," he added, changing the subject rapidly.

"Lord Stoneforth was kind enough to come and say that you required me," nodded Melody. "He is not at home today?"

"Yes, but he is hiding."

"Hiding?"

"Well, he said that he was expecting a most important visitor and that I must apologize for his not being present to greet you because of it, but that is a tremendous whisker, I think." Mr. Attenbury brought his hand from beneath the counterpane and began to play nervously with his fingers again. "Watlow says that they have only been in London since the day I—was shot—so Adam has not been here long enough to know anyone at all important."

"No, I expect you are correct," Melody offered.

"Just so. Adam is hiding in his study so as not to put a damper upon our conversation. That is my opinion. I told him straight out that that was particularly stupid. After all, your mama is here. Why should Adam not be here as well? But he thinks we cannot want him."

"Of course we want him," declared Melody.

"So I thought myself. And so I said, but he would not listen. Adam is a hero, you know," added Mr. Attenbury, his fingers ceasing to intertwine and his eyes abruptly blazing with pride as he looked at Melody. "He is a hero several times over, Adam is. And he is likely the most formidable swordsman of all time. They fight with swords, you know, the dragoons, and so they must learn to be excellent with them. They cannot stand off behind a hill somewhere and toss grenades at the enemy. No, they must be right up face-to-face with the foe over and over again."

"You admire your brother greatly," smiled Melody.

"I should think I do."

"You are fortunate to have him home with you."

"Yes, and he is not going back to the wars ever again."

"He is not?"

"No. He has sold out and I am enormously glad of it too. It is because of his eye, you know."

Melody thought perhaps she had misheard that statement. "His eye, Mr. Attenbury?"

"Yes, his right eye. Adam has lost the sight in it. It happened while he was in the midst of a fray at a place called Albuera, did it not, Sergeant Watlow?" Attenbury asked as Watlow entered the chamber with the gentleman's tonic.

"Aye, Albuera," nodded Watlow, pouring the required dose into a glass and giving it into Mr. Attenbury's hand.

"He rode down upon the French to support Colonel Montague's Blues, who were being severely beaten. Adam was the very first of his regiment to leap from his horse, and there were French all about him and rain coming in buckets and mud so deep that it came up over the top of Adam's boots," Mr. Attenbury continued, after he had gulped the vile medicine down. "Is that not so, Watlow?"

"Aye," agreed the sergeant, relieving the young man of the glass, and winking at Melody. "Wishin' ta hear the tale agin, are ye, lad?"

"Yes, but it is only because I want Miss Harriman to know how brave Adam is and how he lost the sight in his eye and so had to sell out."

"Ter'ble outnumbered we was," Watlow began in his gruff, gravelly voice. "But the colonel, he were a reg'lar demon ta behold. Stood an' fought, layin' them Frenchies out lef' an' right with a parry here and a lunge there and a thrust home, thrust home!"

"But no sooner had he laid them low than more appeared," inserted Mr. Attenbury, his handsome face thoroughly aglow with excitement. "Like flies, the Frenchies were. Kill three and seven took their places."

"Aye, an' all aroun' him, for all o' us it were the same. One regiment o' dragoons we was, standin' against hordes o' Frogs in support o' Colonel Montague's Blues."

"Yes, and Adam would not give it up," declared Mr. Attenbury proudly. "He would not surrender so much as an inch of the ground he stood upon, nor order his regiment to retreat!"

"Not on yer life," agreed Watlow, "not the colonel. 'Stan' fas', me lovelies!' he roars fer all o' us ta hear. 'Ponsonby will be with us soon and with him an entire brigade! Fight on! Fight on!' "

"And just as Ponsonby did indeed come over the hill and rode down into the fighting, Adam spun about to engage another Frenchie, slipped in the muck and went down beneath Colonel Ponsonby's horse and got himself kicked in the head," Mr. Attenbury ended the account with somewhat bemused finality.

"Oh, my goodness!" Melody exclaimed, and from the chair before the window where Lady Harriman sat came a tiny gasp.

"An' that be why the colonel kinnot see nothin' out o' that eye. On accounta gettin' kicked in the head by Colonel Ponsonby's 'orse." Watlow, the bottle of tonic in his hand, looked from Melody to her mother and back again, enjoying their amazement.

"Yes, well, it was a wretched disaster, Adam says," offered Mr. Attenbury. "There ought to have been six thousand Anglo-Portuguese troops at Albuera, but the weather and the swollen streams and the flooding delayed the most of them and made mincemeat of the battle plans."

"Aye," nodded Watlow. "Would not 'ave engaged the enemy at all, the colonel, but fer the fac' that Colonel Montague's Blues was already upon the field and bein' speared an' gutted. Seemed ferever that we was fightin' alone, just us an the Blues against thousands o' Frogs."

"Yes, and when Colonel Ponsonby and the others did at last arrive, Adam did not get one good look at them. Not one, because he was lying unconscious beneath Colonel Ponsonby's horse."

"Unconscious beneath Colonel Ponsonby's 'orse," agreed Watlow with a sad shake of his head. "An' would 'ave died there, too, had not me an' Dickens an' Carvelle seen Colonel Ponsonby a signalin' fer help an' gone ta stand over the colonel an' keep him free o' Frogs till we could at last drag 'im up the hill."

Melody sat in astonishment, her lips slightly parted, her eyes filled with wonder. She had grown up the daughter of a diplomat. Never before had she heard even one account of the actual fighting that her father worked so hard to bring to an end in favor of Great Britain and its allies.

"At any rate, now Adam cannot see anything with his right eye, though the surgeons think the eye itself is not damaged. It is something inside his head keeps him from seeing."

"Aye," Watlow nodded. "Somethin' touchin' upon somethin' else what it ought not ta be, they says. Says as how he won't never see out o' it agin likely." And with an awkward bow to Melody and Lady Harriman, Watlow excused himself and carried Mr. Attenbury's remaining medicine with him out of the chamber.

"What a courageous gentleman your brother must be, Mr. Attenbury," said Melody quietly.

"Well, I should think so," nodded Tobias Attenbury. "Quite possibly the most courageous gentleman in all the world and his men as brave as they can stare."

"You want me to do what?" quite possibly the most courageous gentleman in all the world asked, astounded, in his study two floors below.

"Abduct an opera singer and see she is safely smuggled out of England—as far as St. Petersburg," drawled Stoneforth's visitor. "Will you do it?"

"Really, Castlereagh, you are hoaxing me, are you not?"

"No. Not at all. Her name is Miss Tallia Gorsky. Her grand patron is Tsar Alexander. And word has come to me that she is likely to be assassinated at any time."

Stoneforth ran his fingers through his hair, setting his black curls leaping about in all directions. "Assassinated? An opera singer? Are they not—I mean, why would anyone—even if a Tsar is fond of her, I cannot believe—" His words tumbled to a halt. He rested his arm along the mantelpiece and he peered down at Castlereagh, who was leaning back comfortably in one of the chairs before the grate. "This is all fun and games, eh, Castlereagh? Some sort of jest, no doubt."

"No, I swear not. But I think that perhaps you departed England at too young an age and have been away far too long," Castlereagh chuckled.

"Why? Cease snickering and tell me."

"Well, I mean, I have just caught on to it myself, Stone-forth. I said opera singer and you immediately got the queerest look upon your face. You are thinking Miss Gorsky is a lightskirt. You *are* thinking that, are you not?"

"That is what it means—opera singer."

"No, Stoneforth. Opera *dancer.* That is what they call the lightskirts. An opera singer is a lady who sings opera and the lightness of her skirts does not come into consideration. Miss Gorsky is a great celebrity of the Russian opera and has condescended to perform at Covent Garden. Well, she has not actually condescended to do so. She begged to do so because she is madly in love with the writings and music of Mr. Herbert Van Cleef, and his comic operas are performed only there."

Stoneforth's lips twitched upward. "My mistake. But even so, Castlereagh, why me?"

"Because you are here, Stoneforth, and I know I can trust you and the thing must be planned and carried out, I think, like some maneuver upon the battlefield, instant by instant with cunning and malleability and because, well—"

"I owe you a considerable debt of gratitude for all you suffered by getting me into Almack's?"

"I have not suffered for that yet," sighed Castlereagh. "But I will, I assure you. By now Emily Anne has spoken with her friends and knows that I was there—without a ticket—and that I brought you with me without a ticket. I shall not hear the end of it for weeks and weeks. I expect I shall be dining at my club for the remainder of the Season. But truly, Stoneforth, it is most important to avert this disaster. Miss Gorsky's death while in London would prove an immense disaster for all of England and its allies." Castlereagh stared up at the gentleman with the most hopeful look in his eyes, but behind the hope lay a darkness, a tinge of despair that Stoneforth readily perceived and interpreted correctly. Such a look had often been reflected back at him from his own looking glass. The very existence of it in Castlereagh's eyes gave Stoneforth pause and he said nothing.

"You will not then." Castlereagh's words broke the silence. "No, do not say a word. It is a great deal to ask of a man who has done so much for so long already. I ought not to have mentioned it, Stoneforth. You are just arrived upon our shores after years of fighting. Why should you wish to throw yourself back into danger yet again?"

"Because a friend asks it of me," murmured Stoneforth.

"I am hardly your friend. An acquaintance barely."

"Odd. I had the distinct impression that you were acting like a friend all that night at Almack's. Have you suddenly changed your mind then? Have you thought about it and decided that you are too high in the instep to cry friends with a lowly dragoon, Castlereagh?" Stoneforth abandoned his place before the mantel and strode across the chamber to a low credenza. He unstoppered a crystal decanter, turned two glasses upright and poured a golden liquid into them. "Enough nonsense. I know a friend when I meet with one," he growled, carrying both glasses back across the room and sliding down into the chair beside Castlereagh's. "Take the glass and drink—to our friendship."

"To our friendship," whispered Castlereagh, who had thought for years now that he never would learn to make a friend. He held the glass in a visibly unsteady hand and raised it to his lips.

"And to the safe rescue of Miss Gorsky."

"Are you certain, Stoneforth?"

"About our friendship? Indeed, and privileged to think that you will have me. About Miss Gorsky? I will make the attempt. That is the only promise I can give you."

* * *

Melody did not think that the astonished trembling of her heart would ever cease. On the way home in the coach it flitted and fluttered most annoyingly inside of her.

"You are overcome," said her mother, and she leaned forward to give Melody's hand a pat. "I thought to request Mr. Attenbury and Sergeant Watlow to cease their narrative, but I wished to hear the whole of it and I could not think that I had raised you to be so missish as to faint away at one tale of war."

"I was not about to faint away, Mama. I was simply amazed. I have never thought of the war in such a way before. Man against man in the rain and the mud, I mean. It has always been simply something Papa and the other gentlemen went off to discuss. Something quite far removed from my own existence."

"As it still is. The war will not come to England, nor you ever go to the war. Even now your papa and the others are working to convince the Tsar to abandon his alliance with Napoleon and to throw in his lot with the allies, which will most likely end the foul thing at last."

"Even so, Mama, did you ever hear such a tale? Oh, if those are the sort of tales that Uncle Frederick relates to Bea, no wonder she is so very enthralled with Lord Stoneforth. I can just picture him, Mama, in the mud and the rain, surrounded by enemies determined to fell him and yet encouraging his men to 'Fight on! Fight on!' "

"Indeed," smiled Lady Harriman. "It would make a most incredible painting would it not? Such a tall, straight, broad-shouldered gentleman with sword in hand, and likely those diabolical black curls of his dangling limp with rain across that most aristocratic brow. The very thought of it makes my heart beat erratically, let me tell you."

"Mama!"

"Well, can you not see him in the midst of battle,

Melody? Would not such a sight make your heart flutter?" Lady Harriman smiled the most infectious smile.

"It has been fluttering for some time now," giggled Melody.

"Yes, I thought it might be. Mr. Attenbury is very proud of his brother, did you notice?"

"One would need to be blind and deaf not to notice, Mama. Why his eyes lit up so and his voice sounded so filled with—with—admiration and—"

"Love."

"Yes, love. I am certain he loves Lord Stoneforth dearly though they have not been together, Mr. Attenbury says, for years and years."

"Mr. Attenbury is a remarkably fine young gentleman," nodded Lady Harriman. "And he is handsome as well. Quite delightfully so. And though his brother bears the title, Mr. Attenbury is not without his own resources. Both his uncle, Lord Sanshire, and his brother have provided well for him—very well."

"Mama!" Melody sat back against the squabs and stared wide-eyed at her mother.

"What, dearest?"

"How do you come to know how Mr. Attenbury is provided for?"

"Why, I posed a question here and a question there."

"Mama, you did not!"

"Well, when a gentleman in a raging fever calls for my daughter, declaring all the while that he loves her, I do think it is incumbent upon me to discover if he is an eligible gentleman or not."

"And is he an eligible gentleman?"

"Oh, most eligible. My goodness, will you look at that," declared Lady Harriman as the coach rolled to a stop. "Our doorstep is overflowing with gentlemen. Poor Higgens must be going wild to have so many come at one and the same time."

"Allow me," offered a deep voice as the coach door was opened and Mr. Davies smiled up at them and let down the step. He gave Lady Harriman his hand to help her descend and then did the same for Melody. "Every eligible bachelor in London has apparently picked this afternoon to visit you," he grinned. "And I daresay that your butler is the least bit discomposed, though he attempts not to show it."

"You have all come to call upon the triplets, I think," offered Melody, immediately removing her hand from Mr. Davies' arm. "With which one of my cousins are you infatuated, Mr. Davies, if I may be so bold as to ask?"

"Why, with them all, Miss Harriman, though I do think that Miss Beatrice is by far the sweetest."

Melody had the most difficult time not to fall into whoops. Bea, sweet? Oh, she must inform her cousins of that statement directly. Why, not even Uncle Frederick, who loved his daughters above all things, had ever once referred to Beatrice as sweet.

Though she is certainly a charmer in her own way, thought Melody as the throng of gentlemen parted, allowing her and her mama to enter through the front door.

"Glory be!" exclaimed Lady Harriman as they entered the vestibule. "Higgens, are you all right?"

"Madam! Yes, I am f-fine."

"You do not look fine," grinned Melody. "You look to be at *point-non-plus*. Let me help you, Higgens, do."

The Harriman's butler, leaning against the long mahogany table, a vase of wild flowers in one hand, a dozen long-stemmed roses resting upon his arm and another posy in that hand as well, with any number of posies and cards piled precariously about him, struggled to appear unruffled but failed completely.

"Where are James and Matthew? They ought to be here to help you," Lady Harriman said softly, taking the

roses from Higgens' arm and handing them to Melody.
"You cannot possibly accept all of these offerings and
turn away all of these gentlemen by yourself, Higgens.
It is quite too much for one man."

"I am discovering that, madam. But James has gone
to take the letters to the mail and Matthew to walk behind
Miss Lange and Miss Kate and Miss Bea in Green Park.
We thought that all the gentlemen had come and gone,
my lady. And the young misses desired to have some air."

"Yes, well, you were wrong," Lady Harriman said with
a merry gurgle. "Apparently all of the gentlemen had
not come and gone. Barely any of them, I think, for there
cannot be many more gentlemen in all of London than
are upon our stoop at this very moment. Melody, take
those roses and as many more of the posies as you can
carry to the kitchen and I shall gather up what I can and
follow. Higgens, you must simply accept the gentlemen's
cards and then turn them away. Say that the young ladies
will be pleased to speak with them at Almack's tomorrow
evening. That will send them off in good humor. Oh,
and add that we shall be at home on Thursday to receive
morning callers."

"We shall?" asked Melody when she and her mama
had reached the kitchen and given the flowers to the
little scullery maid to arrange in vases.

"We shall what, Melody?"

"Be at home on Thursday to receive morning callers?"

"Yes, dearest, I think we must, do not you? I cannot
deny the gentlemen entrance to this establishment forever. They are all of them bound and determined to
spend time in the presence of your cousins. You do not
mind, Melody, if the triplets become all the rage? You
will not be jealous of them?"

"Oh, great heavens no!" exclaimed Melody, her eyes
alight with laughter. "It is exactly what we hoped would
happen when we decided to write you and ask for permission for them to come."

"Very good. Very good, indeed. Because now all the gentlemen shall come into our home and they shall make your acquaintance as well, and they will discover that you are a perfectly lovely young lady with wit and poise and without pretensions, and no longer will they be guided by the despicable Lord Wentworth."

"Be deviled if I will go and stand about upon their stoop like some pigeon waiting to be thrown a crust of bread," mumbled Wentworth to himself. "Let Davies make himself a fool. Let them all act like simpletons. I will not be led into beggary by some chits from the country, and that's a fact!"

He was dressed in the most wonderfully fitted puce morning coat and buff pantaloons. His Hessians gleamed in the sunlight and his silver spurs glinted and jangled as he walked. A high-crowned beaver perched at a most rakish angle upon his golden curls, and he tapped his cane against the flagway at every other step, the cane's tap joining in the formation of a sort of rhythm with his spurs. "I do not care ever to enter the Harriman's house," he muttered as he followed the path toward the little farmhouse that nestled in the midst of Green Park. "I shall just go down to the farm and purchase a glass of fresh milk and enjoy the afternoon in solitary splendor. Yes. And I will not drive anyone about Hyde Park this afternoon either. The Promenade is a dreadful bore."

Everything is a bore, he thought then, gazing about him at the shrubbery. If it were not for my bet with Boylan-Jolnes, I should die of ennui here and now.

The bet. His mind wandered over the terms of the bet. He was to make his way into the cellars at the new Covent Garden Theatre and purloin the stock of wine that The Beefsteak Club had once again entrusted to Mr. Kemble. It would be a great lark, actually, if he got away with it. The Beefsteak Club had lost their entire stock of wine when the old theatre had burned to the ground in '08 and it had taken Kemble four years to get the club to entrust him with the wine again. And now, it would simply disappear. Truly, the uproar would prove most entertaining. The members of the club were not celebrated, after all, for their gentility but for their enormous appetites and foul mouths and recklessness. The very thought of the uproar they would make etched a smile upon Wentworth's face. He continued to smile to himself for at least another ten steps, whereupon he was rudely and abruptly knocked to the ground and pummeled about the head, shoulders, stomach and thighs by lace gloves and a remarkably pretty striped apricot skirt filled to the brim with wiggling legs. His smile disappeared. He grunted and wriggled and pushed and then he was unceremoniously trod upon by a very fine pair of jean half-boots.

"Of all things!" exclaimed a voice that was rapidly becoming most familiar and most unwelcome to Wentworth's ears. The half-boots attempted to scutter off him but kicked him in the ribs while doing so. "I did not expect you to help me, but you might have moved out of my way. Now I shall never get it back!"

Wentworth raised himself up on his elbows and glared into the fine gray eyes that frowned down at him. "What the devil do you think you are doing?" he shouted angrily. "Cannot a gentleman stroll through the park without being attacked?"

"Oh, do be quiet," grumbled the voice behind those most remarkable eyes.

Wentworth gained his feet and began to brush at the grass and dirt, straining to look over his shoulder at the back of his clothing and grumbling inaudibly.

"You are totally useless and annoying to boot, Wentworth, and now I cannot possibly catch it," declared Bea.

"Catch what? What are doing running about like some wretched urchin? I vow, Miss Beatrice, you are totally without—"

"Without what?"

"Decorum! Now what the deuce?" he added as he turned to look her straight in the eye and discovered tears glistening in them both. "What are you crying about? You cannot be injured. I am the one was knocked full to the ground and trampled upon."

"I am not c-crying," protested Bea, swiping at her eyes with one fist. "It is the wind merely. Oh! Oh! There it goes!" she cried, pointing.

Wentworth's gaze followed the direction of her finger to discover a wide-brimmed straw hat sailing across the lawn in the mouth of a most distasteful-looking cur, the hat's apricot ribands trailing over the dog's behind. To one side of the beast, but quite far off, a footman was loping in its direction, and from the front of it and to the other side, Miss Bea's sisters were attempting to catch up with the animal as well.

"They will never catch it now," sniffed Beatrice. "I almost had it. I did. I would have had it had you not strolled directly into my path and cut me off."

"Never mind," grumbled Wentworth. "You may buy yourself a new bonnet."

"No, I may not!" cried Beatrice most petulantly, one lace-gloved hand becoming a fist and punching a thoroughly astonished Wentworth in the arm. "I have spent most of what Papa gave me and I have not enough remaining to buy another!" Beatrice threw a second angry punch at Wentworth that landed solidly in the pit of his stomach and doubled him over.

Seven

"Devil! I am sorry!" gasped Beatrice, putting an arm around Wentworth's hunched shoulders before he could straighten up. "I did not intend to do that! It is just that I am most upset. And when I am most upset, I do strike out at the nearest object."

"So I observed," mumbled Wentworth, straightening with a groan. "Where the devil did you learn to punch like that? I thought Jackson had laid a solid hit upon me."

"I am very good at fighting," Beatrice informed him with some pride. "I have always been. Papa did never have a son, you see, and so, when I showed signs of interest in—in—fighting and such—why Papa was quite eager to explain to me how it was done and to help me learn properly. When a gentleman has three daughters he is not overly concerned that one of them leans toward boyish interests, because the other two more than balance her out, you see."

"By gawd, you are more than a match for any boy," muttered Wentworth. "Where has my hat got to?"

"It went flying when I knocked you down."

"I am certain it did. Which way did it go?"

"I did not see. I shall help you to look for it, shall I?"

"No. Definitely not. Likely you will hit me again because we find mine and do not find yours."

"Well then, find it yourself," Bea replied. "So much for attempting to be kind to you. I vow, Wentworth, you are the most contemptible person in all the world."

"Do not call me Wentworth," growled the earl, attempting to straighten his neckcloth. "Young ladies do not refer to gentlemen in such a fashion. Has no one taught you even that much?"

"Balderdash! That is a rule made up by gentlemen to keep ladies in a state of subservience! Your friends call you Wentworth all the time. I will lay you odds upon it. Yes, and your enemies call you the same. And I will do so if I please, because I am just as much your equal as any gentleman in London."

Wentworth's eyes widened, his jaw dropped and he stood speechless upon a little square of green with his golden curls blowing wildly in the wind, his clothing stained and disheveled, and his seemingly endless ennui completely dispelled.

"I am so very sorry, Beatrice," Ally called as she hurried toward the two of them. "We could not catch the wretched animal. Not even Matthew, with his long legs, could outrun the cur. Your hat has gone down through a veritable jungle of shrubbery and totally disappeared. Good afternoon, my lord," she added, with a perfunctory curtsy in Lord Wentworth's direction. And then she halted all speech and turned slowly to look Wentworth up and down. "What on earth has happened to you?" she asked, stunned.

"I bumped into him and knocked him to the ground," Beatrice explained. "I did call to him to make way for me, but he did not step so much as one foot to the side. I did attempt to stop in time, but I could not. We collided most violently and it was all his fault."

"I did not hear you call," mumbled Wentworth.

"Well, you certainly ought to have heard. I yelled as loud as I could. You were preoccupied with thoughts of how dashing you looked, I expect, and could not be bothered to notice what was happening all about you. You are so very fond of yourself that you do not even know anyone else exists."

"Beatrice!" exclaimed Ally. "You go much too far. It is most unladylike to call any gentlemen a self-centered, egotistical dandy to his very face. Papa would be most ashamed of you."

"I beg to doubt that," replied the lovely Kate as she swished to a halt beside her sisters. "Papa is never ashamed of Bea, only considerably shaken by her from time to time. Oh, what a run! I have not had so very much exercise since the time we entered the foot race at the Wicken fair. Good afternoon, Lord Wen—what happened to you?"

"I knocked him down," muttered Beatrice. "And I do not care to go through the explanation again. No, I do not wish to speak of it at all anymore—not one more w-word." And to everyone's astonishment, Beatrice burst into tears and immediately hid her face against Ally's shoulder.

"Shhh, dearest," whispered Ally, enfolding her sister in her arms. "Tell me what it is. Lord Wentworth did not injure you?"

"Me? Injure her?" fumed Wentworth. "It was she knocked me to the ground and then trampled all over me and—" Beatrice's sobs notably increased and Wentworth, with two sets of equally appalled gray eyes staring at him, could not think that he ought to go on with his description of what had actually occurred.

"I sh-shall never have another like it," sobbed Beatrice into a tense silence. "Th-they do not have such b-bonnets in Wicken! I vow I shall never want another bonnet again."

"Is that all that makes you cry?" soothed Ally. "But they do make such bonnets here in London, dearest. I shall write a letter to Papa and ask that he send you a bit more money so that you may purchase another just like it."

Beatrice began to wail.

"Honestly, Ally," declared Kate, her hands going to her hips, "did you need to suggest precisely that? What will Papa think to hear that Bea has fallen so in love with a straw hat with apricot ribands that she cries over it and must have another just like it? He will think that she has lost her mind, that is what, and he will likely come rushing directly to this metropolis to take us home with him."

"Your hat, my lord," whispered a voice in Wentworth's ear.

"What? Oh! Thank you," replied Wentworth, taking the proffered beaver from the footman's hand. It, like the rest of Wentworth's clothing, was somewhat the worse for the experience, having come to a stop in the midst of a bramble bush whose nettles had pierced it clear through in several places. Combing his hair back into place as best he could with his fingers and without the help of a looking glass, the earl placed the hat upon his head, bent to pick up his cane from the spot on the grass where it had fallen, and then stood and stared in the most confused manner at Bea, who continued to sob in Ally's arms.

"If you wish to mend matters with Beatrice, I know precisely what you can do," whispered Kate in Wentworth's ear, and taking him by the arm, she tugged him a few steps apart from Ally and Bea. "I know just the thing."

"What?"

"Well, it is quite simple, actually. You need simply go to Madame Gallier's in Bond Street and request that

she make another hat just like the one Miss Beatrice
Lange purchased from her last week. The straw with
the wide brim and the apricot ribands. She will remember it, I am certain, because even she thought it particularly attractive upon Beatrice. And when it is ready,
you must simply fetch it and bring it to Bea at Harriman
House and she will be all smiles again and thank you
most sincerely and not blame you one bit for the hat's
having gotten away from her. Most likely, she will even
forgive you for seeing her cry."

"I will do no such thing," protested Wentworth with
great indignation. "Go into some female boutique and
purchase a bonnet? For that—that—hoyden? I think
not!"

Stoneforth looked up from the book he was attempting to read and stared at his uncle's butler. "Lady Jersey,
Forbes?"

"Yes, my lord. I have sent for tea and requested that
she await you in the small drawing room."

"Tea, Forbes?"

"Indeed, my lord. She will expect it, I assure you."

Stoneforth's brow wrinkled in doubt as he placed the
red riband with the tarnished silver medal dangling from
it inside the book to mark his place and rose from his
chair. "It is not acceptable, I thought, for a lady to visit
at a bachelor's establishment. It was not used to be acceptable."

"No, my lord. But Lady Jersey is a married lady, my
lord, and quite an important one at that, and conces-
sions are regularly made in such cases."

With long even strides, Stoneforth made his way along
the ground floor corridor, took the staircase to the first
floor two steps at a time, hurried along that corridor and

turned, feeling oddly warm under the collar, into the small drawing room. "My lady," he said, bowing.

Lady Jersey turned away from the window through which she had been gazing and fairly beamed sunlight upon him. "My dearest Lord Stoneforth!" She strode to meet him and offered him her hand, which he accepted, though he thought twice and decided he would not place a kiss upon the back of it.

"A most unexpected pleasure, my lady," Stoneforth said, escorting her to a chair and taking the one across from it for himself. "I cannot think what brings you here."

He was everything that Sally Jersey remembered—his shoulders as broad, his back as straight, his legs as muscular and his countenance as seductive and alluring. "I have come to discuss your presence at Almack's on Wednesday last," she purred in a low, husky voice and was most amazed at herself to hear it.

"I see." The corners of Stoneforth's lips trembled toward a smile. "We are found out, Castlereagh and I, eh?"

"How did you ever get past Mr. Willis? It has never been done before, I assure you. Was it your brother's ticket you handed him? It is against all the rules, you know, for Mr. Attenbury to have given his ticket into your hands."

"Toby had a ticket?" asked Stoneforth, an eyebrow cocking and the smile that trembled upon his lips flashing into being and out again in a moment. "What a dunce I am! I never thought to look about the house to discover if Toby might already have a ticket. Even Ridgeworth did not think of it."

"You did not use Mr. Attenbury's ticket?"

"No."

"But then how did you—?"

"I have no idea. I put myself into Lord Castlereagh's hands. Your Mr. Willis was somewhat hesitant to allow me to enter, but then Lord Castlereagh took him aside and whispered a word or two in his ear and *voilà*, like magic, I was in."

As Forbes entered at that moment with the tea tray, Lady Jersey was left to consider in silence what words Lord Castlereagh might have whispered and how any words could have worked such magic with the generally dependable Mr. Willis. "I shall pour out, shall I?" she asked as the butler departed.

"Indeed, my lady. I am not to be trusted with pouring out. All thumbs, you know."

"I cannot think that you are all thumbs at anything, my lord. Will you have sugar? Cream? Lemon? Oh, what remarkable tarts!" she exclaimed, taking a most ladylike bite of the pastries that had accompanied the Bohea. Really, Sally thought, what a perfect ninny I sound. Anyone would think me out of the schoolroom only yesterday and attempting for the first time to make polite conversation with a gentleman. But he is such an enticing gentleman! He positively sets my heart to racing.

"About your assembly rooms," began Stoneforth, sipping at his tea and then setting it aside. "I hope you will not hold my entrance into your splendid club against Mr. Willis, nor against Lord Castlereagh either. I am the one instigated it all, I assure you. I was desperate, you see, to be introduced to Miss Harriman as soon as possible."

"Miss Harriman? Little Miss Harriman's presence brought you to Almack's?"

"Indeed. I—"

"Lady Harriman's girl?"

"Precisely."

"Oh. Well, and now that I think of it, Robert did introduce you to her, did he not? And you waltzed with her too," observed Lady Jersey, her eyes large with wonder.

Why in heaven, she mused in silence, would this perfectly splendid man be so drawn to little Miss Harriman that he would induce Robert to violate all the rules just so that he might be introduced to her on Wednesday night rather than Thursday morning or Friday? Great heavens, what have I and the others overlooked about the girl? There must certainly be something. Not that it is any of my concern. "You are much taken with Miss Harriman, then, Lord Stoneforth. How nice that Robert could be of assistance."

The considerable bafflement and disappointment in Lady Jersey's tone did not slide by Stoneforth, and the imp that Nora Huston had long ago aroused inside him began to leap delightedly about. Stoneforth's lips tilted upward. His eyes began to glow with humor. And the fact that Lady Jersey began to squirm upon her chair when his smile fell full upon her made him smile even more widely than he had at first intended. "She is very young, Miss Harriman, is she not?" he asked quietly, remembering what Lady Harriman had told him about Miss Harriman's being considered upon the shelf. "You are doubtless pondering my interest in such a very young lady, especially in the face of such a mature and true beauty as your own. But then, sadly, you are already married, my lady, and Miss Harriman is not. And while I do wish to make Lord Jersey's acquaintance, I assure you that I do not seek to make it at the point of his sword, and so it must be Miss Harriman and not yourself, I am afraid."

"Oh!" exclaimed Sally Jersey, growing quite warm and fanning at her face with a napkin.

The smile departed Stoneforth's face. "Just so. I hesitate to say it, but I think I must, so that all is truth between us. I became most keenly aware of my—manhood—last Wednesday when you waltzed with me, my lady. Had I been in London and made your acquaintance before Jersey had the opportunity to do so, there is no telling but what I—But alas, Jersey is the luckiest of gentlemen and I, a dour old soldier without hope." He gazed at her from beneath slightly lowered lids, the hooded sultriness of those midnight eyes sending Sally Jersey's blood boiling past her eardrums. "You will forgive me for remarking upon it, I hope, but you are a remarkably—alluring—woman, my lady, and no gentleman can hope to ignore that fact, especially not a gentleman such as I who has been absent so long from such pleasing Society."

Lady Jersey near choked upon the fearsome lump that had risen to her throat. Her fingers fiddled unconsciously with the perfectly pressed pleats of her carriage gown. Her eyelashes whispered down across her blushing cheeks and then whispered upward again as her eyes returned to meet his. "I—I—I have come to solve your problem," she gasped with a fluttering heart. "I h-have come to present you with your own vouchers to Almack's so that you may obtain tickets and attend without raising one eyebrow. And I shall tell Emily Anne—Lady Castlereagh—I shall tell her that Maria Sefton gave you the vouchers for last Wednesday night and then forgot all about it. Maria is always forgetting things. She will not remember whether she did so or not and it will not amaze Emily Anne to hear that she did. It will save Robert a good deal of fuss at home, and you may come with or without him on any Wednesday you like."

"How kind you are. Beautiful and kind, a rare combination."

"Yes," breathed Lady Jersey as if she were seventeen again. "I mean, no. No, I mean it is of not the least import, my lord."

"It is of the greatest import, I think, though I do not fully understand as yet the significance of your club. It is a most important gathering place. That is clear. And not only do you free Mr. Willis and Lord Castlereagh of all guilt for allowing such an interloper as myself inside, but you make it possible for me to return without the least fuss. I daresay that you are without equal, my dearest Lady Jersey."

"Sally."

"Sally? No, but I could not call you so. Lord Jersey would be most jealous, I am certain."

"Bother Jersey," murmured her ladyship.

"Something I shall definitely attempt to avoid doing," grinned Stoneforth. "Indeed, I shall most certainly attempt to avoid bothering Lord Jersey ever, but by Jove, I shall be hard-pressed in the doing of it, let me tell you."

Melody sat upon the window seat in the front parlor gazing out at the street, awaiting the triplets' return from Green Park. Her sketchbook lay neglected in her lap. She had intended to begin sketches for a watercolor of the truly lovely picture Hanover Square presented on such a gloriously bright afternoon in springtime, but her mind would have none of it. Her mind carried her instead far beyond the prospect of a London square with a bright sun beaming down upon well-ordered houses and well-scrubbed stoops, delightfully blooming trees and flowers upon the verge. It carried her into the almost mythical and nightmarish environs of a Spanish countryside drowning in rain and mud and blood. She saw Lord Stoneforth again as she had imagined him that afternoon in Sanshire House. Saw him feinting and parrying and lunging and thrusting home. A chill wandered through her, making her shiver as though she were there in the midst of the storm and the battle and the cold, pouring rain.

And then, in the most absurd manner, her imagination skipped from that dreadful, yet inspiring, vision to a most realistic picture of Mr. Attenbury with his cherub's face and sky blue eyes, a red cravat tied adorably around his neck, while he sat in his bed surrounded by pillows. Truly, he was a most handsome young gentleman, Mr. Attenbury.

And he loves me, Melody thought in wonder. Whoever would have guessed at such a thing?

She never would have guessed it to be so. If Lord Stoneforth had not come to speak with her at Almack's, if he had not explained about Toby's calling for her, if he had not requested her to go to his brother, she would never have guessed that Mr. Attenbury loved her. In fact, even when she had heard her name over and over upon Mr. Attenbury's fevered lips she had had the greatest difficulty in accepting that somehow she had engaged that gentleman's heart.

"But he is so very young," she whispered to the scene beyond the parlor window. "He is two years younger than I and most certainly cannot as yet know his own mind. And yet, when he lay in the throes of that fever, practically upon the verge of death, it was I for whom he called. Oh, I do not know how I ought to feel at all. No, nor what I am to do about it. What am I to do?"

"About what, Melody?" asked Kate from the threshold behind her. "What are you to do about what?"

"Nothing," Melody replied, turning with a shake of her ashen curls and a slow smile. "I was simply remembering a scene from one of your papa's comic operas. You are back from the park so soon. Did you enjoy your stroll?"

"Well, I did," nodded Kate, "and I do think that Ally had a marvelous time, but Bea says that she will never go there again."

"Why ever not?"

"Because she lost her new straw hat."

"The one with the apricot ribands? Oh, she loved that hat!"

"Yes, and she took it off to let the wind blow through her hair and set it upon the bench beside her and along came this wily beast of a dog and ran off with it. We all attempted to catch the little demon but it was not the least use."

"No use at all," agreed Ally, strolling past Kate into the room and sitting down upon one of the Louis XIV chairs.

"Where is Beatrice?" asked Kate at once. "You have not left her alone?"

"Of course I have left her alone and she is just fine. No one has died; she has simply lost a hat. But it was the oddest thing, do not you think, for Bea to cry about it?"

"Bea cried about losing her hat?" asked Melody, aghast. "Beatrice? Perhaps she is ill, do you think? I have never known Bea to cry about anything."

"Just so, which is why I do not understand it at all," Ally mused. "One would think she would have counted its loss as the price of the fun and walked off laughing, but she did not."

"The price of the fun? What fun?" asked Melody rising, tossing her sketch pad upon the window seat and moving to sit upon the settee across from Ally. She patted the place next to her, and Kate came and sat quietly, with a most perplexed expression upon her face.

"I thought Beatrice would be exceedingly pleased when I saw what happened," Ally murmured. "It was Lord Wentworth whom she trod upon after all."

"Indeed," agreed Kate. "And I did think at first, when she hid her face against your shoulder, that she was laughing."

"But she was not," scowled Ally.

"No, she was not," Kate declared, leaning back and raising her forearm to her brow. "Oh, woe is me, will we ever, ever understand the meanderings of Beatrice's nature?"

"No, never," Ally sighed. "Just when I have decided that I understand her thoroughly, she must go and cry over a lost bonnet like some dainty young thing from the country."

"Bea is a dainty young thing from the country," protested Melody. "Well, she is young—and from the country," she amended as two sets of steely gray eyes stared at her in disbelief. "And if she is not dainty, she has a most sensitive nature."

"Ha!" declared Kate.

"Bea? Sensitive? I do not think so," Ally murmured.

"That is because she hides it behind all that bluff and bravado she has learned from the stable boys and the grooms and the squire's sons—and, yes, from your papa, as well. But her sensibilities are quite equal to those of any other young lady," Melody said. "I am certain of it."

"You are?" asked Ally.

"Yes. But why she should come to tears over a hat, I cannot imagine. And what had the hat to do with Lord Wentworth? And what did you mean, Ally, when you said that she trod upon him? You must tell me absolutely everything. But first ought we not go to see how Beatrice does? Has she gone directly to your chambers?"

"Oh, great heavens!" exclaimed Kate, rising on the instant. "Did she go directly to our chambers? Ally, did she? And in such a state as she must be? Ally, Bea did not bring—she would not go—but yes, she would, because I do not doubt that she is totally frustrated with herself for having given away so—and in front of Lord Wentworth!"

Melody looked from Kate to Ally, who was jumping to her feet and rushing toward the doorway almost as soon as the words began to tumble from Kate's lips.

What were they so excited about all of a sudden? And then Melody remembered. She remembered exactly what it was that Beatrice always did—had done since she was old enough to do it—whenever she was overly excited or confused or—frustrated. "Oh, she would not!" Melody cried, gaining her feet as well and dashing into the corridor immediately behind her cousins. "Not here in London! If she is seen and recognized, she will be ostracized from Society forever!"

"Bea!" Ally called as she hurried toward the main staircase, very nearly knocking Higgens to the floor.

"Beatrice!" shouted Kate at a most unladylike volume as she lifted her skirts and ran up the stairs.

"Steady on, Higgens," offered Melody, reaching out to steady the butler before she, too, spun around the newel post and dashed up the staircase.

"Now what the deuce is going on?" murmured Higgens, staring after the young ladies. "There is nothing Miss Beatrice can do to bring about such panic as that. I shall never grow accustomed to having young ladies about the house, I fear. Never." But he smiled a very comfortable smile as he turned in the opposite direction and strolled off toward the kitchen.

Eight

Stoneforth sat back in the saddle and watched admiringly as the lad gave the chestnut filly her head. The horse and rider were traveling at full tilt in the small valley below him, the boy's dark curls whipped back by the wind, the horse's mane streaming over the hands that held the reins. The young rider leaned slightly forward in the saddle, his knees pressed tight against the filly's side, and the satisfied smile upon his face, though Stoneforth could not see it, was unconsciously reproduced upon his lordship's own as he watched.

Viscount Stoneforth had come to this place because he had discovered that one could not ride full tilt in Hyde Park in the late afternoon. There were far too many horses and carriages cavorting about the park at that hour. Something called the Promenade, Toby had informed him when he had asked. So he had come here to a stretch of land just west of Edgware Road called Crawley's Bottom and he had given the new black his head while at the same time clearing his own. He had bought the black gelding at Tattersall's only the day before and now discovered himself well pleased with his selection. The beast was not as formidable as Seneca had been, but for riding in London where no gentleman's steed need ever react like a warhorse, he would do.

Seneca. Watlow had been the one to shoot Seneca

that wretched day at Albuera, to shoot him where he had fallen in the midst of the muck and the blood, because Stoneforth had already been felled by Ponsonby's Endeavor. "I did never so much as get the chance to bid you farewell, Sen," Stoneforth murmured, remembering the arched neck and the hard-muscled shoulders and the wide flanks with love. "Ten years, and I did not so much as say once how I loved you. But you knew, did you not? You knew. We all know when we are loved, horses and men alike, without the saying of the words. But women and children must hear the words, Nora said. And men like me must learn to say them."

The filly in the valley below leaped clean over a rasper with the lad fully in command, and Stoneforth nodded. "That lad will do. We would be lucky to have him upon the field with our dragoons, that one. Much too young, though, I expect."

Stoneforth was just about to turn the black back toward Hyde Park when the young gentleman apparently caught sight of him and urged the filly in his direction. They ascended the rise, lad and horse, at a gallop and pulled to a halt with a whirring of wind and a flashing of hooves. "You are Lord Stoneforth," the boy announced, thrusting a hand toward the viscount. "It is a pleasure to meet you again, my lord."

"We have met before?" asked Stoneforth as he took the small hand. The black sidled beneath him, nervous at the nearness of the chestnut.

"Yes, at Almack's. Do you not remember?"

Stoneforth studied the lad curiously. From top boots to buckskin breeches to forest green velvet riding coat and perfectly tied neckcloth. "No," he confessed at last, "I do not remember you, I fear. At Almack's, you say?"

"I am Miss Harriman's cousin, Bea."

"By Jove," drawled Stoneforth, looking her up and down, an eyebrow cocked in surprise. "So you are."

"I knew it was you the moment I looked up," Bea declared excitedly "There is a particular look about you, even at a distance. I took great note of it at the assembly rooms. I am so very pleased to meet you again! You are the very essence of a cavalryman, you know. Everyone who joins wishes to be like you."

"I doubt that."

"No, do not, because it is true. Oswald and Geoffrey— they are Squire Conner's sons—they cannot wait to purchase their commissions and ride out to be heroes exactly like you. You have been mentioned in despatches a full twenty-four times and Wellesley swears you are the very best of the lot."

"Odd, Wellesley has never mentioned that to me."

"Oh. Well, it is most likely because he did not wish to embarrass you with such strong praise."

"Most likely," Stoneforth murmured, nodding, a most amused light springing to his eyes.

"Soldiers are like that. They despise to be embarrassed by praise. My papa says that soldiers are the most stoic and practical people in all the world."

"And your papa is?"

"Mr. Frederick Lange. You do not know him, but he is most interested in all that goes on involving the fighting, and he knows all about you. To think that just a while ago I was so distressed as to be crying and now I have the privilege of speaking with *you*, just the two of us! I do think it was Fate caused it. It must have been Fate because I have never, ever, cried like that and disgraced myself so before. Never. But I would never have ridden out had I not. So it must have been Fate, must it not?"

"Oh, undoubtedly," offered Stoneforth, beguiled. "You ride incredibly well."

"Yes, I know. I ride like a dragoon. And I fight like a dragoon too. Well, perhaps that is a whisker, because

Papa does not know the sword exercise and so could not teach it to me and so I do not know precisely how dragoons fight, but I am very good with a sword nevertheless."

"I will wager you are," Stoneforth nodded. "You would like to be a dragoon, eh?"

"Of all things!"

The smile lurking in Stoneforth's eyes slipped away for a moment. "Your papa is most fortunate that you were born a young lady and cannot join. To lose you to a Frenchman's sword would send him into a mourning from which he would never recover."

"Bosh!" exclaimed Bea. "He would not lose me. I would be victorious always."

"No one is always victorious," sighed Stoneforth softly. "We lost well over four thousand men at Albuera alone. Good men. Brave men. Men whose mothers and fathers are grieving to this day. I am bound for home, Miss Beatrice. Will you allow me to accompany you to Harriman House first?"

"Will you talk to me about the war?"

"If you wish."

"You do not think it most improper to speak of the war in the presence of young ladies?"

"I do not have much to speak of but the war," murmured Stoneforth. "War is all I have known since I was seventeen."

"I am seventeen," offered Beatrice, turning her horse in the same moment that Stoneforth turned his.

"I should never have guessed. Will you race with me as far as the road? I have yet to see how this bit of blood does with another horse running beside him."

"You think I shall be able to stay beside you?"

"All the way," nodded Stoneforth. "Every inch of the way."

* * *

He returned her to Harriman House without one eye looking at her askance by skirting Hyde Park at the very height of the Promenade and behaving along the thoroughfares as though she were his brother, speaking loudly and gruffly to her and once or twice slapping her upon the back. No one, he was positive, had taken her for anything but a lad. They approached the Harriman House stables at a trot, the two of them so engrossed in conversation that it took them both a moment to realize that a trio of young ladies was poised in the stable yard regarding them with the greatest relief.

"Lord Stoneforth, I cannot think how to thank you," Melody said, the train of her riding costume falling over one arm. She laid a gloved hand upon his horse's withers and stroked the animal gently. "Ally and Kate and I have just come from Hyde Park. We thought, you know, that that is where Beatrice would have gone. And we were most discomposed when we could not discover her."

"Phoo!" Bea exclaimed, stepping down from the chestnut and handing its reins to a groom. "I took one look at that place and rode right on past. Filled with prissy little ladies and dandies and not one of them able to ride at more than a shuffle. And I would have been held to a shuffle as well the place was so full of them. I asked a little street sweeper where the gentlemen went to put their horses through their paces and he pointed me in the proper direction."

"Yes, and now I am pointing you in the proper direction," announced Melody, allowing the train of her skirt to fall to the ground and placing a hand upon Bea's shoulder, then turning her toward Kate and Ally. "To the house at once," she ordered. "I will follow in a moment."

Stoneforth smiled to see the trio of young ladies, Kate and Ally in proper riding dress and Bea looking quite like their brother, set out across the mews for the rear of Harriman House. Beatrice spun about to wave at him and he waved back.

"I cannot thank you enough for bringing her safely home," Melody said, her attention once again focused upon Stoneforth. "We feared she would discover herself to someone of the *ton* and be shunned for riding out dressed like a boy and without so much as a groom up beside her."

"Yes, I rather thought she might meet with some disapproval for it," Stoneforth replied, holding to the reins of his black and staring down into the most wonderfully serious green eyes. "She wishes she were a lad, you know. Thinks we gentlemen have all the fun."

"I know."

"She will discover soon enough what an awesome privilege it is to be a woman and she will prove to be a strong and remarkable one, I have no doubt."

"So I think," Melody agreed. "If only we can keep her from running off in disguise to join the cavalry."

Stoneforth laughed. He threw back his head and laughed right out loud at the sky above him. His thick black curls rippled about his collar and his broad shoulders trembled and his stern, austere countenance sparkled like sunshine. And Melody's heart lurched up into her throat.

"Do you attend the dancing at Almack's tonight, Miss Harriman?" he asked then, his midnight blue eyes sparkling down at her.

"Yes, my lord. We are all of us to attend."

"And will you waltz with me?"

"I should be most pleased to do so, but it is Bea, I think, with whom you should dance."

"No. Never. Miss Beatrice would never forgive me if I danced with her as though she were just a young lady."

"She would not?"

"No, Miss Harriman. She would like to ride with me

again and would be delighted were I to discover a time and place to fence with her and she would not at all mind to hear me rattle on even more about the war. But for me to dance with her—she would consider that the greatest of insults now that we have come to know each other as equals."

"Never say that Bea sees you as an equal," protested Melody. "You are her hero, my lord, and have been, the girls say, since she was old enough to rattle off your name."

"Oh?" Stoneforth cocked an eyebrow in the most humorous fashion. "Even more reason not to dance with her. One turn about the floor together and I will likely go plummeting down from that pedestal upon which she has placed me."

"Bosh! I cannot think but that any young lady would feel privileged to dance with you, my lord."

"Yes, well, that is because you see me through entirely different eyes than Miss Beatrice. Toby accompanies me tonight."

"Oh! Ought he to be out and about so very soon?"

"Yes, I think so. It is much better for him to be up and about. It is his shoulder merely. It is not as though his leg is broken. The fever has left him and the shoulder will heal if he is in bed or out of it. But he may not dance. I have made him promise me as much. He will likely sit in your pocket the entire evening, Miss Harriman. But I daresay you will not particularly mind that."

"No, of course I will not. I shall be pleased to have his company and I shall do my best to entertain him."

"Yes, well, we shall see you this evening then," Stoneforth replied with the oddest look upon his face. Then he leaned down from his horse and held out his hand and Melody put her own into it. He raised the hand to his lips and pressed a kiss upon the back of it. "Farewell, Miss Harriman."

He was off with a nudge of his spurs against the black's sides, and he did not once look back. And it was a very good thing that he did not, because he would have seen Melody staring at the back of her gloved hand in wonder as her cheeks colored up to a bright pink, and he would have hated himself for being unable to resist kissing her—merely her hand, just this one time—and bringing that most bewildered expression to her face.

"You are going where?" Lady Castlereagh in an outrageous gown of gold silk with an overlay of silver gossamer, a plume of dyed silver ostrich feathers set at a most extraordinary angle in her hair and golden slippers upon her feet, paused in her primping and turned upon her vanity bench to stare in amazement at her husband.

"I do not see why you should stare so, Emily Anne. Are you not always ringing peals over my head for showing not the least interest in your little club? Well, I am showing an interest. I am wearing these confounded knee breeches and the silk stockings that make me want to scratch every time I take a step, and even the jeweled buckles that you bought me for these odious dancing slippers. I look like a court jester, Emily. But I have decided that I will accompany you to Almack's, laugh though people may."

Lady Castlereagh's face did not quite know how to compose itself. Should it smile or frown? Should it arch an eyebrow? Should the lips tilt just the slightest bit in disbelief?

"You were at Almack's last Wednesday night without me."

"Yes, I was. I knew Sally would tell you, too, so it was not intended to be a secret." Lord Castlereagh, shooting his cuffs into a more comfortable position, strolled the rest of the way into his wife's dressing room and came to a halt directly behind the little vanity bench upon which she perched. "What else did Sally tell you?" he asked quietly, placing his hands gently upon her shoulders.

"That you gave Mr. Willis the both halves of your torn ticket to gain entrance and that you arrived with Lord Stoneforth, Mr. Attenbury's brother, upon whom Maria had bestowed vouchers and then promptly forgot to tell anyone that she had. I vow, Maria is a halfwit. Who is this Lord Stoneforth?"

"Mr. Attenbury's elder brother."

"Yes, Robert, but who is he? Why should you accompany him to the club? I have never so much as heard you mention his name."

"That is because he has not been long in London. He has been on the Continent for years, my dear, and has just now returned."

"He is not a soldier? Oh, Robert, a soldier? You are the Foreign Secretary. Why must you choose to go about with a mere soldier when you might linger over wine with men of distinction?"

Castlereagh leaned down and nibbled on the lobe of his wife's ear. He had not done such a thing in almost a year and it made Emily Anne jump.

"Oh, Robert! You will disarrange my hair!"

"Just so, my dear. And I will disarrange more than that if we do not drop this discussion at once and leave this house. And tonight I will introduce you to Stoneforth and you will be most kind and most polite to him."

"Do not order me about, Robert. I am not one of your men."

"I am not ordering you about, my dear. I am merely telling you how you will behave. Stoneforth is not a mere soldier, Emily Anne. He is one of Britain's finest and he has risked his life time and again so that you and your friends may reside safely in London and go on playing your little games. More than that, he is a Lord of the Realm and a personal friend of mine and I will not have him ignored or avoided or condescended to by you or any of the rest of the King Street Cabal."

"I do wish you would not call us names!" exclaimed Lady Castlereagh with an angry pout. "Martha, why are you still here? Go away!"

Lord Castlereagh reached the door before the lady's maid and opened it for her. She hurried past him with head down and quick little steps. He closed the door after her and stood leaning against it, staring at his wife in the most distracting manner.

"If you are not very busy," Mr. Attenbury began, sitting rather stiffly in one of Almack's little gilded chairs, his right arm cradled in a sling made from one of his brother's old black silk neckcloths. "If you are not otherwise occupied, I mean, do you think you might like to attend the theatre this Friday evening? Adam thought we might make a party of it. You and your cousins and your mother, of course, and Adam and myself."

Melody smiled and nodded. "I should be delighted, Mr. Attenbury. Mama," she said, turning a bit upon her chair and giving Lady Harriman's arm a pat.

"Yes, dearest?"

"Mr. Attenbury wonders if we are free to attend the theatre with him and Lord Stoneforth on Friday? All of us."

"What a charming idea. Of course we will accompany you, Mr. Attenbury. We thank you for the invitation." And then she turned back to watch the dancers, her eyes flitting from one to another of her nieces. Truly, the triplets were lovely girls. Her brother Frederick had done a marvelous job to bring them up so perfectly. And their presence certainly did much to bolster Melody.

There are fifteen gentlemen at the very least present this evening who rarely patronize Almack's, thought Lady Harriman. And three of them have come to place their names upon Melody's dance card already. Others will surely follow. Lord Wentworth's wit notwithstanding, once a number of gentlemen come to know Melody she will no longer be considered an unmarriageable spinster, because she is as fine and sweet a girl as any gentleman could wish. And even if Melody does choose to align herself with Mr. Attenbury in the end, it will be so much better for her to come to know more than one gentleman before she decides.

A number of other mothers were also gazing upon the dancers and musing about their own daughters. Lady Skiffington, for one, could not help but ponder the sudden decrease in popularity of her own Elizabeth, who had never once sat out a dance at Almack's but was now warming the seat of the chair beside her. And Mrs. Matherson-Harding could not comprehend why Lord Emery, whom she had considered charmed into submission by her Bella, had abandoned the girl to skip about the floor with one of those abominable Langes. And Mrs. Pascale's face was rapidly turning purple as Mr. Davies, who had all but ignored her Dorothy for the entire week, now laughed delightedly at that absurd Lange child with the short curls who did not deserve to even enter Almack's portals. Why she was barely out of the schoolroom and anyone could see that she had no idea how to go on in Society.

A number of befuddled young ladies who had never once been wallflowers and now sat politely with their hands in their laps were not terribly amused by the situation either. Almack's ballroom was filled with more gentlemen than ever before but apparently unless one were married or betrothed or about to be so, not one of those gentlemen was going to request a dance with anyone not named Lange. Really, it was the outside of enough! And none of the patronesses were doing anything at all about it.

Lady Jersey did think that she and Maria and Emily Anne ought to make some effort to encourage the gentlemen to dance instead of allowing them to stand about, leaning against the walls, staring like simpletons at the Lange triplets. "We cannot allow them to do this," she whispered in Maria Sefton's ear. "We shall take them one by one and introduce them to the other girls, and they will take the hint."

"That will work very well for girls who are accustomed to being without a partner," Lady Sefton agreed, "but those who generally have a plethora of beaux will be most insulted."

Lady Jersey watched as the dancers quit the floor and then began to regroup for the next dance, and a most intrigued smile moved over her face. "Why those rascals," she murmured to herself. "Whatever do they think to do? We shall not interfere for a while, Maria," she told Lady Sefton then. "Only see what is happening. Good heavens, that is Robert!"

"What are you saying of Robert?" asked Lady Castlereagh, who had just then come up beside the two. "Well, for goodness' sake! Who is that chit he is bowing so properly before?"

"Miss Harriman," Lady Sefton informed her, clapping her hands together in joy. "It is wonderful of your husband to lead her out, Emily Anne. She is so often ignored by the gentlemen and I cannot think why. She is a delightful girl."

"She has been ignored by the gentlemen, Maria, because Lord Wentworth chose to make her an object of his wit and they would none of the gentlemen chance approaching her," Lady Jersey explained patiently.

"And only look, my dear, Miss Turnbill is to dance and Lady Constance and Miss DuBoise."

"Oh, my!" exclaimed Lady Sefton. "Are all of our wallflowers to dance this evening? Just see, Sally, Mr. Davies is leading out Daphne Davidson!"

"How dare he!" exclaimed Mrs. Pascale, with the most unbecoming scowl. "Dorothy, what have you done to give Mr. Davies a distaste of you?"

"Nothing, Mama."

"But he does not lead you out. He leads out that unfortunate Davidson chit instead. Where can his mind be to choose her over you? And has Miss Skiffington injured herself? Is that why she does not dance? She is generally upon the floor at every opportunity, you know."

"Yes, Mama, I do know. And I am generally upon the floor as well. But here I sit neglected while Mr. Davies dances first with that snip of a Lange girl and now with Daphne Davidson of all people! And he has not so much as approached me to sign my dance card, Mama. There are barely any signatures upon my card at all!"

"Well, you must have said or done something to give Mr. Davies a distaste of you," muttered her mama angrily. "You would be out there upon the floor this moment else."

"Mr. Davies dances with Miss Davidson because Miss Beatrice Lange urged him to do so," offered a flushed Miss Bergen, leaning over just enough that Mrs. and Miss Pascale might hear her. "I overheard him promise Miss Beatrice to lead Daphne out while we danced this last set."

"She urged him to do so? Why on earth would she think to—"

"I cannot say," Miss Bergen interrupted, "but then, when the figures put her opposite my Donald, she petitioned him to lead out Miss DuBoise. Well, Donald inquired of me if I should be at all jealous and I told him that he might do as he pleased in the matter. We are betrothed, after all, and I can have nothing to fear from Miss DuBoise."

Lady Harriman sat back in the little chair and attempted not to laugh out loud. She hid her smiling lips behind her fan and giggled instead. Truly, it was the most diverting thing, and the look upon Lady Sefton's face was priceless.

"What is it that you find so very entertaining, my lady?"

Lady Harriman turned to discover Lord Stoneforth in Melody's empty chair between herself and Mr. Attenbury.

"It is the delightful look upon Maria Sefton's face. Maria is truly the kindest of persons and she is so overcome with joy. That is she, right beside Lady Jersey, and I know that you know which is Lady Jersey, my lord," she added with a sly glance, remembering the waltz the two had shared the week before.

"Why is she overcome with joy?"

"Well, because apparently all of the young ladies who spend most Wednesday evenings sitting here with the chaperones are to dance tonight and Maria is thrilled for them."

"And are you pleased for them as well?"

"Indeed, though I cannot think how it comes about."

"Your nieces," declared Stoneforth enigmatically.

"My nieces? What can this have to do with my nieces?"

"I know," offered Mr. Attenbury, leaning slightly across his brother. "Haversham whispered it to me not five minutes ago and he is even now dancing with Miss

Elroy because of it. Your nieces, Lady Harriman, are requesting of every gentleman who dances with them that they dance next with one of the girls who is generally without a partner. And further, they have refused to reserve any of the rest of the dances beyond this one. After this reel, any of the beaux wishing to dance with one of the Langes must first have danced with one of the wallflowers."

"Just so," nodded Stoneforth. "Precisely what I was told. And all of the gentlemen wish to dance with one of your nieces, my lady," he added. "Every last one of them."

Nine

"Why did you dance with Miss Harriman?" Lady Castlereagh hissed, grasping her husband's arm as he wandered past her just to the far side of the dance floor.

"Because she is a friend of a friend of mine," offered Castlereagh, staring down into the quite lovely, but scowling, face to which he had grown much accustomed.

"Where, Robert, have you suddenly acquired all of these friendships and why are they people I have never met?"

"I vow, Emily Anne, you are jealous," Castlereagh said, amazed, a slow smile stealing into his eyes. "I never thought to see the day."

"I am not jealous!" exclaimed Lady Castlereagh loudly enough to turn more than one interested glance in her direction. She immediately hid behind her painted fan and blushed.

Castlereagh, with a gentleness long unused, grasped the fan above the point where his lady held it and folded it slowly. Most seductively he closed it, one tiny section at a time. His eyes never left her face. They glowed down at her. "I have not seen you blush in so very long, Emily," he whispered. "You are a veritable vision when you blush so. Listen. Gow is striking up a waltz. Come, Emily Anne, waltz with me."

"It is—*gauche*—for a husband and wife to—" Lady Castlereagh's tongue tripped over her own words.

"Let us be *gauche* then," murmured Castlereagh, placing one strong hand upon the small of her back and clasping in his own, the small hand from whose wrist the fan now dangled uselessly. In three quick, breathless steps, he swirled her out onto the floor.

"Oh, my! Lord and Lady Castlereagh are dancing together," Melody observed to the sapphire stickpin that adorned the center of the knot in Stoneforth's neckcloth as that particular couple twirled past them upon the floor.

"Is that odd? I should think it just the thing myself."

"No, it is not at all the thing." Melody raised her gaze to meet the beautiful eyes that stared questioningly down at her. "Mama says that the married ladies and gentlemen are expected to go their separate ways in public. No gentleman wishes people to think that he is always sitting in his wife's pocket."

"Balderdash," murmured Stoneforth. "I should not marry a woman if that was not precisely where I wished to sit."

"You would not?"

"Never. I daresay Toby wishes to sit in your pocket for the rest of his life. I do thank you for agreeing to accompany us to the theatre on such short notice, Miss Harriman." Stoneforth stumbled the slightest bit as he led her through a turn.

"Oh, my goodness. I completely forgot. You need not spin me so very enthusiastically, my lord. Truly, you need not. Nor so often. We shall adapt the waltz into a new, more elegant dance."

"We shall? Why shall we?"

"Because you are growing dizzy. You must be. I know about your eye. Mr. Attenbury told me. It must be difficult to be spinning about so."

"Difficult," nodded Stoneforth, "but not impossible. Why should Toby mention to you about my eye?"

"Because he is most proud of you and wished to fill me with awe at tales of your courage and skill upon the field and so he told me of Albuera. Mr. Watlow assisted in the narrative."

"No, Watlow did? By Jove, you must think me a veritable barbarian if Watlow added his penny's worth. He is fond of blood and guts, Watlow, especially if I am the one splattering them about the field."

"Ugh," Melody responded, wrinkling her nose. "What a thing for you to say—splattering blood and guts."

"It is truth. War is a grim business. Let us not speak of it anymore tonight."

Melody noted the seriousness of his expression and nodded. "We shall speak of other things, but we shall also not twirl quite so much as we have been."

He stepped into the ballroom in the midst of the waltz, his dancing slippers bedecked with jewels, his waistcoat black but dazzling with row upon row of silver thread etching a forest of trees across the front of it. His neck-cloth was tied in a perfect sentimental and its pristine white together with the white of his shirt collars and the small white rosebud upon his lapel fairly glowed against the black coat and breeches and waistcoat.

Mr. Attenbury saw him at once and made to stand and stroll up to him. And he would have done so, too, if Lady Harriman had not reached out and grabbed him by the coattail and tugged him down into the chair beside her.

"Do not so much as take notice of his existence, Mr. Attenbury, or I shall strangle you with your own sling," she said softly, a smile pasted upon her face. "I mean it. I will not have you confront that gentleman while Melody is present. Have you not had quite enough of Lord Wentworth?"

"You do not understand, my lady."

"I understand perfectly. Your brother told me all that happened between the two of you. But it is finished now."

"No, madam, it is not finished."

"You think not?" asked Lady Harriman with the arching of a particularly intimidating eyebrow. "Look about you, Mr. Attenbury. What do you see?"

"Almack's, madam."

"And?"

"I do not know what you wish me to say."

"Really, Mr. Attenbury, do you not see my daughter dancing with your brother? Did you not see her dance with Lord Castlereagh and Mr. Trent and Lord Wheymore? It is over. Lord Wentworth's wit has lost its power to harm her."

"Do you think?"

"I most certainly do. But should you go to him now and cause a row, Melody's reputation will be sunk beyond repair. No one knows of your duel but your closest friends. Not one word has escaped into the public scandal broth, but if you invite him to fight once more, everyone will assume that the fight is because of Melody, and Lord Wentworth will have ruined her Season again."

"Well, devil—" muttered Mr. Attenbury. "Oh, pardon me, ma'am. I did not intend to say that, but it is most aggravating. I have the greatest wish to tell Wentworth what I think of him and to offer to take him on again if he does not retract all he has said of Miss Harriman and do it right here in front of everyone he knows, too."

"I thought that you had lost your duel with Lord Wentworth, Mr. Attenbury," Lady Harriman murmured.

"I did, but that does not mean that he may go off

Say Yes to 4 Free Books!
Complete and return the order card to receive this $19.96 value, ABSOLUTELY FREE!

(If the certificate is missing below, write to:)
Zebra Home Subscription Service, Inc.,
120 Brighton Road, P.O. Box 5214, Clifton, New Jersey 07015-5214
or call TOLL-FREE 1-888-345-BOOK

Check out our website at www.kensingtonbooks.com.

FREE BOOK CERTIFICATE

YES! Please rush me 4 Zebra Regency Romances without cost or obligation. I understand that each month thereafter I will be able to preview 4 brand-new Regency Romances FREE for 10 days. Then, if I should decide to keep them, I will pay the money-saving preferred subscriber's price of just $16.00 for all 4...that's a savings of almost $4 off the publisher's price with no additional charge for shipping and handling. I may return any shipment within 10 days and owe nothing, and I may cancel this subscription at any time. My 4 FREE books will be mine to keep in any case.

Name _____

Address _____ Apt. _____

City _____ State _____ Zip _____

Telephone ( ) _____

Signature _____ RN1B9A
(If under 18, parent or guardian must sign.)

Terms and prices subject to change. Orders subject to acceptance by Zebra Home Subscription Service, Inc. Offer valid in U.S. only.

We'd Like to Invite You to Subscribe to Zebra's Regency Romance Book Club and Give You a Gift of 4 Free Books as Your Introduction! (Worth $19.96!)

If you're a Regency lover, imagine the joy of getting **4 FREE Zebra Regency Romances** and then the chance to have these lovely stories delivered to your home each month at the lowest prices available! Well, that's our offer to you and here's how you benefit by becoming a Zebra Home Subscription Service subscriber:

- **4 FREE Introductory Regency Romances are delivered to your doorstep**

- **4 BRAND NEW Regencies are then delivered each month (usually before they're available in bookstores)**

- **Subscribers save almost $4.00 every month**

- **Home delivery is always FREE**

- **You also receive a FREE monthly newsletter, *Zebra/ Pinnacle Romance News* which features author profiles, contests, subscriber benefits, book previews and more**

- **No risks or obligations...in other words you can cancel whenever you wish with no questions asked**

Join the thousands of readers who enjoy the savings and convenience offered to Regency Romance subscribers. After your initial introductory shipment, you receive 4 brand-new Zebra Regency Romances each month to examine for 10 days. Then, if you decide to keep the books, you'll pay the preferred subscriber's price of just $4.00 per title. That's only $16.00 for all 4 books and there's never an extra charge for shipping and handling.

It's a no-lose proposition, so return the FREE BOOK CERTIFICATE today!

Check out our website at www.kensingtonbooks.com.

FREE BOOK CERTIFICATE

YES! Please rush me 4 Zebra Regency Romances without cost or obligation. I understand that each month thereafter I will be able to preview 4 brand-new Regency Romances FREE for 10 days. Then, if I should decide to keep them, I will pay the money-saving preferred subscriber's price of just $16.00 for all 4...that's a savings of almost $4 off the publisher's price with no additional charge for shipping and handling. I may return any shipment within 10 days and owe nothing, and I may cancel this subscription at any time. My 4 FREE books will be mine to keep in any case.

Name _____

Address _____ Apt. _____

City _____ State _____ Zip _____

Telephone ( ) _____

Signature _____
(If under 18, parent or guardian must sign.)   RN1B9A

Say Yes to 4 Free Books!
Complete and return the order card to receive this
$19.96 value, ABSOLUTELY FREE!

(If the certificate is missing below, write to:)
Zebra Home Subscription Service, Inc.,
120 Brighton Road, P.O. Box 5214, Clifton, New Jersey 07015-5214
or call TOLL-FREE 1-888-345-BOOK

scot-free for making a jest of Miss Harriman—not just once, but time and time again. No, he may not. I shall think of some way to make him pay, and dearly too. I promise you that."

"I do not think you need concern yourself over it any longer, Mr. Attenbury. I believe he is already beginning to pay. Only see the look upon his face."

The look upon Wentworth's face was a mixture of disbelief, astonishment and disdain. The left corner of his lip curled upward the slightest bit as he looked about him, discovering not only Miss Harriman but all of the wallflowers dancing, while Miss Pascale and Lady Grace and Miss Skiffington and Miss Bergen—the most popular of the ladies—lingered listlessly in the company of the chaperones. "What the deuce is this?" he mumbled.

"Do not wear that particular look upon your face, Giles. It will freeze that way and no one will wish to associate with you ever again," grinned Lady Jersey, taking his arm. "We thought perhaps you were not coming. It is very near eleven."

"What the deuce is going on here?" he asked, freeing himself from her grip and shooting his cuff back down where it belonged.

"I think it is a rebellion of sorts," replied Lady Jersey, attempting not to chuckle at his obvious chagrin. "Apparently, dearest, your biting wit no longer rules the gentlemen within these walls. From what I have been able to discover, you have been overthrown by the Misses Lange. Do not pout, Giles. Mr. Brummell returns soon and he would be certain to overthrow you, you know, in any case."

"Never overthrow me. I shall always bow in deference to The Beau's opinions without the least need for him to overthrow me."

"Yes, I am certain that is correct. We all do bow to Mr. Brummell's opinions in social matters, do we not?

Yet it appears you will not be required to hand back Mr. Brummell his baton, dearest, because you no longer possess it."

Wentworth opened his mouth to protest, but the waltz had come to an end and he discovered himself abruptly surrounded by a number of gentlemen, Mr. Davies among them.

"Yes, yes, do take him off with you," laughed Lady Jersey. "Away, Giles. We shall speak more of it at another time, my dear." And then she was gone, strolling with the most curious look upon her face in the direction of Lady Castlereagh.

"We thought to give up on you, Wentworth," said Mr. Trent with a grin.

"Yes, that we did," agreed Mr. Davies. "We began to think you were going to miss the most fun we have had at this place in years. It is your turn, by the way, to lead Miss Davidson out, Trent. Unless, of course, you wish to abandon your opportunity to dance with Miss Lange and give her to Haversham."

"I shall have the cotillion with Miss Allisandra Lange regardless," Mr. Haversham spoke up. "I have led out Miss Amelia Harcourt to get it."

"Miss Amelia Harcourt? Which is she?" asked Lord Emery.

"The one with the rosebuds embroidered upon her bodice and the brown ringlets with the red riband through them. There, seated just where Castlereagh is now passing."

"Miss Amelia Harcourt?" Wentworth's eyebrow cocked significantly. "I thought you fairly shackled to Miss Matherson-Harding, Emery."

"Pardon me?"

"Shackled. To Miss Matherson-Harding. Won the prize there, I thought I heard you say last week."

"Perhaps. Perhaps not. I have not yet decided if I will

have her, to tell the truth. Oh, Bella is pretty and all, but Miss Kate Lange is a deal more interesting and a good deal more humorous and conversational."

"Yes, and you have already had one dance with her," pointed out Mr. Trent.

"I know, and it is not likely I shall have a second dance this evening because not even Gow can manage to play enough tunes in one night to give us all a second opportunity, and only look at the bevy of gentlemen around them now."

"Yes," laughed Davies. "And all having done their duty by one of the wallflowers, I assume, and placing their names upon the Langes' dance cards."

"Just so. But do you know, I danced last with Lady Constance, and even if she is not at all beautiful, she did say some of the wittiest things. And she danced quite nicely too. And she was not forever seeking compliments from me as Bella does. I think I might give Miss Harcourt a try and discover what she is truly like. It is rather like an adventure, is it not, Davies?"

"A monumental adventure," nodded Mr. Davies. "Go get her then, before someone beats you to it, Emery."

"What the devil is going on?" Wentworth growled as all the gentlemen surrounding him departed along with Emery. Only Mr. Davies lingered. "I vow, Davies, you have all run mad."

"No, not mad. It is a game of sorts, Wentworth. You have missed the most of it I fear, though I have no doubt that it will continue on tomorrow at Harriman House. Which reminds me, I am engaged to dance this set with Miss Harriman. You will excuse me, will you not?" And in the blink of an eye Mr. Davies was gone, leaving Lord Wentworth staring in utter confusion at a ballroom floor filling with dancers, a great number of whom were young ladies he deemed to be quite beneath his notice and the notice of his friends and acquaintances as well.

"Well, I'll be deviled," he murmured under his breath, staring down at the buckles upon his dancing slippers. As the music began he looked up and saw a young lady in a pale blue muslin gown staring at him. She was in the first of the lines and coming down the set toward him. Her short curls bounced as she came and her slim little figure trembled beneath the muslin. She smiled, but in her wide gray eyes lay a most distinct question—a question he could see but could not in the least understand and so could not answer. With a minimum of movement and a deal of grace he stepped aside, removing himself from the line of the dance. With a barely perceptible sigh, he lifted his chin, threw back his shoulders and walked off in the direction of the card room.

There was no one there. Wentworth looked about him in stunned amazement. The tables were set up, the chairs gathered around them and the decks lay upon the tabletops, but the room was empty of people. Except for two gentlemen, he noticed then. They were sitting at the farthestmost table from the doorway and so involved in conversation that they did not take the least notice of his arrival.

Wentworth raised his quizzing glass and peered at them. Then he let the glass fall to the end of its riband. Castlereagh. What the devil was Lord Castlereagh doing at Almack's again when everyone knew he thought it not worth one minute of his time? That made two Wednesdays in a row that he had appeared. And the gentleman with him was Stoneforth. Wentworth's heart stumbled for one beat. He was not at all certain about this elder brother of Attenbury's. If anyone might put an end to him upon the dueling ground, it would be this grim, fearsome-looking soldier.

It was Stoneforth who looked up and noticed Wentworth in the brief moment before he lowered his head and turned away. "Well, by Jove," he muttered to himself, and in an instant he was scraping back his chair and rising to his feet. "Wentworth," he called, but the Earl of Wentworth had already strolled out into the corridor and did not hear him. Stoneforth shook his head as if to clear it of some unimportant thought and regained his seat.

"You are not intending to call Wentworth out I hope," said Castlereagh softly.

"No. I was planning to beat him severely about the head and shoulders with my bare fists—in some more desirable place than this, however."

Castlereagh grinned. "No, Stoneforth, truly?"

"Indeed. But now, I rather think I will not. Not for a while at least. He is an odd one, Lord Wentworth."

"How so, odd?"

"I cannot say. There was the queerest look upon his face before he turned away. He is not very old, eh?"

"Twenty-five. Perhaps younger. Certainly not a year beyond twenty-five. Why?"

"I do not know. I did think that I despised him when first we met. Now I am not so certain that that is the case. There is something in him calls to me somehow. Well, but that is business for another time. We go to Covent Garden on Friday then, Toby and I and Lady Harriman and her flock of young ladies, and I shall see what I can see."

"Yes, and I will expect to meet with you on Saturday afternoon at Westminster. I shall be pacing somewhere about the tomb of Charles the Second."

"Why Charles the Second?"

"I cannot say, Stoneforth. Perhaps because in his way he was a most remarkable gentleman and I should like to have known him."

* * *

Melody kissed each of her cousins good night in turn
and her mama as well and then scurried off into the
privacy of her own bedchamber where she slipped
quickly between the warmed sheets. She lowered the
lamp wick and laid her head down upon the pillow and
smiled and smiled. Ally and Kate and Bea had devised a
plan that had worked. She could barely believe it. Lord
Wentworth's piercing wit notwithstanding, a number of
gentlemen had chosen to lead not only her out tonight
but any number of other young ladies who had been
ignored time and time again. And when she had not
danced, Mr. Attenbury had sat steadfastly beside her and
entertained her with the most humorous and illuminat-
ing observations. At least he had done so as soon as he
had got over a rather devastating attack of shyness.

It was so very odd that Mr. Attenbury should become
suddenly shy. She had never once thought it of him before his illness. Why, he had always been sociable and
congenial, filled with good humor and flirtatious
phrases.

And he still is, she thought then. It is merely that he
has been ill and perhaps he was a bit tongue-tied at first
because he was unsure how to begin now that I know
he loves me.

He loves me.

Melody rolled the phrase 'round and 'round in her
mind. "But he is very young," she whispered then, into
the darkness of her chamber. "He is merely twenty-two.
Perhaps that is too young for a gentleman to truly know
that he loves someone."

But she knew with devastating certainty that it was
not Mr. Attenbury's love she questioned. It was her own.
Until Lord Stoneforth had appealed to her on Mr. Attenbury's behalf, she had not once thought of Mr. Attenbury as a gentleman who loved her and so had not

once considered what were her feelings toward him. And now, she could think of nothing else.

Melody turned to lie on her side and stare into the fire banked in the grate, its coals glowing a soft red. I am most fond of Mr. Attenbury, she mused. I know that I am. And I am grateful to him and I cannot think of anyone more pleasant to sit with than he was this evening. I cannot think of anyone more handsome than Mr. Attenbury, either. He is the most handsome man in all of London—but not the most interesting, her mind added abruptly.

Well, yes, that was true. Mr. Attenbury's sky blue eyes brimmed with humor and charm and a certain innocence that were all most appealing, but they lacked the mystery which lurked deep in Lord Stoneforth's midnight blue orbs. And though Mr. Attenbury's cherub face framed by his dark brown curls was most comely, even enchanting, his brother's weathered tan, combined with his austere and intriguing features, absolutely riveted one's attention. That face positively begged one to envision what hardships and heartbreaks had carved out those linear hollows and soaring shadows. One longed to know what battles he had fought in war *and* in life to produce such a thoroughly mystifying face, and one was absolutely forced to speculate about what battles he might choose to fight now that he was a soldier no longer. "Not that it is any concern of mine what Lord Stoneforth will choose to do or not to do," sighed Melody. "I barely know the gentleman. I am beyond foolish to let every flash of his eyes and crease of his brow set me to wondering and worrying about him."

"But how does one know for certain, Adam?" asked Mr. Attenbury, already tucked up in his bed with a fire blazing to chase away the damp and drafts. "I mean,

Uncle North has always said that I need not marry a fortune and therefore may do very much as I like. And I should like to marry a woman I love. But what is love exactly? I mean, a gentleman ought to be certain that he *does* love a lady, no? But how can he be certain?"

"Love is a particular something that you ought not be asking *me* about," grinned Stoneforth, pulling an armchair close up to the bed and resting his stockinged heels upon the edge of Mr. Attenbury's mattress. "I do not think that I am cut out for civilian life, Toby. No, nor my feet cut out for dancing slippers. I shall need a crutch soon if I do not get back to wearing boots from morning until night."

"You are changing the subject," Mr. Attenbury pointed out promptly. "We did not begin by speaking about feet."

"I realize, Scamp. But I know a thing or two about feet. I do not know much at all about love. And what I do know, I cannot explain very well. It is a—a special thing that grows somewhere deep inside of a person."

"A very good thing, no?"

"At times, and at times it can be a very sad thing, but it is always there and it rules your life."

"Rules your life?"

"In a manner of speaking. When you love a woman, Tobias, you wish to share yourself and all you have with her, to keep her safe, to fill her life with joy. And when the time comes that you discover you cannot do all of that all of the time—well, you are devastated. But you persist in your attempt to do it because in your heart her security and safety and happiness are a deal more important than your own. But you know that. You stood upon the dueling ground for your Miss Harriman, did you not? You were willing to offer your life for her honor. I suspect that true love is actually nothing less than the complete elimination of self-centeredness even unto death itself."

"You do not make it sound at all romantic, Adam."

"No, I do not think it is always, but it is doggedly faithful and will not be turned off no matter how hard a fellow tries. Come, Toby, do not make such a face at me. I told you that I am not the one to whom you should speak. Uncle North would provide you a much better answer."

"Uncle North is from town."

Stoneforth nodded. "I am aware of it. But Uncle North will not remain in the country forever. Parliament is already in session. He is likely thinking of coming to London as we speak."

"You have not written to him, have you, Adam? You have not told him about the duel? Because I do think he will take that news a good deal better if I tell him of it myself."

"I have sent him only the message Watlow penned for me in Portugal that I had sold out and was coming home. That, by the way, arrived here with the mail only yesterday. And no, I will not tell him about the duel. I will leave that to you."

"When you fell in love with Mrs. Huston, did you know all at once that you loved her?"

"Yes. No. I cannot say, Toby. I think perhaps I knew right off, but I did not wish to admit it to myself. I was not—not—intending to love anyone. I did not wish to share all the things I held in my heart with—anyone. But then, after a time, I did share them."

"Was she quite pretty?"

"Other gentlemen thought her plain. I thought she was beautiful. And her voice was the voice of an angel and her eyes—her eyes were a clear and certain pathway to heaven. And that is quite enough for tonight. Why you must bid me speak all of this when you have already given your heart to Miss Harriman, I cannot think," he added, stretching his arms above his head and yawning.

"Well—well—a person does not want to make a mistake about love, Adam. It is a most serious thing to ask a woman to marry you and be your wife forever."

"Indeed, but I am ready to drop in my tracks, Scamp." With a most encouraging smile, Stoneforth let his feet fall to the floor, rose from the chair and turned down the lamp beside his brother's bed. "Tomorrow we will pay a morning call at Harriman House, eh? You will take Miss Harriman a posy and spend some time with her and perhaps even ask her to drive with you in the park," he added, removing some of the pillows from behind his brother's back and helping him to lie down more comfortably. "That will ease your mind on the matter. Now go to sleep." And he crossed the Aubusson carpet to the chamber door.

"But I cannot drive!" exclaimed Mr. Attenbury, just as Stoneforth's hand settled upon the doorknob. "I cannot drive with my shoulder all bandaged up and my arm in a sling!"

Stoneforth turned once more toward his brother. "Does Uncle North still have his barouche?"

"Yes, but—"

"Then I shall play coachman and drive you both. How will that do?"

"I cannot ask you to—"

"You are not asking, Toby. I am offering. There is a great difference between the two. Now go to sleep."

Stoneforth stood staring from his bedchamber window down into the square below. His heart constricted in his chest as though some demon had seized it in a great hand and was clutching it so tightly that it barely found room to beat. "I shall play coachman," he murmured. "I shall play coachman and I shall not listen to a word that passes between the two of them. And I will learn to think of Miss Harriman as my sister-in-law-to-be and treat her with all deference and respect.

"I am a fool," he muttered then, and letting the drapery fall back into place, he turned away from the window and began to pace restlessly about the chamber. The ache in his heart grew to enormous proportions. "Why can I not simply accept it?" he growled low in his throat. "I have lived my life huddled inside a shell. And though Nora fought through to find me, no other woman will ever think to do so. And though I promised Nora to crawl out of the blasted shell on my own, I do not think that I actually can. And even if I do, it is highly unlikely that I will ever be like—like—Toby and his friends. No, I am more like Castlereagh. I can see a great deal of myself in Castlereagh. In his eyes. We share the shadows between the lights, he and I. And even among throngs of people, we are each alone. And I shall always be alone and I must learn to accept it. Only—only—"

With conscious effort he caught himself up short, crossed to the fire and placed more coals upon it. He lit the lamp beside his bed and the lamp upon the writing desk in the corner of the room. Pulling a chair up to the desk, he set a sheet of paper before him, trimmed a pen and sat down. He would make a list of all he thought necessary to discover about Covent Garden Theatre, about the street in which it stood and about the operetta itself and its performers. The task of getting Miss Tallia Gorsky safely out of London and on the road to St. Petersburg before some assassin appeared upon the scene was not going to prove an easy one, he feared. He ought to set his mind to it. He ought to pin all of his thoughts entirely upon that one task. And then the ache in his heart would not seem quite so fearsome. He would not feel the pain quite so much. Its presence would be shuttled to the very back of his mind along with the quite impossible idea that—that Miss Harriman—with her wise eyes and patient, gentle ways—was just the sort of woman who might take the time to seek out and rescue a gentleman who was lost and languishing in the shadows of the night.

Ten

"I reckon as 'ow the colonel, he might be a-needin' of ye, Mr. Toby," offered Watlow the following morning. "Well, an' mebbe not. Mebbe not. 'Pends on whether ye kin write."

"Well of course I can write. Oh, you mean because of my shoulder. But that makes no difference, Watlow. I am left-handed, you see, just like Adam. He needs me to write something for him?"

"Aye. I reckon. I din't ask him. But I seen as 'ow he were 'temptin' ta write hisself somethin' out on his desk las' night an' it ain't readable, Mr. Toby, not at all."

Mr. Attenbury's face, which had been rather dismal-looking all the while Ridgeworth had been dressing him, brightened immediately, as Watlow had intended it should.

Well, an' the colonel would unnerstand too, an' let the lad help. The colonel were never one fer sittin' around doin' nothin', thought Watlow. An' this lad, he be just like him. Don't like bein' waited upon. He wants ta do somethin' needs doin'.

"Is my brother dressed, Watlow?" asked Mr. Attenbury, turning away from the looking glass.

"Aye, sir. Dressed and starin' out his winnow. Wonderin' whether ta ask me ta be a-helpin' him. It don't come easy fer the colonel ta be askin' fer help."

"I shall go to him at once, Watlow. I did not know Adam could not write properly."

"No. He kinnot read neither."

"He cannot?"

"No. Keeps workin' at it, he does, but he kinnot yet."

"Then who—?"

" 'Twas me what wrote how he were comin' home. An' me what has been a-writin' an' a-readin' everthin' important fer him since he fell at Albuera. But he has got a brother now."

"By Jove, you are correct there. He has got a brother now, and I shall be more than happy to assist him," nodded Mr. Attenbury, marching determinedly out of his dressing chamber and down the corridor toward his brother's chambers. He knocked once upon the bedroom door, heard a noncommittal grunt and entered to discover Stoneforth seated sideways upon the chair at the little writing desk, his elbows resting upon his knees and a piece of paper dangling from one hand.

"Sergeant Watlow thought you might wish some help with your writing, Adam. Why did you not say anything? I had not the least idea that you could not write."

"I *can* write," grumbled Stoneforth. "I just cannot read what I have written after I have written it. No one else can either. Damnation, but I cannot think why! I know other soldiers who have actually lost an eye and they can read and write properly."

"Perhaps it has nothing at all to do with your eye," mused Mr. Attenbury, taking the paper from his brother's hand and surveying it. "Perhaps it has to do with being kicked in the head. Might the kick not have made something else happen? Something that you do not know about? What the devil is this supposed to be?"

"It is a list."

"It is?" Mr. Attenbury stared at the paper. The letters ran into one another and the spaces between supposed

words were either enormous or nonexistent and all the
lines slanted upward or downward at impossible angles.

"It is a list of things I mean to discover about the
theatre this evening, and I—I—do not want your help."

Mr. Attenbury frowned. "You do not? Why? Do you
not think I am capable of lending you a hand?"

"No, of course not. It is merely that—I cannot think
I ought to involve you in the thing—that is all, Toby. I
have agreed to do a favor for a friend and—"

"What friend? What sort of favor? And why should
my simply helping you to write a list make the least
difference? Adam? I am no longer a little boy, you know.
You have fallen into some sort of scrape, have you not?
Well, I am twenty-two years old, by gawd, and perfectly
capable of helping you out of it!"

Stoneforth watched indignation flash brightly in Mr.
Attenbury's light blue eyes, and felt a perfect fool. Toby
was correct, of course. He was no longer a child and
might be of considerable help. And though Castlereagh
had warned that the assassin might turn out to be anyone—perhaps even someone in the War Office or the
Foreign Office—the assassin was certainly not going to
turn out to be Toby.

"I apologize, Tobias. You are perfectly correct. Not
that I am in a scrape, mind you, because I am not. But
you are perfectly capable of assisting me with my writing, and likely you would be invaluable to me in investigating the theatre as well, and I would be most
thankful to have your aid."

"Just so," Mr. Attenbury nodded and grinned. Then
he took his brother's place at the writing desk and gathered ink and pens and paper. "Now, you must only tell
me what to write," he announced with pen poised. And
then he set the pen slowly down again and stared up
at his brother, who had begun to pace the chamber.
"Did you say investigating the theatre, Adam? Which

theatre? And why? Why should you wish to investigate a theatre? What the devil is going on?"

The long drawing room at Harriman House buzzed with the voices of gentlemen. Like bees about a honeycomb the morning callers gathered around Melody and the triplets. All four of them looked most enticing, Melody in a walking dress of Spanish fly that made the green of her eyes purely dazzling, and the triplets in matching morning gowns with perfectly delectable cherry-striped skirts and high-necked bodices of cream muslin. The four young ladies were holding court quite competently beneath Lady Harriman's smiling eyes, and Lady Harriman's heart sang to see the lovely smile upon Melody's face as she spoke with one gentleman after another.

"May I sit beside you for a moment or two?" Mr. Davies asked, abandoning the seat beside Beatrice and crossing the short distance to the settee where Melody sat. The seat Lord Henley had just vacated.

"Most certainly, Mr. Davies."

"I should like to apologize to you, Miss Harriman."

"Apologize?"

"For behaving like a wretched coward for weeks on end. No, not a coward, because I do not live in fear of Wentworth's wit like most of the others. But for behaving a good deal less than graciously toward you, which I have done. You are the first in a line of young ladies to whom I must apologize, I think."

"You have never been less than gracious to me, Mr. Davies."

"Yes, I have. I have, in fact, treated you dreadfully, Miss Harriman. And I ought not have done. Apparently, the only true gentleman among the lot of us is Attenbury. He has, from the first, made a point of treating all the young ladies with deference and decorum. I cannot imagine why he is not here this very moment. I expected him."

"Perhaps the evening tired him more then he expected. He has been—ill—of late, you know. And yes, Mr. Attenbury has always behaved like a proper gentleman to me and to the other young ladies who are not belles. Why, he actually spoke with us and danced with us, too, without being coerced into doing so by my wily cousins," grinned Melody. "No, do not look quite so stricken, Mr. Davies. I do admit that I was thoroughly discomposed by the reception I received when first I arrived for the Season, but things are steadily improving, I think."

"Steadily," nodded Mr. Davies. "And improving for others as well as yourself. Last evening was an eye-opener to all of us, let me tell you."

"Mr. Davies, do you mean to say that your eyes were not open before last evening?"

"Completely closed. Will you believe that never once did I see Miss Daphne Davidson as anything but a rather short young lady with spots? And then last evening—well, I discovered her to have the most delightful sense of humor and a most rational mind. And you, Miss Harriman—"

"Me, Mr. Davies?"

"Yes, you. I opened my eyes and discovered that you are a perfectly splendid person."

Melody was so surprised by the comment that she laughed aloud. "Spl-splendid, Mr. Davies?"

"Yes, splendid."

"What is it you want of me?"

"And intelligent as well." Mr. Davies' eyes sparkled with laughter. "What a fool I was not to take the time to discover you all on my own."

"Is it a good word whispered in Beatrice's ear that

you wish from me? She is the one you once called sweet, is she not?"

"Well, I think perhaps I was mistaken there. Sweet is not a word that describes Miss Beatrice, is it?"

"Not precisely, no. Bea is more a kindhearted rapscallion."

"Rapscallion. Yes, that is a much more accurate word than sweet. Miss Beatrice is part scamp, is she not? I knew it the moment she glanced up at me with those oh so innocent eyes this afternoon and thrust her foil directly into my heart."

"She did not," giggled Melody.

"Indeed she did. She remarked quite grandly that any rational young lady of seventeen must look upon a gentleman as elderly as myself as totally ineligible material for marriage. 'Why do you look at me so?' she asked me then. 'Is it not true, Mr. Davies, that what is sauce for the goose is also sauce for the gander?' "

"Oh! Oh! I c-can just h-hear her!" laughed Melody.

"It was a direct hit," Mr. Davies chuckled. "And a most deserved hit, too, which I recognized on the instant. And so I have come to apologize to you and to say that I was a fool and—you will see how intelligent you are—to ask from you a word on my behalf in Miss Allisandra Lange's ear."

"Ally? A word in Ally's ear, Mr. Davies?"

"Yes, because I am beginning to think that I would not be up to actually dealing with Miss Beatrice for more than one day out of seven, but I should like to come to know Miss Allisandra a good deal better than I do."

"Do not look quite so woeful, Mr. Trent. Anyone might think you had lost your best friend," Ally observed. "It is not at all a difficult task we have set you. You did dance with them last evening. It is only proper that you pay them a morning call—and that you take them posies. That is how it is done, you know. Papa told us so, and Papa would not lie."

"Must we all do the same?" queried Lord Emery.

"Indeed. Each and every one of you," grinned Kate. "And you must do it with enthusiasm too!"

A series of sighs and groans met this declaration from the bevy of gentlemen surrounding the triplets. "Well, but you have already paid morning calls upon four of us," Beatrice pointed out cheerfully. "Four with one blow. Particularly expedient of you, I should say."

"Just so," Ally agreed. "And since you have behaved most properly toward Melody and Kate and Beatrice and myself, you will wish to do likewise to the other young ladies as well."

"And merely think what an adventure it will be," Kate added stirringly. "It will be like nothing you have ever done before. I can see you now—all of you—forming a veritable legion of London's finest gentlemen, marching in step from square to square, or driving abreast through the finest thoroughfares, happy and laughing and singing perhaps."

"Yes, singing," murmured Lord Dinsdale. "Now there's a thought. The lot of us gadding about the streets like the chorus of Gypsies in *The Innocent Isolda.*"

"What a lark," laughed Lord Henley. "I can just imagine it."

"But it will take us until six at least to spend time with each of the young ladies we danced with last evening," protested Mr. Haversham, sounding petulant, though a smile teased at his lips. "We shall miss the entire Promenade."

"Oh? The Promenade in Hyde Park do you mean?" asked Beatrice. "But that is nothing. It happens every day. I should imagine you would all be dreadfully bored with strutting about the park by this time."

"Exceeding bored," nodded Mr. Haversham. "But it is like to prove a deal more boring to spend the remainder of the afternoon with—with—"

"The wallflowers?" Ally looked from gentleman to gentleman. "Oh, we know you call them so. They know it, too. But only think, you each danced with them and they are all even now hoping, expecting, you to appear and yet fearing that it was all a dream and you will not. You can make them feel wonderful, my dears, truly you can, and you will be surprised how perfectly marvelous you will feel yourselves when you do."

"Yes, and you need not be nervous about what to say or how to act, because you will have each other's support," Beatrice offered. "Like comrades in arms."

"It is not a war we are sending them into, Bea," giggled Kate. "It is more a—a—"

"Series of skirmishes in a plethora of drawing rooms," Mr. Davies finished for her, as he came to a stop beside Ally's chair with a grinning Melody upon his arm. "And I am all for it. Onward into the fray, I say. But there must be some reward at the end of the ordeal. What, pray, are you offering as bounty for a job well done, Miss Lange?"

"Bounty?"

"Indeed. Last evening it was to dance with you and your sisters. This afternoon it ought to be—"

"A nuncheon *al fresco* along the Serpentine," declared Melody. "For everyone, including any young ladies whom the gentlemen care to invite."

"Excellent," cried Mr. Trent. "We shall all meet here and ride out together, eh? What a sight we will make, the lot of us picnicking in Hyde Park for all to see."

"Better than the Promenade by far," laughed Lord Emery. "I can just imagine it. And we will play games, too, shall we? Blindman's buff? Statues? That sort of thing?"

"Oh, yes," Beatrice cried delightedly, clapping her hands together with joy. "And—and—contests of skill between the ladies and the gentlemen."

"Mama, do you think we may?" asked Melody with an enthusiasm that brought considerable joy to Lady Harriman's heart.

"I think it quite possible," nodded Lady Harriman. "It will be splendid fun and I shall see to it that all we need for a picnic is prepared, but you young people must discover the perfect spot and set the date and bring all you need for games and such. All of that I leave in your hands."

Giggles and chuckles and laughter ruled the room as discussion arose over where the perfect site would be and whether or not some of the gentlemen ought to drive rather than ride to the spot, and which of the ladies they were about to pay calls upon ought to be included in the picnic, and which of the gentlemen was going to invite them to join in. All were so very pleased with everyone else's company and so involved in the offering of plans and observations that not one person besides Lady Harriman took note of the very elegant figure who came to stand upon the drawing room threshold, a most annoyed look upon his proud face and a bandbox in his hand.

Lady Harriman set her embroidery aside and rose. Nodding at the gentleman, she crossed the chamber and bent down beside Beatrice and whispered in her ear. Bea looked away from the conversation, her fine gray eyes focusing upon the doorway. Her rosebud of a mouth opened the tiniest bit in surprise. And then she rose and crossed the room with long, determined strides.

"I would not have come had I known you would be so very much engaged at such an hour. I thought by now that all of your morning visitors would be gone."

"Oh."

"I have brought you this," Wentworth said, thrusting the bandbox toward her. "Take it, will you? I feel an absolute fool standing here holding the thing."

"Wh-what is it?"

"It is your hat. Well, it is another hat exactly like the one you lost."

Bea's eyes widened in disbelief. "You bought me a hat?"

"You were crying. I thought—Well, it does not matter what I thought, does it?"

"I do not cry—not ordinarily. Ordinarily I am a very self-possessed young woman."

"You are a hoyden and a tyrant, and you have a fierce right cross. And you are ungrateful to boot," mumbled Wentworth.

"No, I am not that. Not ungrateful, I mean. I do thank you, my lord, for being so considerate as to purchase another hat for me. Is it precisely like the one I lost?" Beatrice set about to open the bandbox on the spot and tugged from it a bleached straw with wide brim and high round crown bedecked with myriad tulips and apricot ribands. "Oh, it is. It is precisely like!"

That exclamation in the most excited tone turned every head in the drawing room toward the threshold.

"By Jove," Lord Emery observed in a voice that fairly echoed through the room, "Wentworth has come bearing a bonnet! I never thought to see the day!"

"It is a most improper gift," muttered Mr. Trent, his mutter clearly distinguishable to all. "Is that not just like Wentworth? He could not bring posies like the rest of us. No, he must bring his posies connected to a hat."

Melody feared for a moment, when all the gentlemen began to laugh, that Lord Wentworth might challenge Mr. Trent to a duel, but Bea lay her hand upon his arm and smiled up at him and Lord Wentworth merely shook his head and shrugged.

If only I had been with Mr. Attenbury, to quiet him so before he challenged Lord Wentworth, Melody thought. Would I have been able to quiet him so? Why has Mr. Attenbury not yet come? she wondered then. Oh, I do hope he has not taken a turn for the worse. That would be dreadful.

For the first time in as long as anyone could remember, the Promenade in Hyde Park proved to be a sadly unattended affair. Lady Jersey looked about her in virtual shock as the carriage she shared with Lady Castlereagh, Lady Sefton and Mrs. Drummond-Burrell made its way along the track. "Why, you may count the number of riders in Rotten Row on two hands!" she declared at last. "And as for the carriages, why, we are practically alone!"

"Nonsense," snorted Mrs. Drummond-Burrell. "There are any number of carriages."

"Twenty," pointed out Lady Castlereagh with the most dismal little smile. "I have counted them. What on earth can have happened? Has Napoleon invaded our coast, do you think, and we the only ones unaware of it?"

"Nonsense," grunted Mrs. Drummond-Burrell. "We are early. Everyone will arrive in a moment or two."

"We are late," Lady Sefton responded, "and there are no carriages queuing up at the gates."

"Humph!" replied Mrs. Drummond-Burrell.

"Oh! Emily Anne! There is your Robert!" exclaimed Maria Sefton in an excited squeak. "Does he not look exceedingly handsome seated upon that bay? He sees you. He is coming this way. Yes, and is that not Lord Stoneforth on the black beside him and Mr. Attenbury upon the gray? It is! We shall ask them where everyone has gone, shall we?"

"I doubt Robert will have an inkling," murmured Lady Castlereagh. "He has not ridden in Hyde Park at the height of the Promenade for as long as we have been married. He most likely thinks that a handful of riders and twenty carriages are what is to be expected. Why he should suddenly decide to appear—and in the company of that soldier—I cannot understand.''

"Robert, Lord Stoneforth, Mr. Attenbury," grunted Mrs. Drummond-Burrell in greeting, her nostrils flaring the slightest bit and her nose tilting appreciably into the air.

"Clementina," nodded Castlereagh. "Ladies."

Mr. Attenbury nodded and Stoneforth bowed curtly from the saddle. Lady Jersey's heart lurched. Then Lord Stoneforth smiled directly at her and Sally Jersey thought she might just die right there in Maria Sefton's landau.

"We do not mean to interrupt your drive," continued Castlereagh, "but something has come up, Emily Anne, and I must speak to you about it at once."

"And if you will spare me but a moment or two of your time, Lady Jersey," drawled Stoneforth, "I would be most grateful. We thought, perhaps, if you would consent to walk with us a bit—"

"That Mr. Attenbury might escort Maria and Clementina around the park and then the carriage return to pick you both up again here," finished Castlereagh, dismounting and going to help both his wife and Lady Jersey from the carriage.

No sooner did Sally Jersey set foot upon the ground than Lord Stoneforth was at her side. She took possession of the arm he offered instantly and smiled up at him. Really, she thought, I am a perfect simpleton to let that face cause such panic to course through my veins. The other ladies would laugh to know how this man affects me. But Jersey would not laugh. Jersey would not laugh at all.

"Toby mentioned that he recalled your being in possession of a yacht, my lady," murmured Stoneforth as he looped the black's reins over a low-hanging tree branch and led Lady Jersey off along the path. "And Castlereagh assured me it was at one time true, though he did say that you might have sold the thing."

"Why should—you are particularly interested in yachts, Lord Stoneforth?"

"At the moment, yes. Do you still have her? Do you and Jersey take her out often?"

"Jersey and I? Never. She belonged to my grandfather Child. Jersey has not once been upon her. He grows notoriously green when he so much as drives past the ocean."

"Oh. That is too bad. You do not use her at all then. You have probably not so much as seen her in years, eh?"

"No, I do go out upon her whenever we visit Wintergreen. She is berthed at Newcastle, which is very near that particular estate. But I cannot think why you—"

"It is a pressing matter brings me to speak of it—Sally."

Lady Jersey's breasts heaved with an enormous intake of breath. Sally. He had called her Sally and the very sound of her name upon his lips thrilled through her, setting all her nerves a-jangle and her brain into obscurity.

"I know you must think me most forward, but there is something I have promised to do and, well, to tell the truth, I wondered if you would be kind to me once again and grant me the loan of your vessel and your captain and crew. I realize that it is a great deal to ask."

"M-my yacht? My captain? My crew? But why?"

"I cannot say," murmured Stoneforth, leading her along a bit of flagway bordered by jonquils and crocuses. "Truly, I cannot. If you cannot see your way clear to do me this favor, why, you must simply say no. I will not think badly of you for it."

"Lord Stoneforth—"

"Adam. You had best call me Adam, for I cannot possibly ask such a favor of a woman with whom I remain on formal terms."

"Adam," whispered Lady Jersey, and she could quite hear that name floating up into the greening trees above them to be whistled by the sparrows and trilled by the thrush. "Adam, I should be most happy to have you make use of my yacht. She is called the *Terpsichore*. You need only tell me when you require her to be ready and I will alert Captain Farleigh."

Eleven

"Mama, may we not send James around to inquire if Mr. Attenbury is not well?" Melody was fidgeting nervously with the ribands upon her gown as she paced the drawing room which was, at long last, empty of company. "Not only did Mr. Attenbury not come, Mama, but Lord Stoneforth did not either."

"No, but they did send posies," announced Beatrice happily. "I saw them as they arrived. The colonel's batman brought them. I am positive he must have been the colonel's batman for he looked just the part and he spoke like a soldier too. Higgens placed them in the morning room. There are yellow roses from Mr. Attenbury and the oddest little plant from the colonel—Lord Stoneforth, I mean. It has no flowers as yet, the plant, but it does have buds upon it. I think they are buds."

"You think they are buds?" asked Ally with a grin.

"Well, it is very hard to tell. I have never seen any plant quite like it."

"No doubt," giggled Kate. "You never noticed roses before this very spring. You ought to have seen her, Aunt Lydia. She came running into the house demanding to know what were those red things down near the wall, and neither Ally nor I could think of what she spoke."

"Well, they frightened Gretel just as she was about to jump," Bea declared. "At any rate, Melody, Higgens has the cards that accompanied the posies. If Mr. Attenbury has taken ill again, surely Lord Stoneforth will have written something upon his calling card to inform you of it."

"Yes," Melody nodded. "Of course he would have done. I shall go ask Higgens for the cards at once."

"If Mr. Attenbury has taken ill again," Beatrice called after her, "may I accompany you this time to Leicester Square? I will be good, I promise. I will only sit and stare at Lord Stoneforth and not say a word."

"Beatrice, for shame," laughed Lady Harriman.

"But it is most unfair, Aunt Lydia. I am the only one who knows every battle that Lord Stoneforth has fought and when they occurred and how they ended. I am the one who utterly worships him. And Melody is the one who goes to his home and with whom he has waltzed twice at Almack's."

"Yes," Lady Harriman smiled. "I agree. It is most unfair. But tomorrow evening, Beatrice, when we all attend the theatre, I shall see that you are the one who sits beside him."

"You will?" Bea's eyes grew very wide. "Do you mean it, Aunt Lydia? You will not change your mind?"

"I will not change my mind. I shall manage everything, and your sisters will help me, so that you may sit beside Lord Stoneforth while Melody sits beside Mr. Attenbury."

Melody stood in the morning room staring down at the two calling cards in her hands. Mr. Attenbury had scrawled *in deepest gratitude* across his and upon Lord Stoneforth's, in wavering script, was merely his title, *Stoneforth*. She looked at the beautiful yellow roses which had been placed in a cut-glass vase upon the square maple table before one of the windows and then studied the small green plant that stood most humbly beside them. And then she took another two steps and gazed down at the plant. She reached one finger toward it and several of the windmill-shaped leaves closed into tiny balls. Sprinkled about among the leaves, tiny buds showed promise of pink flowers to come.

"Goodness!" came Lady Harriman's voice from the doorway. "Where on earth did Lord Stoneforth discover that? I have not seen one since my own papa brought one home to Mama. I could not have been more than ten at the time. It is not generally a plant a gentleman presents to a young lady." Lady Harriman strolled up beside Melody and placed an arm about her daughter's waist, smiling down upon the unpretentious little plant with a fond light in her eyes. "Do you even know what it is, Melody?"

"No, I do not think I have ever seen one before. Look, Mama, how the leaves close up when my finger comes near to them."

"It is called a heartbreaker."

"The plant?"

"Indeed."

"But why?"

"Well, your grandpapa told me that the very first of the plants sprang from the blood of the heart of Atropos, the Fate who cuts the thread of life. Apparently she wished to alter the inflexible strand of a soldier's life and—"

"What soldier's life? I do not remember any Greek legend about Atropos and a soldier."

"No, dearest, I do not think it actually came from the Greeks. More likely it was a fairy tale composed by a mad Englishman. Still, your grandpapa vowed that Atropos once fell in love with a soldier, and finding that she could not lengthen or transform the strand she had cut for him, she begged Zeus to intervene and to lift the soldier up into the heavens, that she might share with him her immortality."

"And Zeus would not?"

"No. And he told her so upon the spot. The soldier was not one of the favored heroes, you see, nor destined to become a legend as many were. He was as insignificant as are most brave warriors who fight the good fight, and when he died, his name would be buried with his body, never to be spoken again. And so Zeus declared that he could not be bothered with him."

"Oh, how sad," murmured Melody.

"It gets more sorrowful still," replied her mama. "Because the moment Zeus refused his aid, Atropos' heart split asunder and rained down blood upon the soldier as he fought, and at his feet the very first heartbreaker plant sprang up full-grown from the droplets. The soldier set his sword aside and knelt to see the plant more clearly, thinking that somehow this was a gift from the gods. And his enemies surrounded him and stabbed him again and again until he was all but dead."

"How dreadful!"

Lady Harriman nodded. "A most tragic tale indeed. But it does have a happy ending."

"No, Mama, how can it?"

"Well, when Zeus saw Atropos' heart veritably split asunder, he repented his high-handed denial and swept down to the battlefield just in the nick of time. He wrapped the soldier in his cloak of immortality and carried him up to Mount Olympus and presented him to Atropos, whose heart healed immediately. And because of Atropos' love the inflexible thread of the soldier's life was not so inflexible after all and he lived forever in the company of the Fate who loved him and whom he grew to love."

"Oh, I like that," Melody smiled. "It is quite like a fairy tale, is it not?"

"Which is why I think your grandpapa invented the entire thing right there on the spot. Nothing ever happens so simply and forthrightly in Greek myths. Oh, and the little pink flowers are the drops of Atropos' blood, and the leaves close when one approaches because they are meant to gather about the soldier and protect him from his approaching enemies. I do think that is all. At least, it is all that I can remember. But it will be a beautiful plant when it blooms. Do not forget, dearest, that we all go to the Hydes' this evening. Gloria's little parties are always notorious fun. You will enjoy every moment of it." And giving her daughter a gentle kiss upon the cheek, Lady Harriman departed the chamber with a thoughtful smile.

"Why would Lord Stoneforth think to send me such a plant?" wondered Melody aloud when she was once again alone. "Gentlemen do not normally send plants, I think. Flowers, yes, certainly. But not little potted plants. Perhaps he thought that to send me flowers would make him appear to be a beau rather than the brother of the gentleman who loves me? Yes, exactly that. He thinks it likely he will become my brother-in-law and intends to treat me as a sister already. And he most likely does not even know it is called a heartbreaker plant. Why would a gentleman know such a thing? He most likely thought it modest and unassuming and chose it for those reasons."

She will not know what it is, Stoneforth consoled himself silently as he loosed his spurs, dropped them upon the carpeting and sprawled across the sopha in the rear parlor. Nora would have known right off, I expect, had I sent her one, but Miss Harriman will not recognize the thing. She knows nothing at all of soldiering or the legends connected with it. Why would she know what a heartbreaker plant is? No. I am safe enough there. Not even Toby knew what it was when I chose it. But I should not have done, and I will not do anything at all like it again!

Stoneforth leaned his head against a cluster of pillows and allowed as how he was much more tired than he had a right to be. But everything was going well and soon, with a bit of luck, Castlereagh's little opera singer would be safely on her way back home to St. Petersburg. Toby had written to Uncle North and requested that he remain at Witherbe Hall until a coach containing Miss Gorsky should arrive at the door. Then Uncle North was to escort the lady to Newcastle, where Stoneforth would meet them and accompany Miss Gorsky upon the *Terpsichore.*

She will have a maid or a companion, someone to chaperon her, he thought. That will make two ladies I must spirit away. Well, at any rate, we are certain to have the yacht, and she and I and her companion will sail through the blockade upon the North Sea into the Baltic Sea, up into the Gulf of Finland and then into safe harbor at St. Petersburg.

It was not an expedition he wished to make and Stoneforth sighed and closed his eyes against a mounting pain in his head. It would be a long trip and perilous, especially if word of Miss Gorsky's presence aboard the *Terpsichore* should reach the wrong ears. Still it was his duty to do what he could to promote an alliance between the Tsar and Great Britain. And this was what he could do, now that he was useless upon the battlefield. And besides, he had promised Castlereagh to do the thing and to do it quickly, too, before the Little General's assassin—whoever he might be—should discover the means and the opportunity and do away with Miss Gorsky right in the middle of London.

"All I must do now is to discover a way to abduct the

girl in the midst of a performance and spirit both her and her companion out of the city before anyone so much as suspects that she has departed. How the devil I am to do that, I cannot think!"

In fact, he could not think of anything at all for any acceptable period of time without a small plant with pinking buds entering his mind and turning his thoughts in the direction of Miss Melody Harriman.

Thank goodness Toby has got so involved in the plot to save Miss Gorsky that he has quite forgot his intention to call upon Miss Harriman and take her driving in the park with me as coachman. "I likely could not have done it," Stoneforth muttered without once opening his eyes. "I likely would have pleaded a headache and forced Watlow into driving the dastardly barouche. And though Toby would have suspected nothing, Watlow would have known without a doubt."

"I knows wifout a doubt already," proclaimed a gruff voice.

Stoneforth's eyes opened on the instant.

"Ye were speakin' out loud agin," admonished the batman. "I kinnot be held responsible fer answerin' when you are talkin' right out like that, Colonel. An' I knowed the moment ye picked that wretched plant out o' all the others an' tucked it unner me arm ta deliver ta the lady. I knowed wifout a doubt."

"I picked yellow roses to go with Toby's card. Yellow roses are a deuced sight more expensive and a deal more the thing."

"Aye, but you sent 'er the heartbreaker, ye did. Ye could not he'p yerself."

"But she does not know what it is, Watlow. She cannot. Young ladies are not versed in the legends of soldiers. She will consider it nothing but a rather sorrowful little offering from her brother-in-law-to-be."

Watlow studied the gentleman upon the sopha with

a keen eye. "I seed it comin' upon ye the very evenin' when you went fer ta ask her ta visit Mr. Toby. But I did not say a word."

"And I wish you will not say a word now, Watlow. It is of no account. Toby will offer for Miss Harriman's hand and she will accept him and they will live happily ever after."

"Humph!" grunted the batman, crossing his arms upon his chest. "Ain't we the honorable gent."

"Yes, we are, Watlow. You will not get a rise out of me by saying that, I assure you. Besides, I cannot possibly love Miss Harriman. I have not known her for so much as a fortnight put together. It is all a result of some swelling in my brain, some madness come along with being kicked in the head. And if I did send Miss Harriman the heartbreaker plant, it is only because she has been so very kind as not to despise an old soldier who is her beau's brother and for no other reason."

Watlow's face betrayed considerable disbelief at those words, but since Stoneforth was not looking at him, the batman was not harangued for it and was grateful for the fact. "Ridgeworth be awaitin' on you upstairs, Colonel," he murmured, changing the subject with alacrity. "Sent me ta fetch ye. Finished with Mr. Toby an' ready ta begin dressin' you up fer the party tonight."

"Party? What party?"

"Well now, I don't be knowin' exackly. But it be special an' ye did promise Mr. Toby as 'ow he could be goin' if he dinnit be exhaustin' himself exceedin'-like and left when you said it were time. I heered you tell 'im so m'self over breakfas'."

Peter Redding could not believe his eyes. "Now what the devil?" he growled and then pushed back his chair and stood.

Wentworth caught the motion from the corner of his eye, turned in that direction and started immediately for the table behind which his half-brother stood glaring at him. In an instant he slid into the chair opposite Redding's.

"Giles, what are you doing here? You have no business in The Four and Twitch. It is not a place welcomes the Quality."

"No, I know it is not."

"Why are you here then?"

"Because—because I need to speak with you, Peter, and Margery said that you had come here."

"Which she had not the least business to do. I am at the warehouse ten hours a day. That is where you must come, Giles, not to such ragtag places as this." Redding raised his finger at a robust and feebly grinning man with a white apron tied lopsidedly about his sagging middle. "An ale, Jack, for this gentleman," he said loudly. "And do not be all night about it either. Now, what is it that is so all-fired important? Your coach will be ready tomorrow as I promised."

"No, it is not at all about the confounded coach," murmured Wentworth, placing his hat upon one of the empty chairs and running his fingers through his short, blond curls. "It is about something—something—Oh, devil take it! It is about a girl!"

Redding's face creased slowly and silently into a smile.

"I vow, she is the most aggravating creature on God's green earth. I do not understand her at all, and I should like to strangle her, but when she cried, Peter, I could not help myself. I had to go and purchase the confounded bonnet."

Redding cocked an inquisitive eyebrow. "Bonnet?"

"Yes, well, it is not as if I could not afford to buy her

another. And I expect if I had not been in her way, she might well have caught the cur."

"Cur?"

"And how was I to know that the house would be filled to overflowing at such an hour, I ask you. I was not to know. That is the truth. They ought all to have been gone by then."

"Apparently," drawled Redding, as the rotund barman set a glass of ale before Wentworth and departed, "this all makes perfect sense to you, Giles, but it is mishmash and muddle to me. Would you care to begin at the beginning?"

"No. That is—no. I cannot. I do not even know when the beginning was or how any of it has come to be. It is the most lunatic thing, Peter. And she will be at the Hydes' tonight, you may well believe it. And what I am to do, I cannot think."

"She who?" Redding asked succinctly.

"Miss Beatrice Lange. That is her name. She is not even an honorable, Peter. Just Miss Beatrice Lange and nothing more."

"Is she pretty?"

"I expect so. She and her sisters have become all the rage and in less than two weeks, too."

"Ah, she has sisters."

"Two of them. They are triplets."

"I thought it took three to make triplets."

"Yes, it does. Oh, I see. She has two sisters and the three of them together are triplets, is what I meant to say. And they have driven all of the gentlemen of the *ton* completely mad."

"All?"

"Perhaps not all, but a goodly number of them— Trent and Davies and Henley and Haversham and Emery."

"And you."

"No! That is to say, it is only Miss Beatrice who is driving me mad, not the other sisters. She is totally impossible. She has not so much as a semblance of manners. No, nor the least bit of humility either. She is a complete hoyden and no doubt a shrew as well and she punches like a man, Peter. I vow she does."

"A young lady punched you?" A most interested gleam arose in Redding's dark brown eyes.

"Yes, but that is not what I have come to speak with you about. I do not care a fig that she punched me in the stomach hard enough to double me over. That is not it at all. I—the thing of it is—well, I am to attend an entertainment this evening at the Hydes' and—"

"Who are the Hydes?"

"Lord and Lady Hyde, Peter. You know, he is the viscount who stands up in Lords and shouts, "Put a period to it!" whenever anyone's speech is especially too long, and she is the lady who draws faces upon flagways with chalk when the weather is fine."

"Ah, yes, of course. Even I have heard of the Hydes then."

"Indeed. And I am to go to them this evening. It will be a very small party and there will be something incredibly exciting to do—because there always is something exciting to do at one of their parties."

"Then you ought to be looking forward to it."

"I have been for weeks. But now it is a sure thing that Miss Beatrice will be there and—"

Redding's eyebrow cocked again, significantly. "And?"

"I do not know what to do. I mean, I wish to go to the Hydes', but I do not wish to spend any more time with Miss Beatrice because she makes me particularly uneasy and—"

Peter Redding had all he could do to keep from

chuckling. "So, you are as human as the rest of us, eh, Giles? Rather a comedown for you, I expect."

"What does that mean?"

"It means that you can be brought to fall in love with a pretty face just like any other man."

"No, I am not in love, Peter. You do not understand at all. She makes me most uncomfortable and self-conscious and I cannot imagine what she will think to say or do to me next. The very sight of her sets my teeth on edge."

"Just so," nodded Redding. "Love."

Wentworth's eyes widened considerably.

That evening in the Hydes' long, narrow house in Cavendish Square, ten gentlemen and nine ladies gathered about Lady Hyde in the newly furnished Cavalier room. "I have got it all worked out perfectly," declared Lady Hyde, a bright smile upon her face as she stood amongst tea trays and candlelight. "Perceval and I have been busy as beavers the entire week and *this* is the result of our labors."

"That?" asked Mr. Davies with a most disappointed drawl.

"Oh, I know it does not look like much now, but you will be surprised when you see it all together."

"All together?" Lady Harriman, a most beguiled look upon her face, studied the object in Lady Hyde's hand. "But, Gloria, it is nothing but an old gauntlet and it *is* all together."

"Ah, but the gauntlet is merely a piece of the puzzle," grinned Lord Hyde, his bright eyes a-sparkle with merriment. "Gentlemen, if you will give me your assistance. All except you, Attenbury. You cannot be moving furniture about with your arm in a sling. Back. Up against the walls. All of it."

With curious buzzing and a deal of laughter, the gentlemen did as they were told, clearing all the furniture to the very sides of the chamber.

"There, now you can see it perfectly!" Lady Hyde exclaimed. "Well, perhaps not perfectly, because we are none of us up quite high enough to gain the correct perspective, but that will be part of the fun."

"See what?" asked Lord Emery.

"Why the carpet, my dear. Did you not wonder why this is called the Cavalier room? It is because of the carpet."

Eighteen puzzled people stared down at the brilliant red-and-black carpet they stood upon.

"Oh, I see!" Melody exclaimed. "The black outlines a cavalier upon the red. There are his boots and there his sword and right where you stand, Lady Hyde, is his plumed hat."

"Exactly so," laughed Lady Hyde. "Exactly so. He is a most handsome soldier, our cavalier. Perceval and I have named him Sir Gregory the Red. And tonight, we are all going to make him come to life."

"How are we going to do that?" asked Lord Stoneforth, pacing down to where Melody stood at the cavalier's feet. "Yes, I see now. Even his shoulder-length curls are apparent once you know what you are staring at. But make him come to life?"

"Upon Perceval," grinned Lady Hyde. "Percy has always wished to be a cavalier, and tonight you shall all be divided up into teams and help him to become one. Hidden about the house are all the clothes and accoutrements to transform my dearest spouse into a living portrait of Sir Gregory the Red. And you must find them and bring them to us here for Percy to don."

"And just to make it a bit more interesting," added Lord Hyde, "you will be given a specified number of points for each object you bring back. Some are worth more than others, you know. The mate to this gauntlet, for instance, is worth merely five, but the cavalier's pantaloons fifteen, because he may appear without his gauntlets, but there was not one cavalier who would dream to fight without his pantaloons."

"No, and Percy is not going to fight without his pantaloons either," giggled Lady Hyde. "If the pantaloons are not found, I promise that there will not be a living portrait this evening. Now, come, gentlemen. All the ladies' names have been written upon a slip of paper and placed in Percy's beaver and each of you must select one to be your partner."

"Oh, and before I forget," added Lord Hyde, "the prize!" With long, measured strides his lordship crossed to the bellpull and tugged the cord. In the briefest of moments the butler and two footmen appeared carrying an immense and terribly ornate epergne. "It is not the wretched epergne that is the prize, mind you," smiled Lord Hyde. "The prize is hidden within."

"Though you are welcome to the epergne as well," Lady Hyde said. "I should be thoroughly happy to have it disappear from this house, let me tell you."

Twelve

"Miss Harriman, do come out from beneath that bed. The Hydes cannot have intended their guests to crawl about beneath the furniture, do you think?" Stoneforth stared, bemused, at the soles of Melody's slippers as they wiggled and twitched. "I was merely hoaxing you, Miss Harriman, when I said that a cavalier's pantaloons would likely be under the bed in the master's bedchamber. I did not expect you to take me seriously."

I ought not to have done this thing, he thought, when no answer but a giggle was forthcoming. Better I had declined to participate than to wander off unescorted with Miss Harriman upon my arm. He tugged distractedly at the neckcloth that was suddenly choking him. The more Miss Harriman's slippers wiggled and waggled and the more she giggled, the tighter the neckcloth grew.

He had attempted to exchange partners with Toby, who had drawn Miss Katherine Lange, but Toby would not hear of it. "It is merely the luck of the draw," his brother had informed him with a grin. "We must abide by the rules, after all, Adam. You do not dislike Miss Harriman, do you? No, you cannot. She is as fine as fivepence and most interesting."

"Yes, but Miss Harriman is the woman you love and I—it makes no difference with whom I am partnered.

You do wish to be partnered with Miss Harriman, do you not?"

"Well, well, of course! But you have drawn her name, Adam, and I have drawn Miss Katherine, and it would look most odd for us to be exchanging partners. Only think how Miss Katherine would feel to be shuttled about so. Do not look so very serious, Adam. It is only a game, after all."

"It is only a game," Stoneforth whispered to himself. "It is only a game," he said again hoarsely. Nevertheless, Miss Harriman was now beginning to back out from beneath the bedstead, and she was attempting to keep her skirts from climbing up about her limbs as she did so. She could not. The loud pounding in his ears, as he got a lengthy look at a lovely pair of legs in pink silk stockings, belied the fact that it was only a game. Stoneforth's breath caught in his throat and his fingers struggled even more to loosen the knot of his neckcloth. It is a game, a game, a game, he repeated over and over in his mind. She does not so much as guess how a glimpse of her stockings affects me. No, nor does Toby have the least inkling how badly it frays my nerves just to be near her.

"However did you know?" cried Melody as she managed at last to extricate herself and bounced to her feet waving the cavalier's pantaloons at him. "We are going to win, my lord. I do think we are going to win. You are so very intelligent. You know precisely where to search for everything!"

"No, I do not actually. I am simply guessing."

"Well, you must be the very best guesser in all of London, for we have discovered the other gauntlet and the sword and now these. I am so very happy that you are my partner! Are you not excited? I confess that I am. I have never won anything before in all of my life."

"What? Nothing?" Stoneforth gazed down into the prettily flushed face and glorious green eyes and his heart thundered with love. "I find that very hard to imagine."

"Well, but I never have. Not once. I distinctly remember that even as a child I always lost at all the games. Oh, at last I am going to win at something and it is all due to you!" she exclaimed, standing upon her tiptoes and planting a joyous kiss upon his cheek. And then she stood back and gazed up at him, her eyes at once enchanted and puzzled. "What is it, my lord?"

"What is what?" breathed Stoneforth unevenly.

"You are growing most pale. And your hands are trembling. And you are staring at me in the most peculiar manner. Are you not feeling quite the thing? Should you like to cease this nonsense and go back down to the Cavalier room and sit for a while? I shall not mind. Truly, I shall not. It is only a game, after all, and it does not matter in the least who wins."

"No!" protested Stoneforth, juggling the pantaloons she had handed him with the gauntlet and the sword he carried in abruptly sweating and unmanageable hands. "You have never won anything. Tonight you shall win all." And then he dropped the sword and bent immediately to retrieve it.

Melody bent at exactly the same moment and their foreheads came together with a resounding crack.

"Oh, m'gawd!" breathed Stoneforth, dropping the rest of his load and gathering a surprised Melody into his arms. "Oh, m'gawd, I am so very sorry. Are you terribly hurt, Miss Harriman? I am such a bumbling fool! You will have a lump the size of an egg from that blow!"

Melody gazed up at him from the overwhelming coziness of his arms and felt her forehead with one trembling hand. "The s-size of an orange," she giggled dizzily.

* * *

"Well, I cannot think why you expected to find anything at all here," declared Bea with a toss of her head. "Truly, Wentworth, your mind has turned to mush."

"Do not call me Wentworth!"

"I will call you whatever I choose to call you. I am not yours to command. You may think the entire population of London must ebb and flow with your every whim, but you are sadly mistaken, let me tell you."

"I do not need to let you tell me," grumbled Wentworth, peering under a glass-doored bookcase. "You will tell me anyway. There is something under here. Way at the back."

"A ball of dust most likely."

"No. Bring the lamp, Miss Beatrice. Give it to me. Yes, so I thought. Whatever it is glitters in the bit of lamplight that reaches it."

"It does?" Beatrice knelt beside him immediately and gazed under the bookcase. "Oh, Wentworth, it is a gold doubloon, I think. Was there a doubloon in the picture upon the carpet?"

"Several. At the cavalier's feet. Here, let me see if I can reach it. Yes, I have it!" With a triumphant grin, Wentworth withdrew his arm from beneath the bookcase and, opening his hand, displayed the Spanish coin to Bea. "Do you see. I am not always wrong."

"I did never say you are always wrong," proclaimed Beatrice, her eyes shining in the lamplight as she gazed up at him. "I never did. But you are always aggravating."

"How can you know?" Wentworth stared down at her and felt the most unusual knot forming in the verimost pit of his stomach. She was so very small, this obstreperous young lady. Even with both of them upon their knees, he towered over her. And yet, she had nearly felled him in the park, and she *had* felled him at Almack's—she and her sisters had divested him of his power, at least—and this very afternoon she had turned his whole world upside down by forcing him to appear before his friends and acquaintances with a bonnet in his hands. "How can you know," he repeated in a hoarse whisper, watching the lamplight turn her gray eyes to silver, "that I am always aggravating? You are not always with me."

"I know," murmured Beatrice, studying the planes and shadows of his face as the light flickered beside him, "because—because—"

"Because why? You cannot say, can you? Because you do not know it for truth." Gawd, but when she looked up at him that way, with that merest bit of doubt upon her face and her lips pursed in such a way, when her silver eyes showed that tiny bit of hesitation, he wanted to—he wanted to—The gold doubloon slipped onto the carpet. His hands went gently to grasp her shoulders. His head bent downward at an angle.

"Wentworth! There is the wig! There is the wig!" Beatrice cried, jumping up in excitement, the top of her head hitting him smack in the nose and sending him crashing backward to the floor. "Oh! Oh, Wentworth, I am so very sorry. Are you all right?"

"Mfffph!" Wentworth replied, one hand holding to his nose as his eyes teared and he rolled upon the carpet in agony. "Mffph mggle mffleph!"

"La-laaa, la-la-la-laaaa! Onward to glory, lads; onward to the foe; onward to glory, lads, we go!"

Attenbury's jaw dropped.

"No, do not stare at me so, Mr. Attenbury," giggled Kate. "I am just so happy to have found *something*. This belt ought to be worth some points, do not you think? Since we had to lower the entire dining room chandelier to get it, I should think it will be worth a hefty number of points."

"That was from *The Innocent Isolda,* what you just sang," declared Mr. Attenbury. "It is one of my favorites."

"Is it? It is one of my favorites, too. I have loved it forever. It is so—so—dramatic and soul-stirring."

"And you did it perfectly. And your voice—why you might play the part of Isolda yourself, I think."

"Oh, I thoroughly intend to play Isolda someday," Kate grinned, placing the wide black belt over Mr. Attenbury's shoulder and giving his sling a gentle pat. "Or if not Isolda, then Paulina."

"Paulina?"

"Yes, she is Papa's newest heroine and—oh-oh."

"Papa's newest heroine?" Mr. Attenbury's blue eyes widened considerably. "You have loved the 'Soldier's Song' forever, and you thoroughly intend to play Isolda someday, and your papa's newest heroine is Paulina? Your papa is Herbert Van Cleef?"

"I never said that, Mr. Attenbury. You merely assume it." Kate's marvelous gray eyes were alight with humor. "I am not responsible, you know, for anything you choose to assume."

"Your papa *is* Herbert Van Cleef," stated Mr. Attenbury in wonder. "And you are Isolda! I have been to see that particular operetta at least twenty times. It is my verimost favorite of all the plays and mimes and melodramas. I like it even more than Shakespeare. And Miss Gorsky is excellent in the role, but you are the true Isolda, are you not? Yes, you are. I recognize you. When they speak of her eyes like winter mists and her hair like autumn leaves and lips as pure and sweet as cherry wine! It is you, Miss Katherine!"

Kate's laughter trilled through the dining room, a sound very much like the tinkling of silver upon crystal. "There are three of us, Mr. Attenbury, in case you have not taken note, who look quite like that description of

Isolda. But because I already know you to be a most honorable gentleman, I will confess and depend upon you not to let the secret out. Yes, Papa is Herbert Van Cleef. But no one is to know, because it is not at all the thing for a gentleman to write comic operas for which he is paid when they are produced upon the stage. It is much too much like working for a living, you know. Even Uncle Arthur and Aunt Lydia do not know that Papa is Herbert Van Cleef."

"I shall keep his secret, Miss Katherine. I give you my word. Does—does Miss Harriman know?"

"Oh, yes, Melody knows all. Papa has tried any number of ideas out upon my sisters and me and Melody. He sought her opinion whenever she came to visit."

Mr. Attenbury did not know what it was, but he could not seem to tear his gaze away from Miss Katherine. Surely, she was the most beautiful, effervescent young lady he had ever met. And her voice, when she sang, was extraordinary. It was not the voice of a well-bred young lady who performed competently in a drawing room. It was the voice of a diva.

"Truly, we ought to get on about our search, Mr. Attenbury. Everything will be found if we stand here staring at each other much longer."

"I know."

"Come then. Where shall we search next?"

"Anywhere. Nowhere. Will you sing for me again? Just a bit of something? A measure of this or a measure of that?"

"Mr. Attenbury, do come," Kate insisted, placing her hand in the crook of his arm to tug him forward and then forgetting to tug, but leaving her hand there all the same.

Their eyes met and Mr. Attenbury's were as blue and clear and noble as Kate had ever imagined any hero's ever to be, and she found she could not look away from them. She did not wish to look away from them. The merest spark flickered in the depths of her soul. Flickered and flared and then burst into flame. Kate gave the tiniest little gasp as the warmth of it flowed through her. And then she smiled. And then she frowned.

Mr. Attenbury sighed and severed the connection between their gazes. He raised the arm encumbered by the sling, and very tenderly traced the outline of Kate's lips with his index finger. Then he gently twitched at each corner of her mouth, attempting to twitch the smile back onto her face.

Kate giggled.

Mr. Attenbury chuckled. And then his eyes met hers once again. "Your eyes are not at all like the winter mist," he whispered. "I daresay they are much more like the silver stars twinkling in the heavens above. I know they are."

"Mr. Attenbury," Kate managed, at last remembering to tug him toward the doorway to the corridor. "We must get on with our hunt. What will people think if we must admit we have discovered nothing but the cavalier's belt?"

Allisandra was laughing so very hard that she thought she would quite likely never stop.

"Really, Miss Lange, it is not that humorous," Mr. Davies declared, attempting to sound peeved with her, though he was laughing himself. "This is a dastardly thing that has happened."

"Oh, d-dastardly!" exclaimed Ally, laughing all the more and gasping for breath. "I told you not to do it. I only mentioned that the goblet the cavalier holds might be in there. I did not mean that you should—should—it was most irrational of you to even think to d-do it."

"Do not lecture me now, Miss Lange. The door was locked and this was the only way. Help me to get out."

"H-how?"

"Grab me about the waist and pull."

"Oh, Mr. Davies, I could not possibly. That would be most unladylike!" And Ally went off into another round of laughter.

"Miss Lange," Mr. Davies said, attempting to achieve a most stoic tone. "I am stuck in the butler's pass-through and cannot p-possibly get free with-without your h-help," and he fell into a perfect gale of chuckles. "Deuce take it, but the more I laugh, the tighter I am stuck! What the—"

"What the—what?" asked Ally, wiping tears from her eyes with a tiny lace handkerchief.

"Do not go into whoops again, Miss Lange, but there is a cat in here."

"A cat?"

"Yes. A most curious thing he is, too. He is coming right up to look at me. By Jupiter, I think he is laughing at me. Yuck! Now he is licking at my eyebrows."

"You are making it up," declared Ally, coming up beside him and putting her arms about his waist. "There is no cat. You only hope to convince me to help you."

"No. I give you my w-word. N-now he is licking at my n-nose. It t-tickles!"

Ally could not think if he were teasing her or not, but she found she did not care. Truly, he was the oddest gentleman—so prim and proper and rational one moment and attempting to climb into the butler's pantry through the little pass-through window the next. "Do cease wiggling about so," she commanded, though her voice was still tinged with laughter. "I have got you by the waist. Attempt to relax, Mr. Davies. Let your shoulders slope a bit and I shall see can I tug you back into the kitchen."

"Hurry. I think this beast is simply tasting me and means to make a meal of me once he is satisfied with my flavoring."

"D-do not do that," giggled Ally. "I cannot laugh and pull at one and the same time."

"Ow!" grunted Mr. Davies. "Ouch! Miss Lange, are you attempting homicide? No! Do not get at my ears, you dastardly feline."

"Lower your left shoulder just a bit, Mr. Davies. I think if you lower that shoulder I shall be able to pop you free."

Mr. Davies lowered his left shoulder; Ally gave a mighty tug; and out he popped into the kitchen, hitting his head upon the top of the pass-through along the way. Directly behind him, a tiger-striped cat leaped to the floor and rubbed against his leg, purring loudly.

"It is not a he, Mr. Davies," Ally announced, grinning and stooping to run her fingers along the cat's back. "It is a she and a perfectly splendid animal she is too."

"Indeed," grinned Mr. Davies, rubbing at his head. "But was there a cat in the picture of the cavalier?"

Nine couples drifted back to the Cavalier room two by two, laughing and talking, some smiling in triumph, others shrugging but chuckling in defeat. Lady Harriman came twirling the plumed hat while her partner, Mr. Haversham, flipped one of the gold doubloons rakishly beside her. Lord Emery entered, wearing the slashed doublet with Lady Grace Thresher upon his arm, the cavalier's lace collar fitted elegantly over her gown. Lord Petersham and Miss Bella Fretingale had discovered the whereabouts of one of the broad-topped boots and Mr. Boylan-Jolnes and Miss Abigail Dunkin the other. Miss Clarissa Wilkes and Lord Manset had only the goblet between them, but they had filled it with wine and were quite satisfied with themselves and the evening.

"Great Caesar! What in the world happened to you?" asked Lord Hyde as Wentworth entered with a piece of beefsteak held gingerly upon his nose.

"Had an acthident," Wentworth replied with as much dignity as he could manage from behind the meat.

"But we found one of the doubloons and the wig!" exclaimed Beatrice joyfully. "We had to stop searching after that and search instead for something cold to take the swelling down, but we have found these at least." And she placed them merrily upon the table before Lord Hyde with all the other offerings.

"And we have got the belt and the cuffs," announced Kate, swirling into the room with Mr. Attenbury behind her.

"Not another accident," breathed Lord Hyde, as directly behind them Mr. Davies entered the chamber rubbing woefully at his head and grinning.

"A most dreadful accident," acknowledged Ally. "Mr. Davies was caught in the butler's pass-through and whacked himself in the head escaping it."

"And I thought *I* wath in dire thraits," chuckled Wentworth, which bit of humor brought Beatrice's gaze upon him.

"Goodness, and after all that you found nothing, Davies?" asked Lord Hyde.

"Oh, poor Charles," sighed Lady Hyde.

"Well, we did find this," chuckled Mr. Davies, turning about, reaching out into the corridor and producing the purring cat, "but I do not think there is actually a feline in the picture, is there?"

"There is now," laughed Lady Hyde. "I shall say there is and give you five points. Cavaliers were fond of cats as I recall."

"Rode upon them," mumbled Wentworth, then grunted as Bea poked him in the side with a lethal elbow.

"Actually, they kept cats to convince the Roundheads that they had witches upon their side," offered Stoneforth as he entered the chamber, one arm supporting a Melody who held a silver knife to her brow and the other balancing their booty.

"Now, what? Miss Harriman, what has happened to your head?" Lady Hyde queried. "Great goodness, this was intended to be a game, not a massacre."

"We s-simply had an unexpected meeting of minds," giggled Melody. "Or at least, heads. I am perfectly f-fine." And she urged Stoneforth to relinquish his hold upon her and deposit the pantaloons, the sword and its scabbard, the second gauntlet, and four more doubloons upon the table.

"By Jove, no wonder we could find but one boot," exclaimed Lord Petersham, "Miss Harriman and Stoneforth have got most everything else!"

"I suspected a dragoon might have some notion of where to locate a cavalier's pantaloons," chuckled Lord Hyde.

"Indeed, he knew right away that they would be under the bedstead in the master's bedchamber," declared Melody proudly, and all of the gentlemen in the room fell into whoops.

Amidst the laughter Lady Hyde took stock of who had found what and tallied up the points. "Miss Harriman, Lord Stoneforth," she said when the gentlemen had quieted, "the prize is yours. But you cannot have it until Perceval dons all this garb and presents it to you properly as a living portrait should. Go, Percy. Become my cavalier at once."

"We have won," whispered Melody, abandoning the silver knife upon a small table and gazing up at Stoneforth happily. "Oh, I cannot believe it. We have actually won!"

"But what have we won?" whispered Stoneforth, gazing in distrust at the epergne.

"I do not care. Whatever it is, I shall treasure it always."

It was the oddest thing, but the joy shining up at him from those glorious emerald eyes made Stoneforth's ears redden and his neckcloth again grow inordinately tight. His blood raced, singing, through every vein. He knew very well that what he wished to do more than anything was to reach out and take Miss Melody Harriman again into his arms and this time kiss her right there before everyone. But he knew he could not, and with a slight growl, low in his throat, he stepped away from her as the others gathered about to offer their congratulations and to ask how she felt and to laugh over all the places they had searched and what they had found.

Melody's gaze followed him as he stepped aside and wandered across the chamber to pet the cat which had leaped up upon the credenza and was sniffing and mewing about the epergne. Why ever did he wander off? she wondered. It is he deserves all the congratulations. It is he won the prize. "Mr. Attenbury," she murmured as that gentleman smiled down at her, "go to your brother. Something is wrong, I think."

"Wrong? With Adam?"

"Indeed. He became suddenly most silent just now and has put an entire chamber between himself and the rest of us."

With long strides Mr. Attenbury crossed the room to his brother's side. "Are you not feeling just the thing, Adam?" he asked quietly. "Do you wish to leave? I shall not mind going."

"No, we will stay until Miss Harriman has her prize."

"But Adam, if you are ill—"

"I am not ill. What makes you think—"

"Miss Harriman says you became silent so suddenly and then came over here to be away from the rest of us."

"I only came to pet this dratted cat. She is a fine young lady, Miss Harriman. It was you should have been her partner."

"Yes, and then she would have come back with meager pickings, let me tell you. Miss Katherine and I had the worst luck. But she is quite amazing, you know, Miss Katherine Lange."

"Amazing?"

"Yes. She sings."

"Innummerable young ladies sing."

"Not like Kate."

Lord Hyde swept back into the chamber, costumed and coiffed and swaggering in the most audacious manner to the very center of the room, where he stopped to pose in the precise posture of the cavalier upon the carpet.

Kate? thought Stoneforth. He calls her Kate?

"Oh, Lord Hyde is truly the cavalier come to life!" cried Lady Grace Thresher. "It gives me goose bumps to see it."

"I do wish gentlemen still dressed that way," sighed Miss Dunkin, her brown eyes wide with wonder.

"I like the hat especially," Lady Harriman laughed. "And when you are done with it, Percy, I should like to have it for myself. Arthur would think it absolutely wonderful."

"And do you know," grinned Lord Hyde, "I feel absolutely splendid. Exactly like a knight about to ride into battle."

"On a cat," muttered Wentworth, and then dodged away from Beatrice with a smile twitching at his lips.

"Come, Miss Harriman, give me your hand. By Jove, Stoneforth is already over there. Letty, Letty, stop sniffing about, do, or you will give all away, dearest," he added, leading Melody to the credenza and then lifting the cat and setting it upon the floor. "And now," he proclaimed, "to our winners go the spoils!" And with a flourish worthy of the cavalier he portrayed, Lord Hyde doffed his hat and made a most elegant leg, then straightened and removed the top of the epergne. With one gauntleted hand he reached inside.

Thirteen

Melody woke to a soft little paw batting at her nose and smiled. "Go away, do, Atropos. This is not the way to endear yourself to me, I promise you."

"Mrrr," replied the tiny black-and-white kitten, peering curiously at Melody's lips as they moved and laying a paw questioningly upon them.

"But it is barely sunrise," Melody protested, scooping the kitten up in both hands and holding her high in the air, little kitten feet dangling. "What a rascal you are going to be. I can tell. I could tell last evening when you came from the epergne, scrambling up Lord Hyde's gauntlet all upset dignity. And your brother is going to be a handful as well. I do hope that his lordship is up to the challenge. Did you see his lordship's face, Atty, when you and your brother came tumbling into the room?"

Melody hugged the kitten to her and petted it gently as she sat up in the bed. "His face absolutely crinkled into laughter to see the two of you. I do think he is fond of cats. Well, he must be, for he did not once hesitate to accept your brother as his prize. And that is most odd, for gentlemen are not generally fond of cats, I think. And did you see the way his eyebrow jerked when he said he would name your brother Soldier and I said that then I shall name you Atropos?"

"Brrr-phft," Atropos responded, squiggling out of

Melody's arms and pouncing on one of the embroidered roses upon the counterpane. "Brrr-brrr-phftf!"

"Yes, my thoughts exactly. He knew the entire legend behind that plant when he sent it to me, Atty. But it was most obvious that he did not think that I would come to know it. I think it embarrassed him to discover that I had."

Melody threw back the covers and, tying her robe around her, wandered across to the washstand, the kitten bouncing gleefully behind taking mighty swipes at the hem of her night rail. "I do think Lord Stoneforth is the most wonderful gentleman, Atty. I cannot think that I know a nicer. I cannot help but like him, even if he does have a head as hard as stone," she added, peering at her brow in the looking glass and giving thanks that only a small bruise showed and there was no lump at all.

"Mrr-mrrr-mfpht!" observed the kitten, scrambling up the runner to the verimost top of the washstand and placing its front paws upon the bowl to peer down into the water Melody had poured. Then, most carefully, Atty reached down with one tiny white paw to feel the liquid. Melody grinned to see it.

"If you do not disappear from my sight this instant, I shall chop off all of your legs with my broad sword and set you out back for the dogs to feast upon," growled Stoneforth.

"Mrrr-pft!" replied the tiny beast, staring bravely up at him through eyes quite as green as Miss Harriman's. "Mrrr-pft, fffph-ffpht!" Whereupon the kitten took a bold swipe at the tassel on one of his lordship's Hessians, leaped up into the air, tumbled backward and then came charging again, full tilt, straight back at the tassel. Tiny claws caught at the leather strands and the kitten rolled over in midair, clinging and hissing and fighting most courageously with the many-armed thing.

Stoneforth grinned and shook his foot. The tassel swung from side to side carrying the persistent kitten with it.

"I vow, you are the stubbornest thing. I must have been out of my mind last evening to have accepted you. Especially when Hyde declared I might have the blasted epergne instead."

"Phffft-ssss-phffft!" the kitten replied, leaping free of the tassel and scrunching down upon the carpet, its little striped rear in the air, preparing to pounce again.

"Oh no, you do not," laughed Stoneforth, scooping the feline from the floor. "You are a perfect rascal and I will never finish dressing if I do not discover some way to keep you occupied. Ah, I know." With the kitten in one hand, squirming to be free, Stoneforth made his way to the japanned dresser and, opening the top drawer, withdrew a much-battered cherry wood box with a cover inlaid with tiles. He flung the cover off, picked up a handful of ribands and, strolling back across the room, tossed ribands and kitten onto the unmade bed.

"Now, grant me some peace, Soldier. I have other things to think of besides yourself. I do hope Miss Harriman's Atropos is better behaved than you are or she will not manage to get dressed until tonight when it is time for the theatre, if then."

The thought of Miss Harriman, laughing as the kittens scurried out of the epergne and leaped to the floor in the middle of the Hydes' Cavalier room, made Stoneforth chuckle as he strolled back to the looking glass and began once again to tie his cravat. Truly, she had looked so completely charmed and charming. One might have thought she had won a thousand pounds instead of one slightly cross-eyed, tiny black-and-white kitten.

And he had shared in that charming and charmed

happiness. The thought stilled his hands and made him turn back to watch the kitten on the bed with a great deal of thankfulness. Whatever was to happen for the rest of his life, for one brief moment he and she had shared a triumph and a joy just between the two of them. And if he was never to have her to himself again, if he was forever after to be merely her brother-in-law and to share only in what she and Toby wished to offer him, at least for one brief moment he had felt what it would be like to have a part in making her happy, and he would always have Soldier to remind him of it.

"And she named her kitten Atropos," he murmured. "I told her I would call this fellow Soldier and she said immediately that hers would be Atropos. She knew all the while about the heartbreaker plant."

"Ye got not the least respect," observed Watlow, entering the chamber at that moment with a stack of neatly pressed neckcloths. "Them be medals on the ends o' them ribands."

"Yes, I know, Watlow. And they were doing nothing at all but lying neglected in a box. Now they are kitten-pleasers. Look at that, Watlow. I have never seen them put to such good use since first I had sight of them."

Watlow grinned a toothy grin as he watched the kitten rolling about among the bedclothes, tossing the medals into the air with all four feet, pouncing upon them, fighting them as though it stood alone against an entire battalion of fiends.

"I do apologize, Watlow, for adding to your work, but I could not refuse to bring the thing away with me. Hyde was depending upon it. And besides, how much trouble can a kitten actually be?"

Wentworth, dressed to the nines in a sky blue riding coat, a canary yellow waistcoat and buff breeches, strolled into the warehouse in Newgate Street, his spurs jangling. He fairly leaped up the stairs to the office and with a wide smile and a flourish, he placed a stack of bills upon Redding's desktop.

"I daresay you are in a fine mood this morning," mumbled Redding, gazing up at the earl.

"Feeling fit as a fiddle, fine as fivepence, fortunate as flying fish!"

"Fortunate as flying fish?"

"Well, to keep in the *f*'s, you know. Good as gold would not have worked at all, Peter. Is my chariot ready?"

"Indeed. You do not actually intend to drive it out of here in broad daylight, do you? Really, Giles, it is pure ugliness."

"Ah, but profitable ugliness, I assure you."

"Profitable?" Redding's eyebrow cocked as significantly as any aristocrat's might. "May I ask in what way profitable?"

"No, you may not. It is not a bit of your concern."

"I see. May I ask then, instead, how your evening turned out, Giles? With the young lady, I mean."

"Splendidly. We came to an understanding of sorts."

Peter Redding smiled abruptly. "An understanding? Truly, Giles? Am I to wish you happy?"

"No, not that kind of an understanding."

"What kind then?"

"If I do not continue to plague her by being a self-centered dandy, she will not hit me again."

"Giles, that is not at all the manner in which one—in which one—deals with love."

"Well, I did attempt to kiss her last evening—just the barest kiss—but before I could, she clunked me in the nose with the top of her head and sent me to the floor. She did not realize I was intending to kiss her, I think, but still—I cannot believe that I am in love with the girl, Peter. She is the most exasperating child!"

"Child?" Redding chuckled and rose from his chair. He stepped forward and put an arm comfortably around Wentworth's shoulders. "I should think she must be seventeen at least, to be out and about, Giles."

"Barely seventeen."

"Yes, well, you are barely twenty-four, which makes me think of you as a child from time to time. But you are not, are you?"

"A child? Me? I should think not!"

"No. And I doubt your Miss Beatrice Lange thinks of herself as a child either."

"No," sighed Wentworth resignedly, "she thinks of herself as a dragoon."

Castlereagh grew more and more jittery the closer the clock approached to six. He could not think why he had told Emily Anne that they must attend at Covent Garden this evening. He was not at all fond of the theatre. Still, he did feel it his duty to be present at the place in the event that his presence might prove useful to Stoneforth.

"Miss Gorsky is yet unaware that she requires rescuing," muttered Castlereagh to himself as he paced the vestibule, awaiting his wife. "I expect telling her so must be incorporated into the plan or the poor woman will think that Stoneforth means to kidnap her. I had better mention that when we meet."

"I cannot think why you think we must attend an operetta, Robert," declared Emily Anne, appearing at the top of the staircase in an opera dress of apple green satin with a *faux* Elizabethan frill at the high neckline and long, tight sleeves ending in cuffs of Brabant lace. The dress had five flounces and was considerably embroidered about the bosom. She wore elegant slippers of lemon yellow with jeweled toes and a glimpse of pink stockings met Castlereagh's eyes as she descended the staircase.

Castlereagh blinked and blinked again. "What the deuce is that in your hair, Emily? I have never seen anything quite like it. It is nothing alive?"

"Do not be absurd, Robert. Of course it is not alive. It is stuffed. It is a stuffed hummingbird upon a golden tiara and the diamonds are meant to resemble flowers."

"Oh."

"Truly, Robert, you have not the least sense of fashion these days. You do only remember what women wore when first we met. You have not taken a bit of notice since," scolded Lady Castlereagh, sliding on her short, lemon yellow gloves and allowing the butler to slip a shawl of Brabant lace over her shoulders. "Not that you should. You go out so rarely into Society. But that is because you are always so preoccupied with your work. I do wish you had never begun at the War Office and I wish even more that you had not accepted the position at the Foreign Office."

"I thought you liked that I am Secretary of Foreign Affairs, Emily Anne," Castlereagh replied as he took up his cane and offered her his arm to lead her to the carriage. "I thought it gave you a considerable amount of prestige among your friends."

"Well, it does, but it is—it is—forever keeping you away from home. I cannot think how you have managed to discover so very much free time of late. Why, you have been to Almack's twice and gone riding in the park and now we are off to the theatre. It is most unlike you."

"Yes, but I did ask you if you would be free this evening and you did say that you would."

"And so I am," nodded Lady Castlereagh—very carefully—so as not to throw her hummingbird off balance. "I was to attend a rout with Cecil, but I informed him that I would not."

Cecil Artentrout, Castlereagh knew, was an ardent admirer of his wife's and forever appeared upon their doorstep to escort Emily Anne to one function or another. He was a dappled dandy of a little man with apple cheeks and a nose like a plum and Castlereagh could not bear the sight of him. "Artentrout is the world's greatest bore, Emily. I do not understand how you can bear to be with him," he muttered as he took his place across from her in the *vis-à-vis*.

"You are quite off there, Robert," she replied with a pout that was intended to appear particularly pitiful. "You are the world's greatest bore of late. You are never home. And when you are, you never wish to do anything."

"Ah, but tonight we are doing something, Emily Anne. We are going to hear Miss Tallia Gorsky sing. And you will like that, will you not?"

"Yes, I shall like to appear at Covent Garden, especially with my hummingbird, for it will cause all sorts of excitement. But I am not particularly fond of Miss Gorsky's singing. It is so very loud, Robert."

Stoneforth stared about him in amazement. "This is Covent Garden?" he asked his brother in a low whisper, as Lady Harriman and the young ladies swept before them through the Greek Doric portico and into the lavish vestibule.

"Do you like it, Adam? It is most impressive, I think."

"Yes, but what happened? It is not at all what I remember. I only attended twice, of course, but I am positive that it looked nothing at all like this."

"Burned down," answered his brother succinctly. "To the ground. This one is nicer."

"Hmmm," nodded Stoneforth, staring about him at the pilasters and the Grecian lamps as they followed

the ladies up the elegant staircase and into the ante-
chamber that led to the lobby of the lower tier of boxes.
"Must have cost a king's ransom."

"I expect so."

"What do you expect, Mr. Attenbury?" asked Melody,
ceasing to goggle at the extravagant furnishings of the
interior and centering her gaze upon Stoneforth.

"I expect this building cost a king's ransom to build.
Adam is amazed at it."

"So, too, am I. I have never seen such an establishment. It might well be a palace."

"Oh, no, it is nothing at all like a palace," laughed
Stoneforth, his eyes shining down upon her.

"And are you familiar with palaces, my lord?"

"A considerable number of them. Though, when I
saw them, they were necessarily a bit run-down."

"You never did see a palace," protested Beatrice,
stepping back from the entrance to their box to join
them. "You never fought anywhere near a palace."

"Yes, I did. Near one in Egypt any number of times.
Rode my horse directly through the portico into the
great hall and directly up the staircase."

"Balderdash," laughed Melody. "I do not believe a
word of it. You are jesting with us."

"Yes, but I might have seen a palace," grinned Stoneforth, "if I had allowed myself to be taken captive at
Alexandria. Of course, I highly doubt I would be here
to speak of it today."

"I am so very relieved that you have ceased to be a
soldier," declared Melody. "Now that I have come to
know you, I should worry about you, were you away at
the war."

"No, would you?"

"Every moment of every day," nodded Melody.

Mr. Attenbury gazed at her with the most curious

expression and then he smiled and, opening the door to their box, urged everyone inside.

"I am to sit beside Lord Stoneforth," Beatrice declared, moving past Melody to take that gentleman's arm. "Aunt Lydia promised that I might."

With a rustle of silk and satin, a slight murmuring, and a shuffling of feet, the four ladies and two gentlemen arranged themselves upon the chairs and began to look about them at the slowly assembling audience. Mr. Attenbury whispered a word in Miss Harriman's ear and she turned her head to gaze at the couple entering four boxes down from them to their right.

"Whatever is Emily Anne wearing in her hair?" asked Lady Harriman, following her daughter's and Mr. Attenbury's gaze. "I vow, Lady Castlereagh dresses more oddly as the weeks go by. Arthur always did say that he thought her more than a bit fey."

"It looks like a bug," Kate observed. "Does it not look like a bug to you, Mr. Attenbury?"

"No, a mouse rather."

"Oh! A mouse? No one would wear a mouse in their hair."

"No one would wear a bug either. It must be something entirely different. Perhaps it is a diamond butterfly, eh?"

"Oh, there is Mr. Davies," Ally pointed out to no one in particular as she gazed down into the pit. "And only see how handsome he looks with his high-crowned beaver and his cane."

"And Lord and Lady Jersey are to be present as well," offered Melody. "See, they are just entering their box."

"Did Miss Harriman say that Lord and Lady Jersey are here?" asked Stoneforth, glancing quickly to see in which direction Miss Harriman looked.

"Yes, but that has got nothing to do with anything,"

protested Beatrice. "You have promised to tell me all about Alexandria, my lord."

"And so I will, but first—ah, I see her now."

"Lord Stoneforth," demanded Beatrice, giving his coat sleeve a mighty tug, "are you in love with Lady Jersey? You cannot be, you know. She is a married woman."

Stoneforth's smile encompassed his entire face and Beatrice was profoundly struck by the charm of it. "No, my dear, I am not at all in love with Lady Jersey, I promise you. But I do find her a most appealing and attractive woman."

"You do?"

"Um-hmm. Now, why do you look so pensive?"

"What is it makes her appealing and attractive?"

"I—that is to say—she—"

"She is most arrogant and filled with her own importance and not very beautiful, and she talks on and on and cannot be silenced. Everyone says so."

"Well, but that has nothing at all to do with it. That is to say, there is something—something about her that draws my admiration. I cannot say precisely what it is. I expect the same thing drew Lord Jersey's admiration as well."

"Can you not tell me what it is?" asked Beatrice with the most plaintive sigh. "I do not understand. Not any of it."

"Not any of what?" Stoneforth queried, quite unsure whether he ought to be as amused by Miss Beatrice's questions as he felt.

"Not anything. I do not understand anything. I came to London to put an end to Wentworth. It was to be a war and I the dragoon sent to bring him down. And now I find that I—"

"Wentworth? You came to London to put an end to Wentworth?"

"Yes, because of the manner in which he treated Melody. And I have engaged him several times and we have lunged and parried and thrust at each other, and I am much better than he at the thing, but I find that I cannot—cannot—actually bring myself to thrust home and send him plunging to the depths."

"Miss Beatrice," began Stoneforth, his eyes growing intensely serious. "My dear Miss Beatrice, you are speaking figuratively, are you not? You and Wentworth have not actually engaged in swordplay?"

"Oh! Oh, no! Though I am certain I could best him at that."

"Thank God," sighed Stoneforth.

"It is merely with words and actions that we fence."

"Just so."

"But—but—I do not wish to do it anymore."

"I see," nodded Stoneforth. And one blind eye or not, he did see very well. "Except that you actually do wish to do it and continue to do it and find it most exciting."

"Yes. Exactly so. I find that I enjoy parrying with Wentworth immensely. He is truly the most aggravating gentleman. Yet, at times, I think I love him. He makes me so very angry that I wonder, how *can* I love him? But just when I am angriest, he will do something foolish or sweet or most unexpected and I will know that I love him and wish with all my heart that he loved me. But he will never love me because he does not find me at all appealing or—or—attractive, as you said about Lady Jersey."

"I see."

"And—and I wish you will tell me how to go about it."

"To go about what?"

"To go about becoming appealing and attractive."

Luckily for Stoneforth the performance began at just that moment and his gaze fixed immediately upon the stage, though he gave Bea's hand a comforting pat.

Miss Tallia Gorsky did not appear until the second scene of the first act and when she did, she did so to rousing applause. Stoneforth studied her as best he could. She was not so large and well endowed as he had suspected. In fact, she was quite tiny. Almost as tiny as the young lady beside him. But she had a voice that could shatter crystal.

Mr. Attenbury's gaze fastened upon the stage as well, and though Melody whispered a comment upon Miss Gorsky's voice in his ear, he did not appear to hear a word of it. Melody could not think why he should be so suddenly entranced. He had told her himself that he had seen Miss Gorsky perform this operetta any number of times. And then she noticed him take a pencil and a small paper, much resembling a calling card, from the pocket of his coat and begin to write upon it.

What on earth can he be doing? she wondered, and leaned to the side to peek at what he wrote. There were numbers and arrows indicating left and right and up and down, and dotted lines. And at the very end of Miss Gorsky's first aria, Lord Stoneforth leaned across Beatrice and said, "Write that she exits upon the final note and be certain to mark how long before she returns, Toby. We must have at least three minutes, I think."

Melody's eyes turned immediately upon Stoneforth but he had instantly returned his attention to the stage. Three minutes? Melody thought befuddled. 'We must have at least three minutes?' Three minutes for what? And then, quite abruptly, she remembered that Miss Gorsky was a favorite of Tsar Alexander, whose every loyalty her papa was at that very moment working hard to gain for Britain and her allies. And it popped into her mind that if anything should happen to Miss Gorsky, all of her papa's hard work and that of the other members of the mission would be for naught. And if someone were taking notes upon Miss Gorsky's performance—notes upon where and when she entered the stage and where she stood and how long before she exited and returned—well, it might mean—it might mean—Melody blinked her eyes slowly in disbelief and then stared from one to the other of the brothers. It might mean there was a conspiracy in the making and that Miss Gorsky was the object of it!

But they would never, she told herself, frowning. Mr. Attenbury is much too sweet and noble and certainly Lord Stoneforth is a hero and a gentleman of honor and courage. I am being totally absurd. They would never think to abduct Miss Tallia Gorsky! Yet she could see that Mr. Attenbury marked carefully the point of Miss Gorsky's exit and was even then gazing down at his pocket watch, noting the number of minutes before her next entrance.

Fourteen

"I thought to be here just in case," murmured Castlereagh in the long corridor behind the boxes. "Is there anything I can do?"

"Yes," Stoneforth replied. "You can buy a bag of oranges for us. Toby and I have used that as an excuse to the ladies for departing so precipitously at the beginning of the very first interval. I doubt we shall be able to return before the performance resumes if we must go rushing about in search of an orange girl as well as discover what we need to know about this theatre. And if we come back without the oranges, the ladies will likely become suspicious."

"Where are you bound?"

"Backstage. To look about. There is a rear entrance somewhere, I presume, for the actors and such. I should like to know where it lies and how accessible it is."

"Adam thinks it may be possible to take Miss Gorsky from the stage at some point during her performance and directly out of the theatre and into a waiting coach," offered Mr. Attenbury, "but I do not quite remember how close we may bring the coach to the rear door. And we are discussing the possibility that she may need to hide upon the floor with a rug covering her until we are out of the city. That will be safest, do not you think?"

"You know all about it?" asked Castlereagh with a curious glance at Mr. Attenbury.

"Yes, everything. There are lists to be made and notes to be taken, you know, and Adam cannot read or write properly because of his eye."

"He cannot?"

"No, I cannot just yet. Do not look so doubtful, Robert. Toby is my brother. He is to be trusted, I assure you."

"Well, I do not doubt that. I only worry that now I have involved two Attenburys in something that could prove to be extremely dangerous. If something goes wrong, your uncle, Sanshire, will have my hide for certain."

"Balderdash, Uncle North will be proud as a peacock even if we are both killed, because we do it for England. But nothing can go wrong," Mr. Attenbury declared with the confidence of youth. "You could not have picked a better man for the job than Adam."

"Well, I know that, Attenbury. I have every confidence in him—and in you as well. Go on, then. Get to it. I shall fetch a bag of oranges and meet you here. By the way, Stoneforth—"

"Yes? By the way?"

"Miss Gorsky has not got the least idea that her life has been threatened or that any of this goes forward. I expect you must take her aside and explain everything to her at some point. If our villain or villains should see me speaking to her they will become immediately suspicious, I think. Emily Anne is already suspicious because I have brought her to the theatre. I seldom make an appearance in such a place and she has been badgering me for an entire hour to know why I have come tonight."

"I shall attempt to explain what goes forward to Miss Gorsky when Toby and I have discovered all we need to know. There will be another interval in the production will there not?"

"There are three altogether," offered Mr. Attenbury.

"Good. We ought to be able to speak with her during one of them, I think, even if we must take her aside in the green room. You do know where the green room is, do you not, Toby? Yes, so I thought. All young men seem to know where those particular places lie. Go and fetch the oranges, Robert, and do not waste another thought upon Miss Gorsky. By the time we leave this place tonight, Toby and I will have enough information to devise a proper plan and, I assure you, Miss Gorsky will understand exactly what we intend to do and why and she will be pleased to cooperate with us."

Oranges notwithstanding, when the gentlemen returned to the box mere moments before the end of the first interval and exited it again immediately upon the beginning of the second interval, Melody could not but be certain that something was afoot. And though a number of gentlemen came to visit the girls during that break in the performance, she made certain to gaze about at the other boxes to discover where Lord Stoneforth and Mr. Attenbury might have gone. Her first thought was to discover his lordship across the way in conversation with Lady Jersey, but he was not among the visitors there. Nor were he and Mr. Attenbury to be seen in any of the other boxes. Well, where have they gone then? Melody wondered. Are they truly in the lobby procuring champagne? But they ought to have returned by now if that is the case.

They did arrive with the champagne just as the performance recommenced, but when they departed again at the third interval, Melody slipped into the chair beside Beatrice and murmured into her cousin's ear,

"They are off again. Something havey-cavey is going on with our two escorts, Beatrice. This is the third time they have disappeared upon some ridiculous errand."

"Yes. We have had oranges and champagne already. Now it is sweets they claim to be seeking. I, too, think something is not quite upon the up-and-up. Aunt Lydia," she queried, turning to Lady Harriman, "may Melody and I step out into the corridor?"

"Without a gentleman beside you? I think not."

"But I do so need a breath of air."

"There is Mr. Attenbury motioning to me to accompany him!" exclaimed Melody, as the door to the box opened and several gentlemen entered to pay their respects to the ladies within. Melody gazed most convincingly beyond the men and then she waved as if Mr. Attenbury were indeed standing just outside in the corridor. "Apparently Mr. Attenbury wishes me to take a stroll with him, Mama. May I please? And I shall take Beatrice along to play chaperon. That will be quite unexceptionable, will it not?"

"Well, if Mr. Attenbury is to be with you, there can be no harm in it, but you must just stroll as far as the lobby and back. You must not actually go anywhere or stop to visit at any of the boxes. What is acceptable for the gentlemen is not equally so for young ladies."

"Thank you, Mama," smiled Melody. "We will be most discreet, I assure you." And taking Bea's hand in her own, Melody hurried past the beaux who had come to visit and out into the corridor.

"Oh, good show, Mel," Beatrice whispered. "There they are," she added tugging Melody to the left. "They are just going through that door at the end of the corridor. I cannot guess what they are about. Hurry, or we shall lose them."

"You do not think the door leads into someone's box?"

"No. It faces quite the wrong direction for that. Why, a box that is entered from that direction must lie behind us on the wide end of the horseshoe if anyone in it wishes to see the stage."

"When they returned with the oranges, they both appeared to be out of breath. Did you notice?" asked Melody as the two made their way through the throng of ladies and gentlemen who meandered up and down the passageway. "And when next they returned with the champagne, Lord Stoneforth's neckcloth was disarranged and Mr. Attenbury's coat was unbuttoned."

"And Lord Stoneforth had the merest bit of mud upon one shoe," said Beatrice.

"He did? I did not notice that. They went out of the theatre during the second interval then."

"Yes, so I think."

The door through which Lord Stoneforth and Mr. Attenbury had gone revealed to the young ladies a set of narrow but well-lighted stairs. They paused for a moment at the top of them to allow the door at the bottom to swing closed.

"They are just ahead of us still," Melody whispered. "We must not follow too closely, or we shall be discovered."

With the greatest caution, Melody and Beatrice made their way down the stairs and along a narrow corridor that led to a large, rectangular area filled with scenery and costumes and all manner of paraphernalia. Any number of people were milling about, speaking to each other, tugging upon ropes, pushing furniture about, and producing a general hubbub in which two young ladies would likely not be noticed if they kept to the shadows. Which they did attempt to do and still keep Lord Stoneforth and Mr. Attenbury within their sights. They tiptoed behind this and climbed over that and in general scuttled about like two little mice seeking the cheese and attempting to avoid the cat at one and the same time.

And just as they saw the two gentlemen they followed open a door far ahead of them and disappear down what seemed to be another corridor, Melody tripped upon a thick coil of rope and fell forward with a tiny gasp. Beatrice was quick and nimble enough to save her before she tumbled to the floor, but it did give Melody a start and she took a moment to recover.

Wentworth handed the reins to the groom who had accompanied him and leaped from the box of his new coach. He landed with heels clicking and spurs jangling upon the flagway and strolled to one of the windows to grin in at the four tremendously large footmen who sat cramped inside the vehicle. "I shall return shortly, men. You must simply await me here. If anyone questions your presence, you must only say that you are in the employ of the Earl of Wentworth and no one will think to question you further. But I doubt anyone will so much as appear at this hour."

With a distinct bounce in his step, whistling merrily, Wentworth climbed the stoop to the great oak door, tried the latch and found it open, as he had suspected he would. It was going to be an enormously pleasant evening. He knew it. His eyes sparkled with good humor and his imagination filled with the most delightful visions. What a coup this was going to be. Not only would he collect his pony from Boylan-Jolnes but he would set the members of The Beefsteak Club upon their collective ears and Kemble would go positively berserk to think that he had lost The Beefsteak Club's stock of wine once again.

Of course, it was going to be the devil of a job to haul all of those bottles from the cellar of the theatre up to the rear door and out into the coach, but the footmen were exceedingly muscular and good workers as well. And they would do the job with incredible enthusiasm, because he had promised them each ten pounds if they proved successful.

And we are in good time, too, Wentworth thought as he entered the backstage area of the theatre. He nodded at two of the actors whom he recognized at once. "The final interval, eh, Marcus?" he called to one.

"Indeed, my lord. Ten minutes until the final act. The green room is filled with gentlemen if that is where you are bound."

"Just so," nodded Wentworth, taking a step in the direction of that notable chamber, which was a readily available backstage gathering place in every theatre, and then halting again to watch the actors disappear from view. Perfect! Everything was going splendidly. In ten minutes the entire cast and crew would be thoroughly engrossed in the final act. Already the gentlemen who intended to visit backstage before the end of the performance had reached their destination. Better and better and better! There would be no one in the long, shadowy corridor to take note of four hefty men carrying crates of bottles out of the theatre cellar. And it would be a simple matter to pack them out of sight in the coach, too. He had been extremely wise there. Peter thought the vehicle a travesty, but it was perfect.

From the outside Wentworth's new coach appeared perfectly normal if not stylish, but inside, where there ought to have been considerable room for the occupants, there was barely room for two persons to sit in any comfort. The seats had been moved close together, leaving little room for a person's feet, and the backs of both seats could be opened to reveal large compartments. The one behind the rear-facing seat was high and wide, sloping upward to the top of the vehicle and traveling back under the box in one direction and under the seat in the other. And the second compartment, under the front-facing seat, sloped in a like manner toward the back of the vehicle, which had been elongated to accommodate an incredible number of bottles. And still a third chamber lay under the slightly raised floorboards and stretched from the front to the rear of the coach.

Quite enough space to store the wine—well, most of the wine. Wentworth was not certain how many bottles there might be. The Beefsteak Club, after all, had only begun to replenish the stock they had lost in the fire three years earlier. That first stock of wine they had accumulated over a period of fifteen years and more. And so much wine as there had been then could certainly not all have been stolen, but Wentworth doubted there was so much now that his coach could not hold it, especially since he intended to pack only the bottles and leave the crates behind.

Wentworth truly felt like dancing. He would make his way to the green room and lounge about until the beginning of the act and then he would saunter off toward the stage door saying, if anyone asked, that he had forgot an appointment with his friends. He would check the corridor along the way to be certain that no one kept watch over the cellar entrance—but they would not. They never did. No one had stolen even one bottle of The Beefsteak Club's wine in all the years they had stored it in the theatre. No one had ever dared to do it—until now!

"They went right through there," whispered Bea, pointing, as soon as Melody had caught her breath.

"Yes, I saw. Shhh, someone is coming this way."

Melody grasped Bea's hand and tugged her quickly behind an enormous curtain with a forest painted upon the opposite side where they huddled in silence as a cacophony of voices grew rapidly louder, then began to fade. Melody poked her head around the side of the curtain. Bea did the same upon the other side.

"All clear," Melody announced in a hushed whisper, and with quick steps the two young ladies bounded from behind the curtain, across an expanse of bare, unpolished plank flooring and into the corridor down which Stoneforth and Attenbury had disappeared a full two minutes before. "I doubt we shall find them now," sighed Bea. "They have too much of a lead."

"Unless they have turned into one of these chambers. We shall just listen outside the doors. Perhaps we will hear one of their voices."

"And then what will we do?" asked Beatrice, gazing with interest about her. "Knock and enter and ask them what is going on? I cannot think that they will tell us."

"No, I do not expect that they will. But if we do happen to hear their voices, we shall simply keep our ears against the door until we have heard all that they have to say. Something havey-cavey is going forward, Bea. I know it. Mr. Attenbury has been taking notes upon the operetta and when I asked him why, he had the nerve to tell me that it was because he intended to write one himself, which I do not believe for one moment."

"Well, he might intend to write an operetta. Kate says that he is most interested in music and talked to her all night at the Hydes' about Papa's operettas and how he came to write them."

"Mr. Attenbury knows about your papa?"

"Yes, but he will not let it slip. Kate is confident he will not. She thinks he is quite the most kind and honorable of gentlemen and the most handsome as well."

"Yes, well, he is all those things, I am sure."

"Anyone would expect *you* to think so. You are going to marry him, after all. But Kate is not easily impressed, you know, by gentlemen—unless, of course, they are actors in a play. She adores actors in a play. But only because she would so like to be an actress."

"Shhh! Is that not Lord Stoneforth's voice?"

Beatrice pressed her ear against a rough wooden door right beside the spot where Melody had pressed hers, and nodded in silence.

"I cannot think it will do to stay until the final performance, Miss Gorsky. In fact, we ought to move at once, before anyone suspects that word has gotten out."

"And how are you to spirit me away?" asked a husky female voice. "Always after a performance are my admirers standing outside that door, waiting for me to make my bows to them and gather their offerings into my arms."

"That is just the thing," replied Lord Stoneforth. "We are thinking to take you from the stage to the coach at some point during the performance. A point when you exit naturally and no one will suspect you have gone anywhere until you are late for your entrance. Your admirers will not gather outside until the performance is over, eh? Well, we will be a good way from the theatre by then."

"What the devil are you doing here?" whispered a harsh voice in Bea's ear, which made her jump and knock into Melody, who banged noisily against the door. "That is Miss Gorsky's dressing room. Why the devil are you and Miss Harriman eavesdropping upon Miss Gorsky? And where are your escorts? You cannot be prancing around down here alone."

Before Bea could so much as look up at the gentleman who spoke or form one word in answer, the door flew open and a strong hand seized upon the first thing it touched, which happened to be the shoulder of Melody's opera gown, and gave it a tremendous yank, ripping the seam and propelling Melody, instantly and with a deal of violence, into the room.

"By Jupiter, Miss Harriman!" exclaimed Stoneforth. "What the deuce are you doing here?"

"We are—l-lost!" cried Beatrice breathlessly as she rushed into the chamber to discover Melody, in somewhat of a panic, standing before Stoneforth, her gown torn, her cheeks aflame and his lordship's ears burning a bright red. "We thought we heard your voice, Colonel, and came to see if you would escort us back to our box."

"What a whisker that is!" exclaimed Wentworth, coming to a halt upon the chamber's threshold, his gloved hands upon his hips, his feet spread wide, and his hair glistening gold beneath his beaver in the candlelight. "They were eavesdropping is what they were doing. Both of them. Though I cannot think why. Evening, Miss Gorsky, Attenbury. I came upon them just now with their ears pressed against the dressing room door."

"It is none of your business, Wentworth, what we were doing!" Beatrice exclaimed angrily. "You are a thoroughly detestable man!"

As he ignored the interplay between the young people, Stoneforth's arms found their way protectively around a trembling Melody. His lips moved close beside her ear. "I am so very sorry, my dear. If I had known it was you outside the door, I would never have—I thought it might well be one of the assa—someone else. My gawd, I have torn your dress. You are not harmed in any way? Lord bless me for a fool to have jerked you inside so roughly when I had not the least idea that—not the least—"

"Well, by gawd!" exclaimed Wentworth, his eyes widening as he stared at Stoneforth. "Do something, Attenbury! Your brother is kissing Miss Harriman!"

"He is," observed Beatrice, stunned. "Mr. Attenbury, your brother is kissing your beloved."

"And very thoroughly he is kissing her, too," nodded Miss Gorsky with a smile. "That I like, how he slips from ear to cheek to lips so much tenderly and without the commotion. I shall ask Paul to put such a kiss as this in place of the one we do at the end of scene five."

"She is kissing him back," whispered Beatrice, horrified. "Mr. Attenbury, Melody is kissing your brother back!"

"And a demmed good job she does of it, too," remarked Wentworth, somewhat mystified.

"Wentworth, do something!" urged Beatrice, turning to tug at his arm. "Stop them!"

"Stop them? Why?"

"Because—because they are kissing each other right here in front of Mr. Attenbury!"

"I do not think that Attenbury minds," Wentworth offered, glancing surreptitiously at Attenbury.

"Of course he minds, you ninny!" Beatrice exclaimed. "He fought a duel and was gravely wounded and called for Melody over and over when he was dying and—"

"I do beg your pardon," interrupted Wentworth. "Attenbury was not dying. Had he been dying, he would not be standing here grinning like a fool at this moment. He would be dead."

Beatrice turned from the scene before her to glare up into Wentworth's eyes. "That is not the point and you well know it! And do not look so very smug, either. You would not look so if Lord Stoneforth were kissing your intended. I vow, you are the most unfeeling, self-centered person ever to walk upon his hind legs!"

Wentworth attempted to glare back down at her, but he could not help himself and burst into whoops. "H-hind legs?"

Beatrice scowled at him with great contempt, but he continued to laugh.

"H-hind legs," he managed again. "A-Attenbury, I

am w-walking about upon m-my hind legs!" And he did
the most amazing little jig without moving from the
spot. Attenbury could not help himself and he too burst
into gales of laughter.

"Men!" declared Beatrice. "They are all of them
mad!"

"Just so," whispered Stoneforth, his lips at last releas-
ing Melody's. "I am completely mad." He freed her then
from his embrace, but he took her hands into his own
and held them gently there. "I do beg your pardon. Truly
I do. You were so very close, you see, and I whispering
in your ear. And your gown was torn and your cheeks
flaming and your eyes like emeralds in the candlelight.
And you had a look upon your face like a frightened
fawn. I could not help—I merely wished to—I am sorry,
Miss Harriman. Truly I am." He lowered his gaze to the
floor and freeing Melody's hands, rubbed at the back of
his neck. Then he tugged at a bright red ear and cleared
his throat and peered up at Mr. Attenbury. "I do beg
your pardon as well, Tobias. I cannot but think that you—
Toby, what the deuce are you laughing about? Have I
offended you so greatly as to send you into hysterics?"

"W-Wentworth is w-walking upon his hind legs,"
managed Mr. Attenbury, attempting to subdue his
chuckles. "No, do not look at me so, Adam. I am sorry.
I shall—be—over this in a m-moment."

Stoneforth felt a gentle tug upon his sleeve and
turned to meet Melody's befuddled gaze. "Why did you
kiss me like that?" she asked softly, amazed at the rapid
beating of her heart and the tightness in her throat and
the sincere longing that coursed through her to have
him kiss her exactly the same way again.

"B-because—" The turmoil that boiled inside Stoneforth was evident to all who looked upon him at that
moment. The battle that raged deep in his soul shown,
clearly and shockingly, upon his face and in the trem-

bling of his shoulders and in the blazing depths of his eyes. Attenbury and Wentworth ceased to laugh at once. Beatrice's hand went to her lips. Miss Gorsky made the tiniest little noise deep in her throat.

"I will say it," he growled at last, pain and hopelessness most evident in his tone. "I will. I kissed you so, because I have come to love you, Miss Harriman. I have no right to do so. My heart has made me a traitor to my own brother and to you. I will finish what I must with Miss Gorsky and take myself out of your lives forever."

"Oh," squeaked Melody.

"Just so," nodded Stoneforth gravely. "Toby, will you be so good as to escort Miss Harriman and her cousin back to our box and say to Lady Harriman that I was taken ill? I will finish with Miss Gorsky and then take myself out of your sight. I shall put up at an hotel, Tobias, until our plan is carried out, and then you need never see my face again."

Fifteen

"Never see your face again? I think not," declared Mr. Attenbury. "You may find this odd, dear brother, but I wish to see your face every day until the very end of our lives. I have lived too long already with only a miniature of that wretched face of yours by which to remember you."

"But I have just—" Stoneforth began, bewildered.

"There is much confusion, no?" giggled Miss Gorsky in the most appealing manner. "Love is everywhere turned about think I. Just so is it with my Isolda. All turned about."

"Isolda! What time is it? The interval must be near half over!" Stoneforth exclaimed. "Toby, you must return the ladies to our box at once, before anyone misses them. I shall finish explaining our plan to Miss Gorsky."

"What plan?" asked Wentworth.

"These so kind gentlemen, my Lord Wentworth, to rescue me from a plot formed by my Alexander's oh too charming friend, the emperor, have come."

"Do you mean Napoleon?" asked Wentworth, his eyes widening. "That madman?"

"Just so," Miss Gorsky replied. "A plot has this Napoleon concerning me. To thwarz him these two gentlemen intend."

"Thwart him," offered Wentworth. "Well, by damn! Whoever would have thought?"

"I ought to have done," a sonorous voice replied from the open doorway. "Was that what Lord Castlereagh came to speak with you about, my lord? Ah, how I should like to have known. I might have discovered some means to eliminate your involvement. Still what is done cannot be undone, I think."

"Ridgeworth?" Attenbury stared at his valet, flabbergasted. "What the devil are you doing here—and with a pistol in your hand? Put it aside at once."

"I think not, Mr. Attenbury. No, do not move, gentlemen. Simply stay where you are and give me a moment to think, for I do not wish to put a period to anyone's life, certainly not to yours, Lord Stoneforth, or to Mr. Attenbury's. And I shall not like at all to harm the ladies or Lord Wentworth. Miss Harriman, how unfortunate that you and your cousin should be here. This young lady is one of the cousins Mr. Attenbury spoke of, is she not? Come, close and lock this door behind me, Miss Harriman. Do it slowly please. The final act to *The Innocent Isolda* is scheduled to take place offstage this evening and I do not wish to involve any more innocents than are already present."

Melody felt Stoneforth stiffen perceptibly beside her. She reached out and gave his hand a quick squeeze before crossing the chamber and turning the key in the door lock. "I do think," she said, moving back to stand beside Beatrice, "that you are making a great mistake, Mr. Ridgeworth."

"No, I am not. I shall have a fortune in gold when I have done this thing. A man does not care to be a poor valet all of his life, Miss Harriman. A man has desires."

"Yes, certainly. But for a man to desire himself hated by all of England and Russia alike and forced to live abroad until he dies does not seem a very intelligent desire to me. You will be lonely and despised, Mr. Ridge-worth."

"I shall have enough money to set myself up in business, Miss Harriman, and no one on the Continent will have the least interest in how I have come by it."

"No matter how much money you have, it will prove a very lonely and depressing existence. You will miss your country, Mr. Ridgeworth, and your friends. You will always be an outsider in a foreign land. And England will never take you back. Not once you have done this dreadful thing."

Ridgeworth wiped the hand that did not hold the pistol along the side of his breeches nervously. "It makes no difference. No one in England cares the least thing about me."

"What a whisker, Mr. Ridgeworth!" Melody declared. "Mr. Attenbury and I are beyond grateful to you for all you have done to help make him well. We care about you. And Lord Stoneforth is most fond of you and wishes you only well. And Mr. Watlow has confessed to me that he has come to admire you. I cannot imagine that you actually wish to abandon such inroads as you have made with us and sail off to begin again in a foreign country all alone. And when you are alone, you know, you must stare into the looking glass every day for the rest of your life at the face of a murderer—and for the sake of money merely."

"M-murderer?" stuttered Ridgeworth.

"It is not a pleasant thing to stare at yourself in a looking glass and think that you have killed someone," muttered Wentworth, placing an arm protectively about Beatrice. "I could barely tie my cravat all the while Attenbury lay ill. If he had died, I should be the one who had murdered him and I should have hated myself forever."

"It was you shot Mr. Attenbury?" exclaimed Beatrice, thrusting his arm from her. "What a dolt you are, Wentworth!"

"Yes, just so. A dolt and worse. I prayed day after day for Attenbury's recovery so that I should not be forced to acknowledge every time I gazed at my own face, that it was the face of a murderer—that I had actually murdered one of my friends. At least, we once were friends, Attenbury and I, and might yet be if I were not always so—"

"Arrogant," provided Beatrice in a loud, clear voice.

"Yes, that and—"

"Outrageous, inconsiderate, without a thought for others, a self-indulgent boor!" Bea's voice rose dangerously high. Her eyes flashed. Her hands formed themselves into angry fists. "You are the most ill-mannered, inconsiderate person on the face of this earth, Wentworth! You are detestable!" And Beatrice slammed one tiny fist into Wentworth's stomach and the other into his jaw.

Ridgeworth's mouth fell open and he stared, mesmerized by the sight of Wentworth doubling over in pain. Melody thought at that moment to throw herself at the man and seize the pistol that wobbled, forgotten, in his hand. Attenbury actually took a step in Ridgeworth's direction. But before either could do as they intended, Stoneforth was across the room and upon the valet. Wentworth straightened up and tugged both Beatrice and Melody aside, then gave a long, low whistle as the pistol flew out of Ridgeworth's hand and exploded against the far wall while Ridgeworth sailed into the air and crashed against the locked door. It was over in the blink of an eye, and from the chair before the looking glass in which she had been sitting the entire time, Miss Gorsky applauded enthusiastically.

Stoneforth stalked to the valet, seized him by his cravat and lifted him to his feet. But instead of hitting the man again, he unfisted his hands, straightened Ridgeworth's collar and cravat and coat, and sighed. "I should pummel you to within an inch of your life, Ridgeworth," he said so softly that no one else could hear. "But I cannot. You did your best to save Toby's life; you instructed me how best to meet Miss Harriman; you helped Toby and me in any number of ways. Toby might well be dead now without you. And I should be dead as well from the grief of losing him. My debt to you is greater than you realize. But still, I cannot allow you to harm Miss Gorsky."

In Mr. Attenbury's box Lady Harriman was growing more and more uneasy. As the beaux departed one by one, the tiny hairs upon the back of her neck began to pulse and tickle. Where were Melody and Bea? Mr. Attenbury ought to have returned with them by now. "Darlings," she murmured quietly when all of the gentlemen except Mr. Davies had departed, "I must step into the corridor and look about for Mr. Attenbury and Melody and Beatrice. They cannot have gone far, do you think? Likely they are merely speaking with someone in the lobby. Still, I cannot like it that they should be away so long."

"Attenbury?" Davies asked. "Attenbury has gone to the green room. I saw him heading that way, he and Stoneforth both."

"They would not dare escort Melody and Bea to such a place!"

"No, ma'am, they did not. They were alone when I saw them."

"Alone?"

"Yes, quite. I only caught a glimpse of them strolling toward the rear staircase, but the young ladies were not with them. What is it, ma'am? You are turning quite pale."

"No, no, it is nothing, Mr. Davies, I assure you."

"It *is* something," Ally inserted with a frown. "We may trust Mr. Davies, Aunt Lydia, I promise you. Melody and Beatrice were to have gone for a stroll with Mr. Attenbury, Charles. I heard Melody say that he waved for them to join him. That, obviously, was a farradiddle."

"Do you mean to say that they have wandered off alone?" asked Davies.

"Yes," nodded Kate. "I expect Beatrice has gotten herself into some sort of scrape, and this time she has taken Melody right along with her."

"We must find them," declared Lady Harriman as the color slowly returned to her cheeks. "The final act will begin shortly."

"It ought to have begun already," murmured Mr. Davies, glancing down at his watch. "Something has held things up backstage, I expect."

"It ought to have begun already?" asked Ally in surprise. "Good heavens, and Lord Stoneforth and Mr. Attenbury are yet absent as well. Come, Charles. You and I shall go for a stroll and see what we can discover."

"I am going as well," declared Kate.

"And I," nodded Lady Harriman, rising and moving toward the door. "We must not make a great to-do of it," she whispered to the girls and Mr. Davies. "We do not wish for everyone present to notice that something is amiss."

"Of course not," agreed Mr. Davies, holding open the door for Lady Harriman and the girls to pass through into the corridor. "We shall be most discreet, I assure you. Look, there is Castlereagh standing about outside his box with his hands full of sacks. We shall wander that way, eh, and ask if he has seen any one of them?"

Lord Castlereagh recognized instantly the ladies and the gentleman who approached and the sacks slipped from his hands.

"Allow me," offered Davies, stooping to retrieve them. "Oh, sweets. I am afraid some of them are smashed, Castlereagh. You have not had sight of Stoneforth, have you? Or Attenbury?"

Castlereagh did not answer. He tugged his watch from his pocket instead. "Great thundering hogs' heads, is it that late? I thought I had been standing about far too long," he muttered, ignoring the sacks Davies offered him. "The operetta has not yet resumed. I can hear that much. Something has gone amiss."

"Amiss? What can have gone—? Have you had sight of Mr. Attenbury or Lord Stoneforth, my lord?" asked Lady Harriman.

"No, no, and I should have had by now. Davies, escort the ladies back to their box. I shall go and have a look for them myself." And so saying, Castlereagh stuck his head through the door to his own box, muttered a few words, then turned on his heel and marched down the corridor toward the rear staircase.

"Be deviled if I shall be dismissed so!" Lady Harriman muttered under her breath and marched off right behind him, Kate, Ally and Mr. Davies not slow to join the parade. "If Lord Castlereagh knows where the gentlemen have gone, quite likely the girls know as well and have followed."

"Why the deuce was Castlereagh standing about with sacks of sweets?" murmured Davies, setting the sacks upon a table that stood near the staircase door.

"Oh! I know the answer to that, I think!" Ally exclaimed, taking his arm. "He was holding them for Lord Stoneforth to bring back to us. Sweets are what Lord Stoneforth claimed he was leaving to procure. There is something havey-cavey going on, Charles. I do hope Beatrice and Melody are not caught up in the midst of it."

"Mr. Ridgeworth, I cannot understand why you should think to murder Miss Gorsky," sighed Melody. "If you feel so strongly that you must have more money and your own business, why, there are any number of other ways to go about it. I am quite certain that—"

"M-murder?" stuttered Ridgeworth. "It was you, miss, and Lord Wentworth spoke of murder, n-not I. I could never m-murder anyone. I merely wished for time to think of what I must do to keep the lot of you from stopping me."

"Never murder anyone?" asked Stoneforth, standing away from the man and shoving his fists into his pockets. "You came with a pistol into Miss Gorsky's dressing room but did not intend to murder her, Ridgeworth?"

Ridgeworth nodded. "I was m-merely to ab-abduct the woman," he whispered, choking. "No one said the—the least thing about—about—murder."

"Well, but that is what the payment Napoleon offers is for, Ridgeworth—for Miss Gorsky's violent demise upon English soil."

"No one t-told me that," the valet whispered. "I was merely to take her off before the final act so that the performance would be disrupted and everyone would know that she had disappeared. No one said anything at all about m-murder. There are—there are—others involved in it, my lord," he managed. "They are here tonight. They will notice that the operetta does not resume as it should and yet no alarm is spread over Miss Gorsky's disappearance. They will come looking for me to see what has occurred."

"They are in the audience?" Mr. Attenbury asked. "Where?"

"In the pit. Two of them. They are to exit when first news of Miss Gorsky's disappearance reaches out into the house and to meet me and Miss Gorsky at the far end of Bow Street. But if no alarm goes forth and I do not return—"

"They will come to check upon you," finished Stoneforth quietly. "Yes, I see. We would have been too late, Tobias. Had we not come tonight, there would have been no use in formulating a plan at all. Miss Gorsky's assassination was to have taken place this very evening."

"Goodness!" exclaimed Miss Gorsky with wide eyes.

"How much exciting becomes my poor little life. Hush," she added and then a fist knocked upon the door.

"You are late, my dear Miss Gorsky. We are ready to begin," called a male voice.

"That is Mr. Kemble," Miss Gorsky whispered. "To what do I tell him?"

"Say you will be a moment more," Stoneforth whispered back.

"I will be a moment more, merely," called Miss Gorsky. "Do be such a sweet gentleman as you are and tell the audience that Miss Gorsky, she is detained."

For the longest time no sound was to be heard other than that of the theatre manager's footsteps fading away. Then the people in Miss Gorsky's dressing room all took a great breath at the same time and that made Miss Gorsky giggle.

"We must get you out of here quickly," Stoneforth said, a grin teasing at his too solemn face. "It is not a game, Miss Gorsky. You ought not be giggling."

"*Nyet*, of this I certain am, but is so much funny how we all breathe at once."

"I shall go out and get John to bring the coach around, shall I, Adam?" Attenbury asked. "It will take a while, I think. The street will be clogged with waiting carriages."

"We cannot take the least chance that the men Ridgeworth mentions will see her," sighed Stoneforth. "If they, too, are carrying pistols, she will be dead where she stands the moment they come upon her."

"My own vehicle," Wentworth said, "stands outside the rear door even now."

"It does?" Beatrice stared up at him, a deal of curiosity in her eyes. "Why should you leave it there? Wentworth, you are up to something, are you not?"

"Merely an attempt to steal The Beefsteak Club's wine. A bet, you know," he added with a quick glance at Attenbury.

"They will have your guts for garters," Mr. Attenbury said in awe.

"No, because now I will not succeed. But I would have done if I had not come upon these two ladies eavesdropping in the corridor. What the deuce is all that pounding?"

"It will be the gentlemen of the pit, my presence demanding," Miss Gorsky advised them. "Their feet they stomping are."

"If I may make a suggestion, my lord," murmured Ridgeworth.

"Yes?" queried Stoneforth with a cock of an eyebrow.

"If I make my way back to the pit at once, I shall be able to forestall Arnold and Sam by telling them that Miss Gorsky has escaped me and run out the door and down the street. I shall lead them south in search of her while you carry her off in the opposite direction in Lord Wentworth's coach."

"Why ought I believe that you would do such a thing for us, Ridgeworth? I wish to believe it, mind, but why ought I?"

"Because you might have killed me, my lord, a moment ago with your fists alone and you did not and so I am beholden to you. And because I might have fired upon any one of you and I did not and would not have done. And because I have this and I have not once thought to use it against you, nor will I."

Ridgeworth pulled from the pocket of his tail coat a knife of considerable size and placed it, handle first, into Stoneforth's hands. "I am not a murderer, my lord."

"No. I hoped with all my heart that you were not. Go then and take the villains as far south as you can. But do not argue if at last they turn back north, Ridgeworth, or they may suspect that you have betrayed them and then they will kill you."

"Yes, my lord."

"And give me your word to return to Sanshire House, eh? I will discover a way by which you may set yourself up in business, Ridgeworth, without becoming either traitor or murderer. I give you my word on that."

Ridgeworth nodded and turned and spun the key in the lock. He turned back. "The pistol, my lord. I must have it or they will wonder where it has gone."

Mr. Attenbury scooped the pistol from the floor and tossed it to him. Ridgeworth gave the merest salute with the tip of it, tucked it away and rushed out into the corridor, leaving the door wide open behind him.

"Bless my soul, how very rude! A person could be trampled to death back here and no one say a word," Lady Harriman's voice echoed from the corridor. "Was that not Mr. Ridgeworth? I do believe that was Mr. Attenbury's valet. Lord Castlereagh, you are walking a deal too fast for the rest of us."

Lord Castlereagh peered into the dressing room, then stepped back and shooed Lady Harriman, Ally and Kate and Mr. Davies in before him. "Stoneforth, what has gone awry?" he asked instantly.

"It is tonight, Castlereagh. Miss Gorsky was to be abducted only moments ago and then killed in the street, no doubt. So much for time to lay plans, eh? Toby, be off after Ridgeworth and as soon as he has led the villains off far enough that they cannot see the rear alley, come back at once. Miss Gorsky, gather what you can of your things. We shall leave directly Toby brings us word that it is safe. Have you a maid? A companion?"

"Veronika, yes. But tonight she does not come. She is most ill, my Veronika."

"Fiends probably poisoned her to get her out of the way," muttered Wentworth.

Beatrice scowled at him.

"Well, it is what I would do if I wished to abduct Miss Gorsky and kill her. Why deal with two ladies when you are only concerned with one? Come to think of it, perhaps this Veronika is in on the plot. Perhaps she wishes the money and has been made to think, like Ridgeworth, that it is merely a kidnapping."

Stoneforth nodded. "Best not to trust in her. Has your coach a driver, Wentworth?"

"No, I drove myself. But it does have something that will prove useful—a secret compartment in which to hide Miss Gorsky. Even if the villains should pass you on the street, they will never see her. Well, it was to put the wine in, Bea," he added at a glare from that young lady. "I shall go open it up and send my footmen and my groom home so they do not see what happens, eh?"

"Indeed. Castlereagh? Lady Jersey is here, is she not?"

"In her box."

"Go and draw her aside and say that I shall require the *Terpsichore* to sail within the week. She must notify her captain to lay stores for a long voyage—a very long voyage. I have not told her anything but that I must borrow the vessel for a time."

"Done!"

"Where will you take her?" Melody asked, grasping Stoneforth's arm and staring worriedly up at him. "How will you keep safe? What will you do if the villains should discover you or you are stopped by the blockade?"

Stoneforth looked down into those flashing emerald eyes and thought that he would not go at all—that he would stay and hope to live forever in their glow if only as her brother-in-law. And then he remembered how he had kissed her and how the heart within him had been torn from its moorings by that kiss, and he knew that he could not remain were he to be anything less than her husband.

"We shall take Wentworth's coach as far as Witherbe Hall and from there my Uncle North's coach into Newcastle, where Lady Jersey's yacht awaits us. We will sail through the blockade on the North Sea into the Baltic. The ships are Russian. They will know the Tsar's favorite diva, I think, and will let us pass. From there we sail to the Gulf of Finland and into safe harbor at St. Petersburg."

"You will be gone for months!"

"Yes, but—it will give you and Toby time to forgive me for—for—to forgive me if you can."

Mr. Attenbury charged into the chamber at that moment, calling that all was clear as the pounding from the pit above grew louder and more frenzied.

"You cannot go off with the girl without a chaperon, Stoneforth," declared Mr. Davies. "You must take some serving woman with you."

"Yes, and you cannot drive all the way to Witherbe Hall and then go traipsing off upon the ocean when Miss Gorsky possesses only one dress and you nothing but your evening clothes, Lord Stoneforth. You know that would be most impractical," added Ally.

"We must not trust Miss Gorsky's maid," mused Lady Harriman. "But Lord Wentworth's coach has a place for Miss Gorsky to hide. Hide her and drive directly to Harriman House, Lord Stoneforth. Mr. Davies, will you be kind enough to drive me home in your carriage?"

"With pleasure, madam."

"Thank you. Miss Gorsky and the triplets are of like size. You shall leave Miss Gorsky at Harriman House, Lord Stoneforth, and we shall gather some of the triplets' things for her into a portmanteau while you go home and have your man pack for you. When you return, I shall send my Evie with you to be companion to Miss Gorsky. Evie is much accustomed to travel upon the sea."

"Are we not to go home with you, Aunt Lydie?" asked Kate.

"No, I think not. If we all disappear and the villains

return, they may well think to look in our direction. You girls shall attend the rest of the operetta and I shall depend upon Mr. Attenbury and Lord Wentworth to bring you home quite properly."

Stoneforth nodded agreement, freed himself from Melody's grasp and escorted Miss Gorsky through the doorway. "You must take Ridgeworth in, Tobias, when he comes home," he called back over his shoulder. "I gave him my word. You will look after Soldier for me, will you not, Miss Harriman, you and Toby both?" And then he was gone and Lady Harriman and Mr. Davies departed close on his heels.

"Except that there will be no final act to the operetta," Ally murmured. "Aunt Lydie and Lord Stoneforth have quite forgot that the performance cannot continue without Isolda and likely everyone will go spilling out into the street."

"And block Adam's way," sighed Mr. Attenbury with a nod. "Or if he is clear, certainly they will delay Lady Harriman and Davies for Davies' carriage is a full block from the theatre at least, I should think."

"But we have an Isolda!" exclaimed Beatrice. "Kate, you know every word and every note!"

"Do you think I dare?"

"Yes!" cried Melody. "Yes, you must, Kate! We must give Adam and Mama every opportunity we can. Mr. Attenbury, find Mr. Kemble at once and have him announce that Miss Gorsky has fallen ill and that a young lady of Quality has agreed to sing her part for this evening only. That will keep everyone in their seats. They will all be on tenterhooks to discover who the young lady is."

Sixteen

They had got safely away. Melody huddled in the bed, tears streaming from her eyes, and told herself over and over that she was most happy that Lord Stoneforth and Miss Gorsky had got safely away as her mama had said. All of her papa's work with the Tsar would not now be overthrown by such a simple thing as Napoleon had thought to do. And Lord Stoneforth, as Beatrice and Mr. Attenbury had told her more than once, was at this moment merely being the hero he was born to be and had been before and he would come to no harm over it.

"But he is driving a strange team with only Watlow up beside him," Melody whispered, pushing Atropos away as the kitten sought to lick at the tears gathering upon her chin. "And he cannot see all that well to drive at night. I know he cannot. And—and—oh, Atty, I fear I shall never see him again!"

"Mrrrowfph," the kitten replied and struggled mightily to reach the salty tears until at last Melody surrendered to the rough little tongue and submitted to having her chin scrubbed.

"I ought to have spoken," Melody whimpered as the kitten finished with her chin and began to lick one burning cheek. "I have allowed Lord Stoneforth to believe that I love Mr. Attenbury when I find that I do not love Mr. Attenbury at all, Atty! It is Adam I love. But I was so amazed to be kissed by him and to hear him say that he loved me, that I was struck absolutely dumb. And then in came Mr. Ridgeworth and all I could think was to keep the man from shooting someone. And quite suddenly the chamber was filled with people and everything was at sixes and sevens and Mama and everyone speaking at once and then Adam was rushing away and I came to discover that I had said nothing at all to him about—about—but he was gone!"

"Mfffphl," puffed the kitten, ceasing to lick and snuggling into a tiny ball beside her.

"And now he drives Miss Gorsky to Newcastle and then he will attempt to sail through the blockade and if he is not captured or killed, still he will not reach St. Petersburg for months. And I do not think—I do not *believe* that he intends to return, Atty," she sobbed, lifting the kitten into her arms and hugging it to her. "He is so solemn and stiff and determined to do what is right and honorable. I know he will not return until Mr. Attenbury and I are married. And Mr. Attenbury and I shall never be married. And Adam will blame himself for that until the day he dies, until the very day he dies."

Melody kissed the kitten gently. "Adam is gone, Atty, and you are all I shall ever have to remind me of him. You and S-Soldier."

The tears began to flow again and Melody, sniffing, set the kitten aside and left her bed, choosing to abandon the attempt to sleep, to wrap herself warmly in her favorite green robe and to sit upon the window seat staring out into the night.

Wentworth and Attenbury had cried *pax*, at least for the remainder of the night, and quite likely forever. Of course, if Wentworth had not taken it upon himself to apologize for his behavior toward Miss Harriman it would not have happened—not quite so soon at least. But he had apologized, and profusely too, to Miss Harriman and to Attenbury. He had not had much choice in the matter. Beatrice had stood glaring at him, tapping one tiny foot, hands on hips, harrumphing until he knew he must do it. And he had wanted to apologize. He had wanted to apologize from the moment that Attenbury's glove had made contact with his cheek that fateful night. He had just not known how to do it without damaging his carefully acquired reputation for incomparable wit. Now, he did not give a fig about his reputation.

"It is near to one o'clock," Wentworth murmured, peering down at his pocket watch beneath the flickering lamplight. "Perhaps we ought to check at Sanshire House again. Ridgeworth may well have returned there by now. Whoever the villains may be, they will not want him around them now that Miss Gorsky has escaped them completely."

"Which is exactly why we must keep searching, Wentworth. My valet will prove an extraneous appendage to them now. They wished to make use of him to get their hands upon Miss Gorsky without being seen. It would have been Ridgeworth's face that people would have remembered. Ridgeworth would have gone to the gallows, not them. But if they decide that Miss Gorsky has actually evaded them, Ridgeworth is of no use to them at all and might very well betray them and so—I think he knew that, too, when he went out to lead them off upon a wild-goose chase."

"I did not think of that—that they would have no use for him now and might well dispose of him."

"No, I did not either. Miss Beatrice pointed it out to me while Kate was singing. I would not have left the theatre in the midst of Kate's performance else."

"She thinks like a deuced villain, Bea does. Sometimes like a soldier and others like a villain."

Attenbury nodded.

"I cannot think what to do about Bea," Wentworth sighed and then he looked about him. "By Godfrey, Attenbury, we are at The Four and Twitch. Let us pop inside for a moment, eh?"

"The Four and Twitch?"

"Just an old alehouse is all. There, across the way."

"You think our dastards have stopped for an ale?"

"No, but I am hoping that my—that a gentleman of my acquaintance—may be there. A third pair of eyes would not come amiss in this search. The later it gets, the more desperate the situation grows, no?"

"Yes."

The two strolled determinedly across the cobblestone street and up onto the opposite flagway. "It does not look at all hospitable," Attenbury mumbled.

"It is not an establishment accustomed to the Quality. It is populated in the main by merchants and shopkeepers. Ah, we are in luck," Wentworth added, pushing open the door. "That is Peter before the fire. Come, Attenbury. If we are to find Ridgeworth and those dastards in time, we shall require Peter's help."

"You are here again?" sighed Redding, glancing up at his brother with a solemn eye. "I have told you over and over that The Four and Twitch is not a place for earls, Giles. You make everyone uncomfortable when you appear so splendidly dressed. And you are especially grand this evening. Who is your friend?" he added, rising.

"Attenbury. Attenbury, my brother, Peter."

"Your b-brother?" Attenbury gazed from one to the other with a question writ large upon his face.

"His half-brother merely and quite illegitimately at that," grinned Redding, shaking Attenbury's hand. "Giles has spoken of you. Come to think of it, Giles has shot you. What the devil are you doing strolling about with him, and in this neighborhood?"

"We are searching for Attenbury's valet," Wentworth murmured. "Sit down again, Peter, and listen. We need your help."

The coach-and-four flew through the night like a thing possessed. With Stoneforth at the reins and Watlow up beside him, Wentworth's bays raced up the turnpike at a pace that turned heads in every vehicle they passed.

"Ye oughtn't ta be passin' the mail," drawled Watlow, lounging against the back of the box and waving at the driver of that vehicle. "The mail is s'posed ta be the fastest coaches in all o' England."

"Says who?"

"Ever'one. These horses willn't make it another two miles."

"No. I expect we shall be forced to stop at the Royal. Uncle North will have a team boarded there. At least, he always did have when I was young. Check on Miss Gorsky and Miss Harriman's Evie, will you? I do not mean to jounce them around so much as to scramble their brains. If they are on the floor, I shall need to slow our pace."

Watlow grasped the side of the box and leaned down to peer into the coach window. "All right are ye?" he asked the two women, who were clinging to the coach straps with both hands, their eyes wide with anxiety.

"Y-yes," managed Miss Gorsky. "Does he always drive like the madman, this Lord Stoneforth?"

"Aye," grinned Watlow upside down. "We be stoppin' soon, ma'am, ta change teams."

"Thank heaven!" sighed Miss Gorsky as Watlow disappeared. "I hope we shall the coaches change as well, Evie. Never I have been in such big coach with so little room, eh?"

"Pitiful," responded Lady Harriman's maid suc-

cinctly as her knees and Miss Gorsky's came rattling
together.

"They ain't on the floor yet, Colonel," Watlow offered and then leaned back to watch the road fly away
beneath them.

Stoneforth nodded. He ought to be in high gig. They
had got clean away, and he would have Miss Gorsky
upon that yacht and halfway to St. Petersburg before
the blasted assassins even thought to look toward Newcastle. The alliance between the Tsar and the allied
forces might well fall through yet, but it would not be
because Miss Gorsky had died violently upon English
soil. And he was doing something useful again, something exciting, something worthy of a soldier.

Except that he was not in high gig and he did not give
a fig for feeling useful or like a soldier. He felt—hopeless.
Desperate. How could I have kissed her like that in front
of Toby? he wondered. How could I have said aloud that
I love her? Oh God, whatever possessed me?

Nora, he thought then. If I had not promised Nora—
and she was wrong! Acknowledging what is in your
heart does not lead to happiness. It leads to the most
dreadful agony. I was correct all along to hide away inside my shell and attempt to forge my heart to steel. I
ought to have kept on with it. But I could not and now
everything is ruined.

A tremendous pain stabbed through Stoneforth's
breast at precisely that moment and a fire blazed down
his arm. He attempted to catch his breath at the searing
pain of it and could not without gasping. He began to
sweat profusely and the road before him writhed and
warped and wandered before his eyes while his cheeks
grew wet with tears. He prayed Watlow would not notice. His breath rattled in his throat as he approached
the Royal. He held on to the reins and drew them tight,
slowing the bays to a gallop, a trot, and finally to a walk,

directing them safely from the turnpike. As he stood
up to toss the reins to one of the grooms a low groan
escaped him. Watlow turned, astonished at the sound.
But before the batman could guess what was happening, Stoneforth pitched headlong from the box onto
the hard-packed earth of the stable yard.

Inside the foul-smelling hackney, Ridgeworth
glanced worriedly from one to the other of the men he
had come to know while frittering away his half-days at
one of the pubs.

"Well, she dinnae go south, by gawd," grumbled Arnold Duggan. "We 'ave looked everywhere south there
be ta look. Been slumguzzled is what I think." And he
pinned a suspicious gaze upon Ridgeworth.

"Aye," nodded Sam Goodwin, "slumguzzled, Duggan. Who woulda thought it o' sich a fine fella as Mr.
Ebenezer Ridgeworth?"

"Me?" Ridgeworth's eyebrows rose in a very good
imitation of surprise, but his heart pounded with fear.

"Ye warned the gal, dinnit ye, Ridgeworth?" growled
Duggan. "Warned 'er as 'ow we was a-comin' fer 'er an'
then led us off on this 'ere li'l game o' hare an' hounds,
just ta give 'er time ta hide on us. Oh, yes, I sees yer li'l
game now, m' fine fellow. How much did the mort pay
ye is what I'd like ta know. How much does ye got sittin'
in tha' pocket o' yers, eh?"

"I never!" Ridgeworth exclaimed. "She never gave
me a penny. I came upon her in her dressing room just
as you said I was to do and escorted her out the rear
door just as you said. And then she knocked the pistol
from my hand, bit me, kicked me, and finally ran off
down Bow Street."

"So ye said," grumbled Goodwin. "But she did not

run ta fetch the Runners, did she, like any sensible mort?"

"No, an' she did not run ta 'er chambers, or down past the Five Crowns or anywhere else south o' the damnable theatre," Duggan added with a sneer. "Foun' out there were more o' the ready involved than we telled ye, eh, Ridgeworth? Keepin' 'er some'eres so as ta do 'er in yerself an' take it all, are ye?"

"I am not!" protested Ridgeworth with a noticeable tinge of self-righteousness. "Of all the things to suggest! Do her in?" he remembered to add, as though this were the first he had heard of it. "Did you say, do her in? You never said a word about murdering the girl!"

Duggan and Goodwin glanced at each other in consternation.

"Now, now, 'tweren't nothin' but a slip o' the tongue, Ebenezer," Goodwin said. "A slip o' the tongue."

"No, it was not," Ridgeworth replied, attempting a most offended tone. "And if the case is that you mean to kill the lady, then you may count me out now. I shall have nothing more to do with it. Signal the driver to stop at once and deposit me upon the curb."

"Aye, I'll deposit ye upon the curb, I will," growled Duggan, sliding a tenpenny blade from his sleeve into his hand. "But ye'll not be runnin' off ta set the Runners on us the minit I does. I'll be makin' sartin o' that. They'll be scoopin' ye up outta the gutter, m'dear. An' do not think ta be a wavin' o' that pistol in m' face, Ridgeworth, ol' boy. Even I knows it been fired. A man kin see that wifout lookin' at all close."

Ridgeworth paled though the coach was so dark that neither of his former associates noticed. Now what am I going to do, he wondered with the most dismal gnawing in the pit of his stomach. I have got to do something. I shall be dead in a moment if I do not. And then he remembered. "Yer best line o' defense when things appears hopeless is ta attack." Watlow had said that over supper one evening when he had been going on about his exploits and those of Lord Stoneforth upon the battlefield. "Don't matter none does they outman you. No. 'Cause the enemy is always rash an' presumin' when they thinks they got ye down. It gives 'em pause, it does, ta see you comin' at 'em all o' the sudden like when no sensible bloke would do it. Gives ye a chance, it does."

"Well, by Jove, if that is not Miss Gorsky scuttling into that doorway, I will eat my hat!" cried Ridgeworth, moving forward upon the seat and pointing out the window.

Two heads turned in the direction he pointed, and at once Ridgeworth was upon them. He landed Goodwin a facer and shoved the man directly into Duggan; then he opened the door opposite the two colliding men and leaped from the moving vehicle.

"What the devil!" cried a voice as Ridgeworth slipped on the cobbles and went spinning into a hard, well-muscled body.

"Ridgeworth!" exclaimed Mr. Attenbury, grasping one of the valet's arms to keep him upright as Peter Redding attempted to maintain his own balance.

"Damnation, Peter, that is the man for whom we have been searching half the night. And I will lay you odds those are our villains tumbling out of that coach after him," Wentworth hissed as he stepped up beside his brother.

"Are they, Ridgeworth?" asked Attenbury.

Ridgeworth nodded and before he could say a word, Mr. Attenbury, Lord Wentworth and Peter Redding were running out into the street to meet Arnold and Sam head-on. Ridgeworth frowned, then scowled, then groaned, then smiled, then cheered. Oh, it was the most extraordinary row, and Sam and Arnold would likely never think to murder anyone again!

* * *

The candles had burned to stubs in their holders and the barest hint of dawn flickered in the eastern sky. Melody had fallen asleep with her head resting against the windowpane. Eyes as blue-black and solemn as midnight haunted her dreams, and a voice, gentle and tender, whispered to her "I love you, Melody," in accents that set her heart to aching. "I shall always love you. I cannot live without you, my dearest, sweetest Melody. I love you with all my heart, mrrrow."

Mrrrow?

"Mrrr-phsst—rrow!" Atropos demanded, jumping up and down upon Melody's lap. "Mrrrow—phssst! Brrr!"

Brrr? Melody's dream was not proceeding in a rational manner at all. "I love you," whispered Adam, "ka-thunk, ka-thunk."

Ka-thunk?

Melody's eyes popped open. Atropos was batting at her and then leaping at the windowpane and then batting at her again.

"Whatever is happening? Atty? Good heavens! What is that?" Melody caught the kitten up in one hand and hurriedly unlocked the window, pushing it outward. Someone was pounding upon the front door below. She leaned gingerly over the sill and stared downward. "Mr. Watlow?" she called. Stoneforth's batman was easily recognizable in the flambeaux that burned beside the front door. "Mr. Watlow, what are you doing here?"

"I comed ta fetch ye, miss," came the reply, loud and clear. "I thought I weren't niver goin' ta raise nobody. The colonel be dyin', miss. His heart jist up an' broked on 'im. An' Miss Gorsky said as how she were goin' ta stay wif 'im, an' I must come an' fetch you an' Mr. Toby. Only Mr. Toby ain't at home, miss, an' I don't know where ta fine 'im." Melody heard the door open and Higgens' familiar voice, coddled with sleep, exhort Mr. Watlow to cease waking up the dead and come inside at once.

Adam was dying? Melody's mind balked at the thought. Certainly she had misheard. Adam had got Miss Gorsky safely away. The villains had been outwitted and Lord Wentworth's coach had gone flying over the turnpike toward Newcastle with Adam at the reins and Mr. Watlow up beside him. It must have done. Her mama had said it was so. But if it were so, what was Mr. Watlow doing here? Melody wrapped her green wool robe more tightly around her and searched hurriedly for her bedroom slippers. What exactly had Mr. Watlow said? Something very odd. Something about Adam's heart having broken. Heavens! thought Melody clearly for the first time. Broken? Adam's heart has broken? Does he mean to say that Adam's heart has failed him?

Ignoring the bedroom slippers she could not locate, Melody rushed from her bedchamber and down the staircase, the kitten dashing madly behind her, mewing loudly.

Mr. Watlow stood, his hat in his hands, speaking excitedly to Higgens in the foyer as she hurried downward. "What is it you said, Mr. Watlow? What has happened to Adam? Did I hear you correctly—that his heart has failed him?"

"Broked!" declared Watlow. "Busted clean in half I don't doubt. Felled offa the box like he was strucked by the hand o' God Hisself, the colonel did."

"Great heavens!" exclaimed Lady Harriman, who had also awakened to Watlow's pounding upon the door. Wrapped in a heavy flannel robe, she descended at a more decorous pace than had her daughter. "This cannot be true, Mr. Watlow. Lord Stoneforth was fit as a fiddle when he left here with Miss Gorsky."

" 'Parently not," sighed Watlow. " 'Parently not. I come ta fetch Miss Harriman and Mr. Attenbury, ma'am. Miss Gorsky an' yer Evie stays wif the colonel at the Royal until I returns. He be a-lyin' there in one

o' the rooms askin' fer Miss Harriman and Mr. Toby
over an over agin. I do reckon as he be dyin' this time,
m'lady," added Watlow, surreptitiously swiping at a tear.
"I dinnit never seen 'im so pale an' shakin' afore, an'
I seen 'im hurt bad through the years, ma'am. I surely
have. An' I kinnot fine Mr. Attenbury," he added in a
husky, bewildered voice. "He ain't home, nor Mr. Ridgeworth ain't home neither."

"You must tell Aunt Lydie and Mr. Watlow not to wait
about one moment for us," Beatrice whispered, tugging
the forager's hat down over her curls. "Uncle Arthur's
old coach barely rumbles down the road at the pace of
a snail. With luck, Melody, Mr. Attenbury and I shall
beat you there."

"I cannot think this is at all an intelligent thing for
the two of you to do," said Ally.

"It has not the least thing to do with intelligence,"
Melody replied, tucking her curls up under the brim
of one of her papa's old beavers. "Adam is dying and
he wishes to see his brother just one more time, and
Mr. Watlow is exhausted. It will take him forever to find
Mr. Attenbury."

"I know precisely where Mr. Attenbury has gone,"
declared Bea. "He is with Wentworth."

"So, we shall ride and fetch him and then go straight
out the turnpike to the Royal. It is almost dawn. Barely
anyone will be about the streets. No one need know we
have ridden out at all," Melody said confidently, stuffing the bottoms of the breeches Bea had loaned her
into her riding boots.

"Except your mama," Kate observed, slipping into
her round gown. "But do not worry. Ally and I shall
think of some way to placate her. She will wish to help
Lord Stoneforth. She has grown fond of him, I think."

Melody and Bea were out the window and down the trellis in the wink of an eye. They had saddled the horses and were away before John Coachman and the grooms had even got dressed and down to the stables. Looking quite like two lads mounted upon their master's beasts, the girls rode south through the sleeping city of London as if the devil himself were after them.

As they reached Bow Street, Beatrice slowed. "We must watch carefully from here on, Mel. Mr. Ridgeworth led the villains south from Covent Garden and Wentworth and Mr. Attenbury will be searching for them."

"I thought you knew precisely where Lord Wentworth and Mr. Attenbury were?"

"Well, not precisely at this very moment. But I did hear Mr. Watlow say that neither Mr. Attenbury nor Mr. Ridgeworth were yet at home. That means that either Wentworth and Mr. Attenbury are still searching for Mr. Ridgeworth or have found that gentleman and are even now delivering the villains up to the Runners—or they are all bound for home even as we speak."

"Beatrice!"

"Well, but I am fairly certain that Mr. Attenbury and Mr. Ridgeworth are not yet bound for home, Mel. We came right through Leicester Square and there was not a sign of life anywhere about—not so much as a hackney cab. Therefore, we must only check at the Bow Street Office and then continue south."

"Beatrice, have you any idea how many streets there are in the south of London?"

"No, but there cannot be a great many, do you think?"

Seventeen

"Who the deuce are those lads and what are they doing here at such an hour?" asked Peter Redding, peering from the hackney window as it slowed and swung in toward the curb. "By Jove, they can neither one of them be more than twelve. Why should twelve-year-olds be lingering about outside the Bow Street Office, eh? The Runners are not hiring them that young, are they?"

"Who? Where?" asked Wentworth, stretching to see around Goodwin and past his brother Peter as the hackney wobbled to a stop. "I say, they look a bit familiar."

"Familiar? Who?" asked Attenbury, tugging Duggan by the collar as he moved to stick his head out the window.

"Beatrice, it is Mr. Attenbury!" Melody cried, recognizing his face in the lamplight. "It is Mr. Attenbury in that hackney! Oh, you wonderful girl! You *knew* they would be here! You were merely jesting about the need to ride through all those streets! Mr. Attenbury, we must speak with you at once!"

"By gawd, that is Miss Harriman's voice," gasped Attenbury, sticking his head *and* one shoulder out the hackney window, dragging the unfortunate Duggan lopsidedly behind him.

"No, do not! You will reinjure your shoulder doing

that," Melody declared, dismounting and leading her horse up to the vehicle. "What on earth? Who is it that you hold so tightly with your other hand?"

"Miss Harriman?" asked Attenbury, amazed. "Wh-what are you doing here? Who is it with you?"

"No, do not say. Let me guess," drawled Wentworth, as the other rider approached nearer the coach. "It could not possibly be Miss Beatrice Lange?"

"Yes, of course it is Bea," nodded Melody, her papa's beaver tipping down over her eyebrows with the action. "I should never have known how to go about finding Mr. Attenbury if Bea had not known to come directly here."

"You are both mad," Wentworth proclaimed with authority. "Riding about the London streets before dawn dressed as stable boys! You are mad as hatters!"

"No, we are not. We have come to fetch Mr. Attenbury. Lord Stoneforth has—has fallen ill and—"

"Ill? Adam? How can you know?"

"Mr. Watlow has ridden all the way back to London with the news. We must go to your brother, Mr. Attenbury," Melody declared. "At once. Have you not got a horse? I thought you would have a horse with you, but you are in a hackney."

"How ill? What has happened?" Attenbury asked excitedly.

"Mr. Watlow thinks that something has gone wrong with Adam's heart," Melody responded. "He lies at the Royal even now in Miss Gorsky's care and he calls for you. You must come with us at once."

"Miss Gorsky at the Royal? How the devil?" grumbled Goodwin.

"Out!" ordered a deep voice that Melody did not at all recognize. "Everyone out!" And both doors of the vehicle opened, disgorging gentlemen and villains and

Mr. Ridgeworth alike from both sides, and in various states of *dishabille*.

"Oh, Mr. Ridgeworth, you are safe!" Melody cried upon seeing him. "I am so very glad of it."

"Of course he is safe," responded Beatrice, crossing to tie her filly to one of the hitching posts and stepping up onto the flagway. "I knew Wentworth would save him. He is quite to be depended upon once he knows what ought to be done. You are not one of the villains, I think," she added, peering up at Redding.

"No. I, ah, am a friend of his lordship's."

"Of Wentworth's? You are? How odd. You do not look the least bit insufferable. Do you know where Mr. Attenbury may procure a decent bit of blood and bone nearby? We must be off. There is truly not a moment to spare."

"No, not a moment," agreed Melody as she followed Attenbury and Duggan around the coach to the flagway, leading her little mare. "We must ride like the wind, Mr. Attenbury. I could not bear to think that Adam needed us and we were not with him as quickly as possible. That is why Bea and I ride astride, so that we may travel full out and without encumbrance."

"Much more expedient to ride full tilt up the turn-pike than to plod along in Uncle Arthur's old coach," nodded Bea, one lovely curl bouncing from beneath her forager's cap directly into the middle of her forehead.

Redding could not help but smile at the sight of the young ladies pretending to be lads. He had never thought to see the day when ladies of Quality would go riding about the town disguised as lads. "Giles," he murmured, "if you and Mr. Ridgeworth will see that these villains are thrust into the proper hands inside, I will borrow this young lady's horse—if I may, m'dear— and Attenbury shall borrow the other and we will fetch us some decent beasts from McCroy's stables. They are merely one street over and a block down," he added with a reassuring glance at Melody. "It will take but a few moments."

"Wentworth, is this friend of yours to be trusted?" asked Beatrice. "He will not steal our horses, eh?"

"Great heavens, of course he is to be trusted," grumbled Wentworth. "Go, Peter, Ridgeworth and I shall look to the villains. I know you can fight well enough one-handed, Attenbury. I have just seen you do it. But can you ride? Fast, I mean, with your shoulder like that?"

"To reach my brother? I should think so," responded Attenbury, removing the sling from his arm and stuffing it into his pocket. "We shall be back in a moment, Miss Harriman," he added, taking Betsy's reins and stepping up into the saddle. "And then we shall be off to the Royal."

The early rising sun peeped in at Stoneforth. It attempted to shine full upon him but was thwarted by a set of damask curtains drawn nearly together across the long, tall windows of the chamber. He squinted through partially opened lids at it, moved his head upon the pillow and groaned.

Melody sprang from the wing chair at the opposite side of the chamber and hurried to him, the spurs upon her boots jangling. "Adam? Adam, can you hear me, my dearest?"

Attenbury, who had rushed quite as hastily from his chair near the door, came to a stop beside her. "Adam? Miss Harriman and I are right here. You are going to be fine. You must only rest a good deal and be most careful not to do anything that makes you at all tired, Dr. Belows says."

"M-Melody? Toby?"

"Yes, we are right here, dearest," murmured Melody, taking one of his hands into both of her own and easing onto the edge of the mattress.

Stoneforth's eyes flickered at her touch and he peered up at her. The corners of his lips attempted to twitch upward into a smile. "I thought never to s-see you again."

"Well, and you almost did not," said Melody softly. "Mr. Watlow was certain that your heart had burst wide open and that you would not live out the night."

"And did I? Live out the night?"

"Well, of course you did," answered Mr. Attenbury.

"I am not d-dead and gone to God, Toby?"

"Not hardly, Adam."

"Then how c-comes there to be an angel holding my hand?"

In the private parlor that the landlord had insisted upon giving them, Redding and Miss Gorsky sat comfortably before the hearth, glasses of wine in their hands and knowing smiles upon both their faces. Wentworth and Miss Beatrice thought, of course, that they were paying them not the least attention, but Redding's ears and Miss Gorsky's as well were practically pointing backward to overhear the conversation occurring behind them.

"You were more than foolish to come rampaging through town in such a manner and at such an hour," Wentworth grumbled. "There is no telling what might have happened to the two of you. What if you had missed us at Bow Street? What if I had got Attenbury home and the two of you were off wandering about London? What then? Attenbury would not even have known to come to the Royal."

"Lord Sanshire's butler knew perfectly well what message to give him if he should arrive at home," Beatrice mumbled. "Mr. Watlow did not intend to stand about waiting upon Mr. Attenbury all night. He intended to return here as soon as possible."

"Yes, but what if after the butler told Attenbury, we had learned that you and Miss Harriman were missing? We could not have come directly here without searching for you. We should not be here as yet. We should be in some wretched alley in St. Giles, no doubt."

"Wentworth, cease and desist! What if this and what if that! It does not matter what if. What matters is that we did find you and that we are here and we are here well before Aunt Lydie's coach too! What matters is that his lordship is not alone. His brother and Melody are with him as they ought to be when he is in such dire straits. He—he will not die—will he?" Beatrice added in a soft, little girl voice.

Redding turned to look at them the moment he heard the jangle of spurs. Wentworth was stepping forward and taking the minx of a child into his arms.

This Miss Beatrice looks the most appealing little urchin in those clothes with her hair all a-tangle, Redding thought. Obviously Giles thinks so as well. And she fits perfectly into his arms. Almost as though she has been sculpted precisely for that purpose. And she seems woman enough to stir up his life and keep him in line at one and the same time. He turned back toward the hearth again before either should take note of his interest and grinned the most charming grin at Miss Gorsky.

"Of course Stoneforth will not die, gudgeon," Wentworth whispered into Bea's ear, his arms fitted around her. "He is Lord Stoneforth and before that Colonel Attenbury, and he is one hundred times the man of any fellow in this inn, including myself, is he not?"

"Yes," Beatrice whispered into the comforting presence of Wentworth's neckcloth. "Yes."

Lady Harriman's coach with Watlow riding alongside arrived at the Royal shortly before seven, and by eight o'clock Beatrice and Melody were dressed most appropriately in morning gowns and slippers. By eight-fifteen, Mr. Redding, with a message to Lord Sanshire and another to Lord Harriman tucked safely into his coat pocket along with Lord Stoneforth's purse, was taking his leave of the company with Miss Gorsky firmly fastened to his arm.

"You must be certain to check upon Harris from time to time for me, eh, Giles?" Redding requested. "He has never been left in complete charge before and I should hate to return to a carriage shop without one carriage taking shape in it or a set of books with greater numbers in the minus column than in the plus."

"I will keep watch over everything for you," Wentworth assured him. "And you must keep adequate watch over Miss Gorsky and yourself. Are you certain that you wish to do this thing, Peter?"

"Who else is there to do this thing?"

"Me."

"Oh, no. I think not. You will take charge of that ship and talk the crew into becoming pirates because you are bored with sailing. Or you will annoy the poor captain so much with your witty observations that he will throw you overboard. No, thank you. I shall be the one escorts Miss Gorsky home. Besides, you must stay and look after Miss Beatrice. There is no telling what scrapes that minx may fall into without you by her side. Fare you well, little brother."

"And you, Peter," Wentworth replied, taking his brother's hand into his own and keeping it there for a very long moment. "I shall not rest easily until you are on British soil again."

And then Redding and Miss Gorsky and Lady Harriman's maid were out the door and into a hired post chaise and off upon the road to Witherbe Hall and Newcastle and places east.

Stoneforth woke several times, but never fully nor for very long until at last he woke to firelight and shadows late that evening. He attempted to push himself up into a sitting position, but groaned and fell back, his head throbbing, his breath rasping and his heart pounding against his ribs in outrage.

"My dear Adam," he heard Melody's voice say, "you must lie very still and rest. You know you must. I have told you so over and over again."

"You have?"

"Yes, she has," Attenbury answered for her. "And so have I. You have not been listening though. You have been a bit odd, Adam, all day long."

"I have?"

"Yes, you have," whispered Melody. "You have been talking to yourself about the most outrageous things. Mr. Attenbury and I have been so very worried, but even so we could not help but laugh at some of what you said."

"You c-could not? Wh-what did I say?" Stoneforth blinked upward, attempting to focus, and discovered his brother to be standing directly behind Miss Harriman, hands upon her shoulders, smiling down at him.

"Before you ask, Adam, Miss Gorsky is on her way to Uncle North's in the company of Wentworth's brother, who has kindly consented to take her all the way to St. Petersburg for us."

"I ought—I am the one—"

"No, you cannot, dearest," Melody interrupted hurriedly, one hand going to smooth the curls from his brow. "Dr. Belows says you are not to do one thing in the least extraordinary or heroic for at least a year or more. Your heart will recover its strength, he says, if you are patient and behave properly and take your medicine as you are instructed to do."

"My heart. I thought it w-was breaking wide open."

"Yes. Mr. Watlow thought the same. But it did not," Melody informed him softly. "Your heart was merely warning you, Dr. Belows said, that you needed to cease worrying about everything and roaring about as though you were a lad of twenty."

"Indeed. I am the Attenbury who is a lad of twenty—well, more or less—and you are the Attenbury who is a good sight older," grinned Toby. "And before you begin again to apologize for loving Melody—"

"I did that? I mean, I intended before I died to beg your forgiveness again—forgiveness from both of you—but I do not remember—"

"You did so just after you muttered that a dragoon had no business to be fencing with foxes and again after you apparently wrecked Papa's carriage by driving it full tilt off a riverbank, and a third time after you admitted to having hidden a puppy beneath your tunic and sneaked it into Wellesley's chamber. Did you truly do that? Sneak a puppy into Wellesley's chamber, Adam?"

"Yes. A very wet, dirty puppy."

"I should like to have been there. However, before you begin to apologize again, I do wish you will pay attention to what Melody and I have to say."

"Will you attempt to pay attention, dearest?" asked Melody, tracing the line of his cheek with one finger.

"Cer-certainly."

"Good. Because we do neither of us wish to hear you apologize again," Attenbury declared, giving Melody's shoulders a squeeze. "I shall begin and Melody will follow. This young woman I presently hold, dear brother, is *not* the woman I love. I care for her deeply and I was terribly infatuated with her from the very first, but the woman I love, Adam, is a bit shorter with curls the color of autumn leaves and a singing voice quite equal to Miss Gorsky's."

"M-miss Lange?"

"Miss Katherine Lange, yes. I thought it quite likely that I did love her after our evening at Lord and Lady Hyde's. But I was not certain then. I am now, Adam. Kate is the woman with whom I wish to share all that I have. She is the one I wish to protect and to do all the other things for that you said I should wish to do someday."

"But I thought that Melody—"

"Yes, we both know what you thought. We have been discussing it all day, Adam," sighed Attenbury. "Had Ridgeworth not come pointing that pistol at us just at the moment he did and the whole world not descended around our ears in Miss Gorsky's dressing room, I should have told you then and there that I did not love Melody."

"Just so," smiled Melody. "And had I not been driven perfectly speechless by your kiss and then immediately threatened by Mr. Ridgeworth, I should have told you then and there that I do not love Mr. Attenbury either."

"You do not love Toby?" Stoneforth's eyes fastened upon Melody with an intensity that sent her heart choking up into her throat, her cheeks to burning and chased the very breath from her lungs. She opened her mouth to reply but could not. She coughed instead.

"I shall leave you alone with him for a moment or

two, eh?" Attenbury whispered in her ear. He gave her shoulders another encouraging squeeze. "I will be back in a moment or two, Adam. I promised Watlow to fetch him when you woke again." And then Mr. Attenbury was gone.

Melody stared down at the gentleman in the bed. Her fingers twisted and toyed with each other. She took a deep breath and sat upon the edge of his mattress and leaned toward him until her lips touched his. She kissed him most tenderly, and then a bit less tenderly, and then, her fingers twisting into his black curls, she kissed him not tenderly at all, but with a passion composed of the sheer dread that he might have died and the great thankfulness that he had not, the exultation of knowing that he loved her and the wonderful certainty that now he must know that she loved him too. "There," she whispered when she had finished, pulling back to hold his hand and look him in the eye. "There, Lord Stoneforth. That is for you. And do not think that I intend to apologize for it either. I do not. In fact, I have every intention of kissing you just like that again and again and again, as soon as you are well, and Dr. Belows assures me that it will not wear you down."

Stoneforth stared up at her in amazement. His lips moved but they made no sound at all. He stopped and started again, this time words spilling from him like water from a badly cracked pitcher. "You cannot mean to say that you love me. It is pity, merely. Pity for a soldier who has evidently outlived his usefulness and made a perfect jackass of himself on top of it. You are the sweetest, kindest, most wonderful woman in all the world and I shall always love you but—"

"Yes, you had best always love me," Melody interrupted, "because I do not intend to marry any gentleman who does not, and I do intend to marry you, Adam Attenbury. You had best set your mind to it right this minute that we are to be married and that you will always, always love me. You do not think that I am being too forward, do you?" she added as an afterthought. "I have been taking lessons from Bea, you know."

Stoneforth stared, then chuckled, then drew her down into his arms. His lips met hers again. When he had finished kissing her, he held her, his soft breath tingling against her cheek. "Yes," he whispered at last, sleepily. "You are entirely too forward."

"Adam!"

"And in case you should care to ask me instead of order me, Miss Harriman, yes, I will be honored to marry you. I will be overjoyed to marry you. And I *shall* marry you, too."

The Wednesday following Miss Gorsky's narrow escape, Almack's boiled with rumors. Any number of Almack's illustrious patrons were of the opinion that Lord Stoneforth, who had not been seen anywhere by anyone since that evening, had run off with the woman to Gretna Green.

"Of course, we know that is not so," murmured Lord Jersey into Lady Jersey's ear as he led her away from the crowd and behind a well-situated potted plant. "One does not require a yacht with enormous stores to reach Gretna, does one?"

"George, if you do not cease plaguing me about that yacht, I shall—I shall—"

"What, Sarah?"

"I will think of something."

"Oh, will you? Why did you give this Stoneforth possession of the *Terpsichore?* You need only answer me that. But you will not though I have been asking you for an explanation since Friday evening. Even I do not have the run of that wretched boat."

"You get *mal de mer* just looking at that wretched boat. I vow, George, I do not know where Adam planned to sail her or why. I did him a favor and that is all. I cannot help that Robert came rushing into our box Friday babbling about the stores and all. If he had not, you would not have known a thing about it."

"Adam? You call the man Adam?"

"That is his name, George."

"And I expect he calls you Sally, eh?"

"Jersey, you are jealous!"

"I will know who this man is to you, Sally. I have heard that you waltzed with him in the most outrageous fashion and that you strolled with him in the park and there are even rumors that you visited with him at Sanshire House!"

Lady Jersey giggled. "Lord Stoneforth is the most incredible man, George."

"Yes?" asked Jersey dryly. "And is he as incredible upon the dueling ground as he is upon the dance floor, do you think? He had best be aboard that boat and far away, Sally. I warn you. Because if he shows his face here tonight, I will meet him tomorrow before dawn and only one of us will return to have breakfast afterward."

"I love it when you are jealous."

"This is not a game, Sally. I am truly angry."

"Indeed, sweetest. So angry that you have come with me to my detestable club and have stayed by my side for over an hour. You are so very wonderful when you are jealous, Jersey." She took his pouting lower lip between her teeth and nibbled at it.

He attempted to stop her, could not, frowned and then began to chuckle. "Sally, you are mad. Someone will see us."

"I find I do not care in the least. Everyone here tonight is mad. Did you not see that Emily Anne and Robert actually arrived together? Good gawd, Jersey!"

she added, peering through the leaves of the plant. "They are waltzing together—again!"

It was true. Lord Castlereagh had not merely escorted his wife to Almack's and waltzed the first waltz with her but he was waltzing with her again.

"I do hope Lord Stoneforth never leaves London," Lady Castlereagh whispered as Castlereagh ceased his explanation of all that had occurred and why it had been so very important to the war effort. She stepped closer to him as they turned in the midst of the dance and sighed. Castlereagh was not at all expecting that. Generally when he even mentioned the war, Emily made some flippant remark and stalked away, no matter where they were at the time. "Are you not feeling just the thing, Emily Anne?" he asked.

"I am feeling quite comfortable, Robert. But I do wish we were at home and not dancing. You have not held me so close as this in years, I think."

"You seldom wish to be held like this. You are always far too busy with your clubs and only longing to be one place or another with your friends."

"Yes, but that is because you have grown so very depressing to be around, Robert. That is why I hope Lord Stoneforth does never leave. He has got you smiling practically every day. Do you remember how you danced and laughed right here last Wednesday evening with little Miss Harriman and made me quite jealous?"

"You *were* jealous. I knew you were."

"Yes. But not anymore. I adore waltzing with you, Robert."

"Do you, sweet Emily?"

"Yes, and if it is not too much to ask, I should like you to tell me what you can about the Tsar and the Russian delegation and who it is escorts Miss Gorsky to

St. Petersburg since Lord Stoneforth cannot. And I should like to know what you meant about Miss Gorsky's maid having pretended to be ill in order to further the plot, too. And when you have finished with all that, I should like you to tell me, Robert, what it is makes you so solemn and crotchety at times and what I may do to make you smile just as Lord Stoneforth seems to do."

In the next moment they were waltzing as slowly and seductively about the floor at Almack's as ever Stoneforth and Lady Jersey had done, and Robert Stewart, Lord Castlereagh, was speaking words he had never thought to speak to his wife before. And with each word and each step of that dance a bridge they had both thought burned to ashes long ago arose again between them and joined them more securely than it ever had before.

They had none of them thought of going to Almack's that Wednesday evening. They had gathered instead at Sanshire House in Lord Stoneforth's chambers to quietly celebrate his return to his home that very day and to keep him company for an evening. And they all looked expectantly up at Ridgeworth when he entered the chamber in answer to the bell.

"I have got the answer, Ridgeworth," Stoneforth declared with a smile, holding tightly to Melody's hand. "We have all thought of it together."

"The answer, my lord?"

"Yes, to your little problem, Ridgeworth," Mr. Attenbury grinned, his arm firmly about Kate's shoulders. "You remember. A man has desires? Well, we have all given it a deal of thought."

Ridgeworth stared abruptly at his shoe tops. "I would be obliged if you would ignore all that I said that evening, Mr. Attenbury, your lordship. I shall be eternally grateful for your not reporting me to Bow Street. That is more than I deserve."

"No, it is not," Wentworth replied, winking at Beatrice, who quite unabashedly winked back. "The truth is, Ridgeworth, you led those fiends off knowing that you might be killed and that deserves more than not being turned over to the Runners. Besides, you do have desires. All men do."

"Just so, and I did promise to help you with the fulfillment of them," added Stoneforth.

"That 'e did," nodded Watlow. "Tole me as much his own self while we was roarin' along the 'pike."

"Indeed," nodded Stoneforth. "What would you think, Ridgeworth, to opening your own shop? Not a tremendously large shop, of course, because I am not quite so rich as my Uncle North, but a decent-size shop, where gentlemen might come to consult you upon their wardrobes and purchase a thing or two?"

"Oh, my lord, I could not!"

"Why not? You need not sew the clothes, Ridgeworth. You would simply study the gentlemen and design clothes for them. I have enough money to hire a number of women to sew for you."

"What he means to say, Mr. Ridgeworth," interpreted Mr. Davies, who sat quite contentedly and very close beside Ally, "is that a gentleman would put himself into your hands and you would be responsible to see that he was properly turned out."

"You can do that, Ridgeworth," added Mr. Attenbury. "You do it every day for me."

"Y-yes, but who would come? All of the gentlemen have proper valets and their favorite tailors as well."

"Not all of the gentlemen, Ridgeworth," Wentworth said. "Did you not look around you when you were in the theatre? The gallery was filled with bankers and merchants and shopkeepers, all of them attempting to dress quite as splendidly as the members of the *ton*. Except some of them do not have the knack, you know. Well, they do not," he added with a teasing smirk at Bea. "Peter, for one, is quite hopeless. But they do have the money, Ridgeworth, and we cannot think why you should not earn your share of it from them."

"Do you think I could, my lord?"

"You would do excellently well at it," nodded Stoneforth. "Provided, of course, that we can lure enough influential cits into the place to begin with. But I think we can."

" 'Course we kin," Watlow grinned. "I gots ideas 'ow ta go about that awready."

"Right. And when you are making a profit, Ridgeworth, you need only pay me back what I have put out on your behalf and we shall call it even, eh?"

"No, no, you shall share in the profits," Ridgeworth breathed, visions of bankers and merchants and shopkeepers begging his assistance and opinion dancing before his eyes. "You must share in the profits, my lord."

"Well, we will discuss it, Ridgeworth. But not at the moment. There is a coach drawing up outside. I can hear it. It will be Castlereagh stopping by after his evening at Almack's. No, do not laugh, any of you. An evening or two at Almack's is good for a man, I think. I intend to dance there again one day—with my charming wife."

"Yes," laughed Melody, "and then with every wallflower in the place. I shall insist upon it. And Mr. Davies and Mr. Attenbury and Lord Wentworth, you will do the same, I think."

"Indeed, he will," nodded Beatrice. "In fact, I believe that we shall go to Almack's next week. It is time, Wentworth, for you to cease being thoroughly detestable and to join in the mutiny against rudesbys with us. You will dance with all sorts of young ladies who are not belles and you will enjoy it too. And you had best not sharpen your wit upon any one of them, or I shall most definitely part your hair with a butcher's knife."

Everyone in the chamber took a very deep breath and held it. Even Lady Harriman did and looked up from her sewing to see what sort of response Bea's words would bring from the earl.

Wentworth stood, turned to look down at Bea and lifted his quizzing glass to his eye with maddening slowness. Then he gazed through it at Beatrice, studying her from the top of her head to the toes of her feet. Then he let it drop and turned to face the other occupants of the room. "I am quite sorry to disappoint all of you," he whispered into the expectant silence, "but I find she is much too nicely dressed to strangle this evening. Tomorrow perhaps." And he sat back down and took Beatrice into his arms and gave her a resounding kiss in front of Lady Harriman and everyone.